"With perfect details, wry humor, an
Jenkins shows us what it was *really* li
that era of free love and openness—wh
its start, handed to us on a plate of h
thought it could be so funny, and so sa

—Sarah Willis, author of
Some Things That Stay and *The Rehearsal*

"A hilarious coming-of-adolescence novel . . . With the wry detachment only an over-brainy eight-year-old can manage, heroine Vanessa Brick steers her way through the bends and potholes of a world that is too lame, too dumb, too scary, too hypocritical—and way too weird."

—Luke Davies, author of
Isabelle the Navigator

"*Mister Posterior and the Genius Child* is like a gentle sorcerer's spell. I was sorry to reach the end, to have to waken from the funny, bittersweet dream I'd been reading."

—Maggie Estep, author of *Soft Maniacs*
and *Diary of an Emotional Idiot*

"A warmhearted novel . . . *Mister Posterior and the Genius Child* reminds us that childhood is no idyll but a time of complexity, confusion, and relentless education in the ways of the world."

—Kitty Burns Florey, author of
Souvenir of Cold Springs

"To an amazing degree, Jenkins has been able to scrub away all the obscuring layers of sentimentality and nostalgia and even irony that settle over childhood. What emerges is startling in its fresh primary colors and so true that it hurts. *Mister Posterior and the Genius Child* returns readers to the lost world of their eight-year-old hearts—scary, innocent, funny, honest, and strange."

—M. A. Harper, author of
The Worst Day of My Life, So Far

"Emily Jenkins takes us on a surprising, nostalgic, and funny ride through childhood, a place where one's friends and enemies seem to change places overnight, and even small decisions can have dramatic consequences."

—Kathy Hepinstall, bestselling author of
The Absence of Nectar

"With lyrical prose, Jenkins evokes a very *specific* 1970s childhood that makes readers of any background long for a lost *collective* past—no matter whether you are fifteen, thirty-five, or seventy-five years old. Simultaneously poetic and dramatic, *Mister Posterior* is a wonderful read that does through fiction what 'classic rock' does through music or Proust's madelines does through cookies."

—Dalton Conley, author of
Honky

"*Mister Posterior and the Genius Child* made me nostalgic for a part of childhood I had almost forgotten. As eight-year-old Vanessa and her single mom wade through the treacherous waters of playground politics, dating, and sexual freedom, you will experience firsthand what it's to grow up in ultraliberal Cambridge in the height of the '70s. *Mister Posterior* is incredibly funny and wise—don't miss out on this unexpected pleasure!"

—Libby Schmais, author of
The Perfect Elizabeth and *Rescue Remedy*

Praise for Emily Jenkins's
Tongue First: Adventures in Physical Culture

"Nothing passes by Emily Jenkins's eye. She is a wry and pungent chronicler of detail."

—Wendy Wasserstein, author of
The Heidi Chronicles and *Shiksa Goddess*

"What a marvelous book! Emily's writing is bold as a bungee jump, smooth as a sweet kiss . . . It will also make you laugh."

—Mariah Burton Nelson, author of
Embracing Victory

Mister Posterior and the Genius Child

Emily Jenkins

BERKLEY BOOKS, NEW YORK

A Berkley Book
Published by The Berkley Publishing Group
A division of Penguin Putnam Inc.
375 Hudson Street
New York, New York 10014

This book is an original publication of The Berkley Publishing Group.

This is a work of fiction. Names, characters, places, and incidents either are the product of the author's imagination or are used fictitiously, and any resemblance to actual persons, living or dead, business establishments, events, or locales is entirely coincidental.

Cover design by Erika Fusari.
Cover art by Lisa Desimini.
Text design by Tiffany Kukec.

PRINTING HISTORY
Berkley trade paperback edition / December 2002

Visit our website at
www.penguinputnam.com

Library of Congress Cataloging-in-Publication Data

Jenkins, Emily, 1967–
Mister Posterior and the genius child / Emily Jenkins.—1st Berkley trade pbk. ed.
p. cm.
ISBN 0-425-18627-X
1. Girls—Fiction. I. Title: Mr. Posterior and the genius child. II. Title.

PS3560.E4835 M47 2002
813'.54—dc21

2002071732

PRINTED IN THE UNITED STATES OF AMERICA

10 9 8 7 6 5 4 3 2 1

For my mother

Contents

Prologue

On line at the deli near my children's school. This other mother—a mother holding a piece of empty Tupperware and wearing a parka made for hiking—asks me to be treasurer of the PTA. To keep track of money. Make sure there's coffee, sugar, and saccharine at meetings. Coordinate cookie-bakers at holiday time. She wants me to organize the annual rummage sale.

I tell her she would be sorry if I said Yes.

"Sorry?" She wrinkles the space above her nose. "Why would I be sorry?"

"You don't want me on the PTA," I say—and I'm not lying. I couldn't do rummage and cookie-bakers and coffee and saccharine and still keep my mouth shut about things I think. If I said Yes, this other mother wouldn't like me for long.

Besides, there is a long, sordid, ridiculous history of me versus the PTA. Not this PTA. One from thirty years ago. It isn't a good idea, I tell her.

She doesn't believe me. I have daughters in the third and first grades. I can string sentences together. My kitchen floor is dotted with crushed Cheerios and cat hair. I return phone calls, and my handwriting is neat. She is sure I'd be perfect. "We can make a difference, Vanessa," she says, as if Difference has a set meaning that everyone agrees upon.

We pay for our coffee, and I buy licorice, too. Out on the street, I turn to walk home. "The bell rings in four minutes," the other mother reminds me.

"I know," I say.

"Is your husband picking up the kids?"

"He's at work."

"Your nanny, then? I don't think I've met her."

Our nanny is a teenage boy with a safety pin through his ear. He comes over on weekends and takes the children to the playground. My older daughter thinks he's glamorous. I can tell by the way she hangs on his leg. He brings her gummy worms and unusual Japanese candies that he buys downtown.

No one else I know has a boy nanny. Especially not for girls.

I tell her our nanny doesn't pick the children up. The children walk home.

"Really? Are you sure that's safe?" We live in New York City.

"They want to," I answer. I have the urge to say it's only five blocks—but I don't. And the older one always stays with the younger—but I don't say that, either.

"They always *want* to do things alone." The other mother's voice sounds challenging. As if to say, That doesn't mean you should let them.

"Don't you love that?" I ask. My youngest wants to read so badly she won't let anyone read her anything. Not until she can do it herself.

"Did you hear about that girl stolen out of her own backyard and locked in a basement for nine days?" the mother wants to know. "The man lived only two doors down. He dressed as a big white rabbit for children's parties, even."

Yeah, I remember that. The trial is in the newspapers now.

"And that was in Connecticut. Vanessa, really."

"What?" I am playing dumb.

"Just consider what could happen. That's all I'm saying."

"I have considered it."

She means well, this other mother. "Wouldn't it just break your heart?" she asks.

It would, I think. It probably would. But I am not sure she and I agree on what "It" is, at all—the "It" that would break my heart. And there is something severely wrong with my heart already. My mailbox overflows with unopened condolence notes; my refrigerator is stuffed with well-meaning tuna casseroles and spice cakes; long-forgotten photographs are strewn across my coffee table.

I cannot see this woman in her hiking jacket clearly. The street goes blurry as my eyes fill. But I know she is looking at me like I am an alien, a bad parent, an ignorant person. And—not the right sort for her PTA, after all.

She hopes I never learn my lesson the hard way, because that would be a cruel thing to hope; but a little part of her hopes I learn it, just the same. She thinks a mother should know better. She thinks I am wrong.

But I am not wrong, because I remember how it was to be eight—and my eldest turned eight just this June. I remember the playground rhymes, the fierce cliques, and the girls we called The Fuckers. That year, 1970, was the year my mother adopted an unprecedented number of cats and dated an ardent nudist. The year I finally found out the truth about my father and his antivegetarianism; and my only close friend became a person I didn't know. It was also the first time I was conscious of myself as a person with secrets, as a free-thinking human being with something to say. Something not everyone wanted to hear.

In Cambridge, Massachusetts, at the start of the seventies, being a free-thinking human being was very popular, especially with the adults of my mother's generation. *Sesame Street* was pretty much new, and Woodstock was only last year. Even people with regular jobs and station wagons were getting in touch with their sexualities, investigating alternative spiritual paths, considering psychotherapy, and passionately advocating liberation from the restrictive laws and social codes that inhibited self-expression and bummed everybody out. So nobody objected to my speaking out *in principle.* People didn't believe children should be seen and not heard. Not anymore. They objected because what I said made them deeply uncomfortable.

And because I made multiple dittos. The year I was eight was the year I became the most notorious child in the history of the Cambridge Harmony PTA.

I.

First Flasher

My most vivid memory of third grade is when a child named Marie pushed me up against the wall in our classroom and showed me her ass.

"You with your cucumber sandwiches!" she screamed, fat round face flaming and hard fingers gripping my shoulders. She shoved me once more, stepped back a few paces, pulled her corduroys down. And mooned.

It wasn't the first bottom I'd seen, but it was the first to be forced upon me.

Why did she care about the sandwiches? Was there something wrong with them? They *were* cucumber, but in my defense, they weren't those delicate little tea things with the crusts cut off and the dark green rinds scraped into the garbage pail. They were made with whole wheat bread that had large sesame seeds in it, and my thick slices of cucumber were burdened with circles of waxy peel.

Marie was new at Cambridge Harmony K through Twelve.

She had only been there a week. The kids in my class had been instructed to open our hearts to her, and we had all sung a special welcome song on the first day of her arrival. Cambridge Harmony was full of ideals. The walls were painted sunny colors, the teachers wore long braids and flat sandals, we studied the American Indian and sang songs like "This World Is Ours to Share" at assemblies. Everyone believed that children were free spirits, really in touch with the essence of life—so we shouldn't be restricted by too many rules and schedules.

When Marie flashed me, I assumed it was my fault. I hadn't opened my heart enough—had done something to anger her. Something to do with the sandwiches, perhaps.

Had she asked me for one? I couldn't remember. I had definitely held her hand like I was supposed to when we had all crossed the street on the way to the library, even though I would have preferred to hold Luke Sherwin's. She couldn't be mad about that.

Maybe it was something to do with bottoms, and that was why she was showing me hers. Had I done something to her in the bathroom, when the girls trooped in there before recess? I wiped, I flushed, I washed my hands so long as a teacher was looking. But it could be I had broken some bathroom rule that no one had ever explained to me, and Marie was inflicting punishment. Or maybe there was something particularly horrible about my own bottom, and she was waving her legitimate one at me in triumph.

I did have an annoying delicacy about me that cried out for teasing and torture. It was pretty easy to make me cry by tying my shoelaces together or sticking a sign on my back. Snowball fights and games of Keep Away made me nervous. So did sports where you had to throw a ball, or those circle games where people have to stand in the center and be It. I was tiny, with frail bones and arms that seemed a trifle too long for my body. I was also an only child and used to a quiet house, so the jostling noise of roly-poly boys often sent me shrinking into the corner of the classroom, where I'd commune with the family of mice that lived there in a Habitrail.

I was a picky eater, too, and despaired of finishing my lunch most days—packed as it was with earnest vegetarian goodies like yogurt swirled with honey. I did have one good friend I'd made back in kindergarten, however: a fast-talking Indian girl named Anu Bhaduri. She gave me the sliced chicken from her lunch box and created a little haze of warmth around my nervous frame. With Anu I became gossipy and extremely verbal, dictating the ongoing adventures of a pair of soggy stuffed rabbits that lived in the "quiet area" of our orange-painted classroom and raising my hand during Circle of Sharing to answer the teachers' questions.

But Anu was absent the day Marie showed me her bottom. She had been absent four or five days in a row, and without her I was a vulnerable target. The shoulders were squeezed, the insult hissed, the ass displayed.

I burst into tears.

"Vanessa, what's wrong?" My braided teacher kneeled down to my level. Marie had vanished, and I was left sniffing and whimpering as a cluster of people gathered around me.

I couldn't answer. The whole thing was so unspeakable. Marie had enveloped me in a kind of intimacy I'd never asked for. Suddenly—although the whole thing had happened right in the middle of the classroom—there was something private between us. She had made it private by showing me her private little butt cheeks, and now that I had seen them, it was nobody's business but our own.

Plus, I knew too much about schoolyard dynamics to risk a public explanation. That's the thing about being a victim of persecution. Talking about it lets everyone know that someone out there finds you worthy of scorn. It gives them ideas.

I didn't tell my mother, either. She noticed my tear-streaked face when she picked me up at 2:15, but she didn't focus in on it very much. She was trying to drive.

"Did you fall down?" she asked me.

I nodded.

"Man. Do you have a boo-boo?"

I shook my head no.

"Well, that's good." She shot her hand out to signal a right turn. My mother always used her hand signals. It made her feel like an especially capable driver. Back then, little kids never wore seat belts, so she was always slamming her right arm across my chest whenever we stopped, then grabbing the steering wheel again real fast so she could wave her left arm out the window.

She was a very liberated woman, my mother—in a limited way. Her name was Debbie Brick, born Deborah May Delancey. She talked a lot about "the establishment" and listened to folk music; her hair was very long and parted in the middle. She earned money by answering telephones and typing in a real estate office, and she called her boss Martin instead of Mister Goldsmith. She had asked me to call her Debbie instead of Mom.

Debbie drove her own car and rented her own apartment, and

when she went to work, she wore very short skirts and clean white stockings. My father didn't live with us. He lived in California, and the subject of my parents' divorce was all but unmentionable. Debbie was never the sort to muse over old photographs, and she rarely indulged in nostalgia about the past. She lived in the current moment—just getting though the day.

I didn't know too much about my father. If I asked her about him, a look would cross her face, and she wouldn't answer. She'd start talking about something else. Vegetarianism, usually.

Debbie became a vegetarian after reading a newspaper article about slaughterhouses and cruelty to animals. It was 1964, and she'd been married for two years. Unfortunately, she read the article on Thanksgiving, and there was a turkey cooking in her oven. She didn't care. She marched right out onto the street and donated our half-cooked bird—roasting pan and all—to a lady who was walking by. The in-laws, who were "totally oblivious people who never read the newspaper," had to eat cranberry sauce and baked potatoes for dinner. There was nothing else.

In response, my father declared shortly thereafter that red meat was the source of virility and the life force. He couldn't live with someone who didn't "desecrate and consume the bodies of animals on a regular basis," said my mother, so he put all his belongings in a van and drove across the country to eat hamburgers and fried chicken. It was only a matter of time before he exploded all over the state of California.

I wasn't even a year old when he left. I hadn't seen him since. I didn't want to, in case he exploded right in front of me.

Debbie had never expected to be divorced. She was the only child of two blisteringly spotless people, whose veneer of shiny white happiness was soiled only by the number of empty scotch glasses that lay in the sink by the end of an evening. Grin, my grandmother, was a tall, stately woman who really did eat sandwiches with her pinky finger sticking out to the side. She wore a lot of discreet diamond jewelry, and men still turned to stare at her, even though she was as old as heaven, or so she said. They listened when she spoke, too, because she had a dishy French accent that came from being raised in the South of France by her adoptive parents. "South of France," that's what we always called it in my family, as if there were no particular cities or regions within it.

Grin had come to the States to go to college, and she met Pompey, my grandfather, when she was only twenty. He loved to tell the story of how he proposed to her. It would change every time he told it, depending on how many glasses were melting their ice in the kitchen sink, and she would pinch his arm in satisfaction and call him Theodore in a scoldy kind of way. One time he proposed to her in a supermarket near the bread bin; another he took her on a rowboat ride and proposed under the August moon. Or he hurt his knee in a skiing accident and proposed when she visited him in the hospital. No matter how he said he asked, her answer was always the same: "Theodore, what took you so long?"

Pompey was a lawyer, which Debbie said meant he helped make the streets safe for children by putting mean people behind bars. It also meant they had extra bedrooms in their house in Chicago, and you could go up on the roof there and sit in deck chairs and look at the lake. Their house had a shelf full of mysterious items: a glass kaleidoscope, thick paperweights with pressed flowers inside, several amethysts and other big stones split in half to display their colored, rock candy insides. There was a small sculpture of a naked lady, and a bowl of ceramic fruit that Pompey would always offer me. But I was too big to be fooled.

So they had this perfect marriage, as Grin called it, and Debbie was expected to have one of her own. She grew up the center of Grin's world, a prom queen, an A student, a popular girl in pastel colors. "I was homecoming queen," she used to tell me, "and I wore a pink dress with a big skirt. They put a crown on my head, and I got to dance with the prince." There was a picture of her from that night, one of the few family photographs I was ever allowed to see. Her hair was puffed up on top of her head, and her dress had sparkles all around the neck and sleeves, and the heels of her shoes were so tiny! She was holding a fat bouquet of flowers. "My date was supposed to bring me a corsage," Debbie said when she showed me the picture. "So I could pin it on my dress. But he brought the bouquet instead. I had to leave it at home. All the girls thought he hadn't brought me *anything*."

"Who was he?"

"Not your daddy," she answered. "Don't go getting any ideas."

The story of how Debbie met my father was never told to me. She went to college but never finished, and we all lived in Boston until the turkey debacle. Then Jordy left for California, Debbie became a divorcée, and she and I moved into the lower floor of a house near Harvard Square.

Pompey said good riddance to that good-for-nothing husband, but Grin still called Debbie "Mrs. Jordan Brick" when she mailed envelopes from Chicago.

Debbie parked the car in front of Katty Sherwin's house, a tiny white duplex with an overgrown yard. She took out a tissue and helped me blow my nose, but she didn't ask *how* I fell down. "You're a big girl now, Vanessa," she said encouragingly. And contradictorily: "It's okay to cry."

Luke Sherwin and I had known each other since we were two, and over the years had developed an imaginary world. We would play dress-up a lot, pulling clothes out of my closet or from a big trunk of old stuff he had in the upstairs of his house. Our favorite thing was a record I had of Mary Martin playing Peter Pan in the Broadway show. We'd run all around the apartment squealing with excitement.

"They're in a frenzy!" Katty Sherwin would say as she ashed her menthol. "A complete and utter frenzy." Katty had red hair and four children. Luke was the youngest, and the other three lived with their dad in a big house that had a trampoline in the backyard.

I don't know how Luke felt, but I felt mildly ashamed and also proud when Katty said we were in a frenzy. It was as if she was admiring our incredible energy, our sheer animal power, but also like she was laughing at us. Like she knew something about our frenzy that we didn't, and was telling my mother she knew. "*Peter Pan* always puts them in a frenzy," she'd repeat, every time it happened.

There was something so thrilling about the scene in which Peter pretends to be a beautiful lady seducing Hook, who wears a big poofy wig and velvet clothes. And about the crocodile who patrols the seas of Neverland in search of another taste of the most delicious flesh he's ever eaten: Hook's missing hand.

We acted out the parts. Luke couldn't be Peter (that was for girls) and he couldn't be Wendy (that was definitely for girls), so sometimes he'd be Hook, and very often he was the crocodile, and every once in a while Tiger Lily or the Lost Boys. Our mothers would smoke in the kitchen and complain that there were no good men anymore in Cambridge, and Katty'd say she was thinking about going out in the woods to beat drums and get in touch with her femininity. My mother would debate shaving her legs again after all these years, and Luke and I would go to Neverland.

The next day at school, however, we'd have nothing to say to each other. Sometimes Luke would come up to me, like when I was swinging on the tire swing and he wanted to get on, but Anu would say loudly, "No Boys Allowed!" and put her arms around me.

"No Boys Allowed!" I would echo, and Luke would walk away as if he hadn't intended to play with me anyway.

That afternoon, though, we didn't listen to *Peter Pan*. The record was at my house. It was a warm October day, so we got out these fat colored chalks and took the best plastic animals out of Luke's room, and sat in the driveway drawing pictures on the hard, black asphalt. Debbie and Katty sat in lounge chairs under plaid blankets, watching us.

"Can you take Vanessa Saturday night?" My mother put her hands together in front of her chest like an angel. "Have her sleep over?"

"This Saturday?" asked Katty. "I don't see why not."

"I'm thinking about screwing Sydney Wheeler."

"Sydney, Sydney, Sydney," said Katty, as if she couldn't place the face.

"The guy with the mustache from the Labor Day picnic," my mother prodded.

"Oh, Syd!" Katty laughed. "Syd who used to go around with Penny Shumacher, right?"

"I think so," answered Debbie in a territorial way, and lit another menthol.

"He's a nice guy. I met him at the ashram."

They were silent for a while. Except for visiting Grin and Pompey in Chicago, I had never slept anywhere but in my own bed.

"So can you take her overnight?" my mother asked. Luke was trying to get a small toy soldier to straddle a rubber duck. I had a horse with plastic hair on the mane.

"Sure," answered Katty. And after a minute added, "But what about the boy-girl thing?"

"What about it?"

"When Malcolm sleeps over, they go head to toe in Luke's bed. Should I do that with Vanessa?"

"Well, they're hardly going to get it on!" My mother cracked up. "Let them take a bath together as far as I'm concerned. Man, I don't care."

Luke was still struggling with the soldier. Its legs wouldn't come apart wide enough to encircle anything but the duck's neck.

What did she mean, "get it on"? I would get on the bed, certainly, if I was sleeping there.

"I don't think so," said Katty, with finality in her voice. "Why doesn't Vanessa bring a sleeping bag? Would you like to bring a sleeping bag, Vanessa?" she called over.

I nodded. That was clearly the right answer.

We all went out for pizza. Debbie didn't eat meat, so we couldn't go for burgers like regular people. The Italian place was right near Harvard Square and had red-and-white checkered tablecloths. College students sat in big groups all around, drinking beer and getting huge pizzas to share. The grown-ups got peppers and onions. Luke and I got a small plain one together. He took all his cheese off so it looked like brains on his plate. He ate that part first, and then he licked the crust.

"Don't play with your food, Luke," Katty said absently. "Debbie, did I ever tell you about Chuck Reddon, that boy I dated in high school?"

"The one who serenaded you?"

"No, that was Michael. Chuck was the one who tried to cook me spaghetti one day when his parents were out of town."

"You never told me."

"It was such a trip. I came over, and he had this bottle of wine. We drank it, and drank it—and one thing led to another on the Hide-A-Bed. He had his hands down my pants, I know that for sure. And then we started smelling smoke."

"No!"

"Yes! The tomato sauce was scorching, and the fire alarm went off, and the neighbors started banging on the door. Chuck's pants were tangled down around his ankles, and he was hopping around trying to get them up again. Didn't know whether to turn off the stove or answer the knock!"

"Freaky." My mother drank some beer.

"Why were his pants off?" Luke wanted to know.

"It's complicated, honey." Katty took a bite of pizza. "I don't think I can explain it." And then, to Debbie, "Will you look at the size of that one?" A football player type was lurching toward the door, surrounded by his buddies.

"I should have finished college." Debbie sighed, wiping her mouth. "I think I really missed out."

"They weren't so big in my day. These guys are enormous."

"They look like meat-eaters to me." Debbie laughed. "Check out the guy in the corner."

I ate the crust first because it was the worst part and saved the nice pointy tip for last, and my pizza was at that crucial moment when it's a little too large to hold easily and very floppy from having no crust—but I looked up to see who Debbie was pointing at. A thin guy in a blue T-shirt was eating a salad. He was talking to a lady in a flowered miniskirt.

"Not my type," said Katty. "You can have him."

"What do you mean, she can have him?" I asked.

Katty burst into laughter. "It's like when you look in the window at the toy store," she explained. "You know how you pick out which stuffed animals you like even though you're not going to really buy anything?"

"Uh-huh."

"Like that. We're just window shopping. And your mommy can have that skinny boy, so long as I get"—she lifted herself up out of the booth to get a better view of the whole restaurant—"that one over there in the Yale T-shirt."

Luke took another piece of pizza and flopped it cheese side down onto the table. He reached for the oregano and sprinkled it all over the doughy underside and then put a little on his head for good measure.

"They're not boys, they're grown-ups," I said.

"They're boys to us," Debbie said, patting my hair.

"Anyway," Katty continued, "Chuck and I broke up about two weeks later. I couldn't take him seriously after that. I always saw him hopping around with his thing hanging out, and the smoke billowing from the kitchen. I never felt the same way about him again."

"He cooked for you, though," Debbie pointed out, as Luke rubbed the upside-down pizza in circles on the Formica.

"I didn't get to eat any of it." Katty shrugged. "So what was the use?"

"Am I going home this weekend?" Luke pulled on his mother's sweater.

For a minute, no one said anything.

"You live at home with me, Luke," Katty almost whispered. "You know that."

"I know. I mean, am I going to Daddy's?"

"No, honey. You're not." Katty took a paper napkin and started wiping up the spilled oregano and tomato sauce. "Vanessa's coming over."

The next day was Tuesday, and I spent the entire morning in a state of terror, lest Marie show any more of her body parts to me. I kept myself safe by sitting at a table right next to the desk of our man teacher, Ron. We had a man teacher and a woman teacher, and at Cambridge Harmony the kids milled around the classroom "making individual choices" and "developing at their own personal growth pace." I didn't actually know the woman teacher's name, even though it was practically Halloween, because I missed the first day of school. She was one of those people who asks children what their names are but doesn't respond by telling them her own. She just assumed we all knew it, like she was famous.

My personal growth pace that day was to sit as close to Ron as he would let me in case Marie attacked again. I was wearing shorts under my dress because I figured she might take it into her head to yank my skirt up, and I had thrown my cucumber sandwich into a garbage can in the hallway before hanging up my coat. I had a reading book to work through, one with a green-and-purple turtle on the cover. I thought it was great. You got to practice the hard words in each story before reading the whole thing. You could also write in it with a pencil if you wanted to, circling things you didn't understand, and there were worksheets in the back that were really easy, but fun anyway. Ron, with his fuzzy brown mustache curling down at the ends and a pencil tucked behind his ear, would check me off each time I finished a section.

"Vanessa." Half an hour before lunch, he looked at me. "I wonder if you might like to go over to the music area and explore?"

There was a music area with a tape recorder and cassettes of folk singers and classical piano. You could put on headphones and listen to "Koombaya" or Minuet in G without bothering anybody, and there were sheets of song lyrics and a bunch of musical theory cards that no one had ever explained to me. No, I didn't want to go there.

"I notice you've been reading a lot," Ron observed.

"I got all the way to the story about the tiger and the red sweater. Yesterday I was only on the one about blue jays."

"Would you like to do some math? Nobody's using the multiplication board."

I shook my head.

"You want to sit next to me, is that it?"

I nodded. "Anu has the chicken pox."

"I heard that. Do you know if she's feeling better yet?"

I didn't. My mother didn't like to call up Anu's parents. She said they were always so formal with her and she never knew what to say. They had Ph.D.'s.

"Well, I'm glad to have you sitting next to me, Vanessa," said Ron. "You can be my special friend today, my special helper if you want to."

"Okay."

"Do you want to?"

"Okay."

"That's my little crumpet." He petted my hair. "You can sit right there near me."

But soon, Ron shook a tambourine to announce the end of Work Period, and then he left the room for a break. We all sat down for lunch with the braided woman teacher.

There was no Anu to give me chicken slices or commandeer the best place in the corner by the mouse cage, so I sat at the end of a table of six. I had only yogurt and some carrots in my lunch box, because I had thrown out the sandwich. Luke was at my table, trading cookies with his friends Will and Malcolm, and he said, "Hi, Vanessa," and did I want a peanut butter cookie? I could have it, even though I had nothing to trade.

I didn't really like that kind of cookie. It was waffle-textured and had a slightly bitter taste of fake nut flavoring, but I saved it for last anyway, proud of being included. At recess, though, the boys from my table burst through the doors into the play yard without a glance backward. They had a game called Lava Monsters. Luke had explained it to me, once, but I was never invited to play. Lava monsters were chasing you, and they were all over the ground. If your feet touched the wood chips, the monsters would burn you to death, in which case you would have to yell, "Medic," and the other kids would carry you to the main climber and nurse you back to health with magic ice power.

I didn't want to play, anyway. I wasn't sure what lava was, even though I had looked it up in the dictionary. The whole idea of liquid rock just didn't make sense.

So I went over by the swing set and stood there waiting for a swing. They had this rule where you could only go on for five minutes at a time if someone else was waiting, and there was even a big clock up in the playground to keep track by, but some people ignored it. Angelique and Didi were on the swings, singing,

Down, down baby,
Down by the roller coaster
Sweet, sweet baby,
I don't wanna let you go!
Shimmy, shimmy coco pop
Shimmy, shimmy POW!
Shimmy, shimmy coco pop
Shimmy, shimmy POW!

Actually, to this day I'm not sure if it was coco pop or coco puff. Puff was a cereal I saw advertised on television, and pop sounded like chocolate-flavored soda. Maybe the song was about something else. It gave me a déjà vu feeling—like I'd heard it long ago when I was a baby, too little to remember who sang it to me. There was something desperate in it, like the singer was going downhill on a roller coaster of despair. His girl didn't love him no more.

"Waiting for a swing." Marie's voice sounded hot and wet in my ear, and she put her thick palm on my shoulder. "Waiting for a swing, waiting for a swing!" She said it like an insult.

"So?" I turned to face her. "I was here first. I've been here four minutes."

"I'm not waiting." She laughed and ran over to the merry-go-round.

Why was it dumb to be waiting? People waited for swings all the time. Or was she telling me I was under her watchful eye, that she knew what I was doing at every moment?

"Come get on!" Marie called. "I'll push you." The merry-go-round was one of those big metal disks with bars on top.

"I'm waiting here," I said. But at that moment, Didi jumped off her swing and grabbed the chain, holding it possessively. "I've been saving it for Summer!" she yelled, and Summer, dropping her jacks on the asphalt with a satisfied smile, ran over and hopped on.

"I was waiting!" I cried, looking back and forth between Summer and Marie. Marie said nothing to back me up.

"So was I," said Summer with total confidence. "I was waiting over there!" She pointed to the square of asphalt where people were playing jacks.

"That's not waiting!" I said.

"Yes, it is," she said, beginning to pump her legs.

"You can't wait and play jacks!"

"Yes, she can," said Didi, standing six inches taller than me and wearing pink.

Down, down baby,
Down by the roller coaster,
Sweet, sweet baby,
I don't wanna let you go!

Angelique and Summer were swinging in sync, now.

He drank up all the water
He ate up all the soap!
He tried to eat the bathtub
But it wouldn't go down his throat!

"Vanessa, get on!" cried Marie.

And so I did.

I sat down near the edge of the merry-go-round, grabbing on to a bar. Marie bent her sturdy knees and pushed. Her red corduroys strained with the effort of her legs, and her tongue stuck out the side of her mouth. I giggled at first, but soon I was spinning much faster than I was used to.

"Slow down!" I called, but Marie's hands went from bar to bar, building up speed. Maybe it would be less dizzying in the middle of the big metal circle. I tried to pull myself up to standing.

"Not so fast!" I yelled. "It's making me sick!" Was Marie just oblivious and trying to give me a really good push? Maybe she was like a big, overeager dog that doesn't know when she's hurting someone. But why wouldn't she stop pushing, then, when I was asking her over and over?

"Stop, Marie! Stop!" I cried, staggering toward the center of the circle. And then my head hit one of the hard metal bars, and

I was vomiting peanut butter waffle cookie and sour yogurt all over the front of my dress.

When the merry-go-round stopped turning, I looked up. Marie was gone. I sat, dizzy, there in the center of the big metal disk, wiping my mouth and feeling the bump above my right ear swell beneath my hand.

The nurse's name was Betty. Her office was cool and white, with posters of kittens on the wall. She had come to our class in September to talk about safety, so I knew who she was. She didn't wear a nurse's outfit like in books. Just regular clothes.

"Did you eat something unusual today, Vanessa?" she asked me, giving me a piece of ice wrapped in a washcloth to put on my head.

"No."

"What did you have for lunch?"

I didn't want my mom to find out about the peanut butter cookie, because I wasn't sure whether I was supposed to have things for lunch that weren't what she packed for me. "Um, yogurt and some carrots," I said.

"That's all?"

"Uh-huh."

"No sandwich or anything?"

I couldn't tell her I threw it away, so I burst into tears.

Betty the nurse came out and talked to my mother near the car after school. She said she was concerned that Vanessa wasn't being given enough for lunch. Hunger and fatigue could make a kid puke, she said.

Debbie didn't comment. She just nodded at Betty and said she was sorry, she didn't realize. She would never intentionally send me to school without enough food.

"Somebody pushed me on the merry-go-round," I said, as my mother waved her arm in a right-turn signal.

"Really? That's great, sugar."

"No, she pushed me!"

"What do you mean?

"She pushed me and I threw up."

"Who pushed you?"

"Marie."

"Who is Marie?"

"A kid in my class. She wouldn't stop." I felt like I was going to cry.

"Did you ask her to stop?"

"Yes!"

"Because sometimes you don't speak up about things, Vanessa. Other people aren't psychic, you know."

2.

Anu, the Way She Was

My participation in Super Duper Spelling would one day lead to my evaluation by psychology professionals and the disturbance of many people's peace—but at the time, I thought it was tremendous fun. We met on Tuesday afternoons, a group of third- and fourth-graders who were ready to spell advanced words. At the end of the previous year we had all taken a test to see who belonged in it.

Me, Anu, and Luke belonged. Every Tuesday at 1:45 we'd follow Ron to a room on the top floor of Cambridge Harmony. There were no spelling books and no worksheets; each of us had a big red dictionary with the word Collegiate on it, and that was it. As soon as we got up there, we'd have a test on the words from the week before.

Notorious.

Precarious.

Precocious.

Nefarious.

Then we'd learn the words for the new week. There was usually some kind of phonic theme.

Measure.

Pleasure.

Treasure.

Azure.

Any word we really wanted to know, we could bring in and learn to spell together. Dirigible. Deluxe. Antidisestablishmentarianism. So far, I had only brought in Herbivore.

Anu came back to school on Wednesday, and I got to teach her the best new word she had missed. Incident: noun. An event that interrupts everyday life. As soon as she got her coat off, we huddled together in the corner by the mouse cage while I explained it to her.

I was a little frightened by how different she looked after being sick. There were chicken pox spots all over her arms and face. Before, I had had a kind of sensual fascination with Anu's warm, brown body—especially her hair. It was long and black like a princess in a storybook, and she tucked it behind her ears. Her hair was what first made me want to be friends with her. Her hair and a pair of sandals she had that were covered with purple plastic flowers.

Now she was the same old Anu with the same hair and the same chicken slices in her lunch box, but her skin was raised in pinky-white scabs. I felt repelled by them, especially the ones on her neck—and later I begged my mother that if I got chicken pox she wouldn't make me go to school until every single spot had disappeared. She wouldn't promise.

Anu didn't mind the pox. Her arms and face were shiny with the vitamin E oil her mother rubbed on to prevent scarring, but she never seemed embarrassed. She'd show me a particularly nasty one every now and then, and I had to pull away a little when she clutched my arm by the mouse cage and whispered, "I had a chicken pock in my throat. All the way down my throat, and it itched and itched! I had to cough to scratch it, and when I drank orange juice, it stung going down!"

"Is it catching?" I asked.

"Not anymore." She shook her head sagely. "You can only get it once."

Later, sitting in Circle of Sharing with the rest of our class, I felt a measure of pride in Anu, mixed with my repulsion. There was a new, benevolent possessiveness in my friendship with her—as if she were a mangled toy that I still loved because I wasn't materialistic. I didn't care if she was ugly and poxy now, even though she used to be so beautiful. I was loyal.

"Anu had a chicken pock in her throat!" I told Luke in the play yard. "She had to cough real hard in order to scratch it."

"Did she have any on her tongue?" asked Luke, picking his nose.

"I don't know."

"Did she have any on her butt?" He bent over in a fit of giggles. "Did she have chicken pox on her butt?"

"She had them all over." I shrugged. But I was secretly worried. Had Luke seen what Marie did to me? Was there some reason people kept fixating on bottoms?

Anu ran over with a small piece of slate she'd found under a tree. "Look at this," she cried, tugging my arm. "It's precious silver."

"Let me see," said Luke, leaning over her hand. He reached out and touched a pockmark on her wrist.

"Get away!" Anu scurried over to another corner of the playground.

I followed, leaving Luke alone. Not even looking back.

"We are a private club," Anu scolded me, over in the corner by a big maple tree that was just beginning to shed its leaves. "No Boys Allowed."

"No Boys Allowed," I repeated.

Anu's hands were cold in the October air. The slate was glinty and rough to the touch.

The next day, I walked home from school with Anu and her brothers. I did it most Thursdays, because Debbie worked late. There were three, two older and one younger: Samir, Ram, and Baby. Samir was twelve and didn't want to walk home with us at all—wanted to stay and talk with girls from the middle school and maybe even smoke cigarettes—but his father made him. Baby was just a baby, only five. Not very interesting.

Ram, however, was a fourth-grader, with Anu's same dark eyelashes. He would say "Hello, Vanessa" in the hallway when the big kids were passing by our lockers. His jeans sat low on his hips in a way that I liked, and his black hair curled up a bit at the back of his neck. He had strong-looking teeth, with a gap in the middle, and sometimes after school he would play board games with us, like The Game of Life, where you drove this little car through all kinds of life events—getting married and winning the lottery—and whoever retired with the most money won. You could have up to four kids, but after that no more would fit in your car.

Once, back in second grade, Ram had said Hi to me in the

hall where Didi and Angelique could overhear. "Vanessa and Ram, sitting in a tree, K-I-S-S-I-N-G! First comes love, then comes marriage, then comes Vanessa with a baby carriage!"

Ram had only laughed and run outside.

Walking home, Anu and I always stayed about ten paces behind the boys, holding hands and chattering.

"There's this clover I know about that you can eat," Anu told me that day. "At the end of this block."

"You can't eat clover."

"Horses eat it."

"That doesn't mean we can." Anu was so funny.

"This is sour clover. It tastes sour, like sour-apple candy. Samir!" she yelled. The boys were hitting each other with sticks. "Samir, we're going where the sour clover is!"

"Okay," he said.

"Wait for us!"

They kept hitting each other, and Anu and I squeezed ourselves through a hedge on the side of the street. There was a gap in it, like kids had been going through there a lot, but I still got leaves on my dress as I went, and a branch scratched my arm a little. Inside, we were in a private corner of a small, empty park. There was a bench about ten feet away, with its back to us, and two big trees on either side. "Like a secret garden!" I said.

"Nobody knows about it."

Anu showed me some clusters of bright green clover nestling by the hedge. "Chew, don't swallow," she said, picking some and sticking it in her mouth. It had a lemony tang and made me squinch up my face. We chewed for a bit, then spat our green lumps gleefully onto the ground. "Sour clover!" announced Anu.

"How did you know you could eat it?"

"Someone told me."

"Who?" I hated it when Anu decided to be mysterious.

"This person I know."

"Who?"

"Just a person."

"Anu!" Samir stuck his head in through the gap in the hedge. "Dad will be waiting."

Anu's parents were university professors, and their house had a wealthy-shabby feel that suggested they were thinking of higher things than home decor, but could still afford a nice couch. Mrs. Bhaduri taught an afternoon class on Thursdays, so she was never home. Mister Bhaduri stayed in his study mostly and let us have the run of the place. He told me the rules the first day I came over: no knives, no dropping anything out windows, no yelling near the office door. We could eat things from the 'frigerator, and there were usually spicy Indian chickpeas in Tupperware and cold apples in the bin; they had dry chocolate cookies in a jar that flaked sugar down my chest when I ate them.

Once, Mister Bhaduri had taken me, Anu, Ram, and Samir to the track. Baby was too little to go. The family owned three race horses, he told me, but they didn't own the whole horse. Just a part of it. Not a leg or a tail, he said—it was more like owning an invisible section of the entire animal, a part of its whole horseness.

The horses were named New Year's Resolution, Bay of Biscayne, and Freedom Fighter. Mister Bhaduri didn't get to name them. They came already named. New Year's Resolution was running the day we went to the track; she was a dark brown horse with a white spot on her face. We got to meet the jockey, who stood the same height as Samir and wore shiny pink and yellow clothes.

After that day, Anu and I were obsessed. We checked out books from the library that showed all the different kinds of horses: palominos, Thoroughbreds, chestnuts, and Clydesdales. We got toy plastic horses with manes and tails of hair that you could braid, and I got a calendar with photographs of foals. We even tried to draw them, which was very hard, although Debbie helped me by showing me I wasn't making their hindquarters big enough.

That Thursday of the week before my sleepover at Luke's, Anu and I did horse stuff up in her bathroom. We filled the tub with water and had the horses taking baths and almost drowning. It was something we did a lot, and Anu always let me pick which one I wanted to play with. I remember we put Barbie outfits on them that day.

When Debbie came to pick me up, Mister Bhaduri came out of his office to offer her a glass of wine. He started slicing up raw chicken right in front of us, while they talked about the upcoming parent-teacher conferences and what they were doing for the PTA's Halloween Fright Fest. They seemed stiff with each other, and Debbie didn't take the wine.

It was the last time I ever played there.

Marie had laid low the first day Anu was back. She did sit opposite me during Circle of Sharing first thing in the morning, but I had avoided her gaze and asked Anu a lot of questions about chicken pox. Then she pretty much kept to herself, working with counting rods on a rug in the math area, or reading in the library corner. On Friday, though, just when I had the courage to leave my shorts in the drawer at home and wear a skirt the regular way, she started in again.

I was working on my diorama for Thanksgiving, which was still a month distant. We were all making them to show our respect for the Indians. (Not Anu's kind of Indians. The other kind.) Mine was made of clay and cut paper.

"You're making your diorama," Marie said, sitting down next to me.

"Yes." I focused carefully on my little statues of a woman and her papoose and another woman making some food over a fire, hoping she would go away. But Marie's fleshy white hand reached in and grabbed hold of my cook, pulling her out into the open air.

"She's making something, right?" Marie was squeezing the clay cook around the middle, putting dents in her belly.

"She's making cornbread in a pan," I explained. "Only she calls it maize. Be careful."

"How did you make the hair?" Marie lifted the hair off the cook's back, where it was supposed to stay attached. It was made of black clay, and a piece of it broke off. She picked it up from the floor and looked at it closely. "Did you roll it?"

"Don't touch it," I said. "You're breaking it."

She set the cook down on the table and took hold of the mother. "You made a baby."

"So?" What was bad about making a baby? Was she making a joke, like I made a baby and that was dirty?

"So it's a baby." Marie laughed. As she shook the mother, making her dance, one of the clay arms came off and fell underneath the table.

I shrieked. The mother had no arm, the baby had an armless mother, the cook's hair was broken, it wasn't dirty to make a baby out of clay!

"Put it down, Marie!" Anu was at the table next to us doing a science project. "We don't touch other people's dioramas."

Marie looked at her, still holding the injured mother in her hands.

"I said, don't touch it." Anu got up and came over. "Vanessa doesn't want you ruining it."

"I'm just looking," said Marie.

"You're breaking it! You're making Vanessa cry!" Anu grabbed Marie by the shoulder and shook her, hard.

Marie screamed. Was I sure she had been making fun of me?

"Give it back!" yelled Anu.

Marie clutched the broken mother, defiant or afraid, I didn't know which.

Kids were looking at us, and I was crying. Ron the teacher came over, squatted down to our level on his haunches. "Is there a conflict here?" he asked.

Marie burst into tears, too. "I'm not in trouble!" she cried. "Not in trouble."

"No one gets in trouble here at Cambridge Harmony, Marie." Ron had on his peaceful voice. "I heard some yelling when I was over in the music area. Anu, was that you?"

"Yes."

"Why were you yelling at Vanessa and Marie?"

"She wasn't." I sniffled.

"I'm asking Anu right now, Vanessa," said Ron, offering me a tissue. "Your turn will come."

"I wasn't," said Anu.

"But I heard you yelling. It looks like Vanessa and Marie are working nicely together on the dioramas. Can you tell me what the problem is?"

"She broke the mother!" Anu waved her arms in frustration.

"I did not!" countered Marie.

"You did, too!" I piped up.

"She made a baby." Marie giggled, wiping the tears from her cheeks. "Vanessa made a little baby."

"Is that Vanessa's diorama piece you've got there?" asked Ron.

"Little baby," said Marie, and handed it over.

"It is a baby, with a mother. That's very nice, Vanessa. Marie, would you like to go to the bathroom and wash your face?"

Marie didn't answer.

"I think that would be a good idea," said Ron. Obediently, Marie disappeared down the hall. "And Anu, would you like to go back to your science experiment? Summer is waiting for you."

"I want to stay with Vanessa." Anu stuck her chin in the air.

"Do you think that's really a good choice for you right now?"

"Yes."

"I think you need to go back to the science table."

"I don't need to."

"Finishing up the salt crystal project would be an appropriate activity for you to do between now and lunch."

Anu stood there, behind my chair, playing with my ponytail. "I don't want to be appropriate. I want to help put the diorama back together."

"Anu, I'm starting to feel frustrated. Don't you want to see what happens with the salt crystals?"

"You keep asking me, but I don't want to."

"Okay, Anu." Ron smiled a fake smile. "I'm not asking you.

I'm telling you. Go back to the science table and do your project with Summer."

When it was just me and Ron with the diorama, he helped me get the hair back on the cook and the arm back on the mother. We used a bit of rubber cement and everything stayed together pretty well. Ron said it was a very good diorama, and I was a talented crumpet, oops, he meant artist. I felt glad of his protection.

"Marie started the whole Incident," Anu said to me on the tire swing at recess. "I don't like her."

"How come?"

"She smells."

"Like what?"

"Like minestrone soup." Anu hated minestrone. We paused, kicking ourselves in circles with our feet, tilting our heads back and staring at the sky.

"Marie did something bad when you were home sick," I ventured.

"What?" Anu turned her head upright and stared at me. "What did she do?"

"Something that's a secret," I whispered. And suddenly, looking into Anu's wide, conspiratorial face, I realized I could turn the whole episode to my advantage. "Something's wrong with her," I said.

I put a spin on the story: Marie had shown me her ass and told me not to tell anyone. She had some weird thing about showing her ass to people. She wanted to play doctor with me but I wasn't that kind of a kid. I wasn't into playing doctor, and besides, everybody knew that was something girls and boys did together, not girls and girls. And you didn't do it right there in the middle of the classroom either. You did it down in your friend's basement rec room, or under the climber where the teachers couldn't see. Marie didn't even know how to play doctor right.

I didn't tell Anu anything about the cucumber sandwiches, or the pushing up against the wall. And I didn't tell her about the merry-go-round Incident, because I didn't come off very well in that story, and I wasn't sure exactly what had happened, anyway. I just told her about that small round bottom, waving itself at me. About the feeling of forced intimacy.

"What a Fucker," she said.

"Fuck fuck fuck fuck," I said gleefully. I knew to say it quietly so the adults couldn't hear. "What do you mean, a Fucker?"

"Someone who's into playing doctor and things," Anu explained. "Like people who have boyfriends and girlfriends. Like Didi, who wears those pink dresses and sits near Malcolm all the time. She's a Fucker."

"Didi's a Fucker."

"Yeah, and Marie is, too. Only messed up. What a weirdo."

"A super weirdo," I said.

I had a twinge of regret. I didn't have the words for it, but part of me realized I had accused Marie of more than I had intended. I hadn't meant to question her sexuality, only to mock her incompetence. (Anu and I, No Boys Allowed, disdained playing doctor but considered ourselves experts on the rules and politics of that kind of activity.) Now there was a good possibility I had branded Marie as an outsider so indelibly she would never, ever make friends at Cambridge Harmony.

Should I take it back?

I felt safe at school for the first time in several days.

Should I venture a few words in her defense?

Perhaps I could just swear Anu to secrecy.

"Hey Summer!" Anu called across the playground. "Come sit with us on the tire! I want to tell you something weird!"

Summer trotted over. Summer the swing stealer. She was the only African-American child in our class, with frizzy hair in two thick French braids across a scalp that I always wanted to touch. She was friends with me when Anu was there, but not if we were alone.

"Marie is such a weirdo. Listen up," whispered Anu, as Summer put her legs in the center of the swing.

Didi and Angelique came, too.

3.

Antelopes and Lemons

I went to Cambridge Harmony on scholarship. I found out when Luke's friend Malcolm came up to me and said, "You go free."

"What?"

"You go free. Your mom doesn't pay."

I hadn't known anybody paid. "Maybe," I said to Malcolm. "Maybe not."

"My dad says its charity."

"So what?"

"So everybody else pays. My dad pays for three kids."

It was true that most of the Cambridge Harmony kids lived in houses with pianos and dads, while Debbie and I lived in the bottom half of a two-story house that was painted a funny green color and had a tangle of herbs in the back. The guy who lived upstairs from us, Terry Mandible, creeped me out. He was always sitting in the front yard, not doing anything at all. He smelled like an old person, even though he was probably only thirty-five, and he was always commenting on my appearance. Debbie said he was trying to be friendly, but I didn't like the way he'd call over. "Hi there, Vanessa. Don't you have pretty eyes? What a pretty little girl she is there, Mrs. Brick."

He worked on and off again as a fix-it man, and came into our apartment sometimes if Debbie needed someone to repair a drip in the sink or to help build a bookshelf. I always waited in my room until he finished, but I could usually hear Debbie offer to pay for the service. Terry would decline: "I'll just take a beer," he'd say. "Beer's enough for me."

They'd drink beer in the kitchen and talk about the weather.

We didn't have enough money to go to the movies very often, and there was never enough to buy sugar cereal no matter how many times I begged, but when I asked Debbie if I went to school because of charity, she told me I went free because they especially wanted me there at Cambridge Harmony. "The teachers and Stuart the principal and everyone want you more than anybody else," she said.

Later I found out they gave scholarships to about 10 percent of the kids to get more diversity. It didn't matter to me, anyway. I just knew that Malcolm had said I was different from everybody else, and it felt like confirmation of something I had known all along.

After school on Friday, my mother took me to a camping store to shop for a sleeping bag, so she could fuck Syd Wheeler on Saturday night. Fuck, fuck, fuck, fuck. I noticed she was wearing blusher, and her lips looked shiny. Debbie was very beautiful then; she was only twenty-eight. She wore low-slung blue jeans and had very dark eyebrows. Her feet had a knobby, twisted look about them and her fingernails were short.

The sleeping bag was puffy and slick; I got to pick the color: minty green.

As soon as we got home, the phone rang.

"Syd!" my mother trilled, lighting up a cigarette and perching on a stool near the kitchen counter. "What's going on? We set for Saturday?"

The sleeping bag was stuffed into a sack that made it very small. I undid the string and pulled it out. Then I crawled in headfirst and lay there on the kitchen floor, letting the sunlight from the kitchen window shine green through the fabric. "No, I don't think so. Vanessa's not ready to meet you," Debbie said into the phone. "No, she's sleeping over with her boyfriend. . . . Yes, she has a little boyfriend."

I decided I needed my antelope, and retrieved it from the bedroom. Now it wouldn't be so lonely in the bag.

"Jordy?" my mother was saying to Syd. Jordy was my father's name. "We like to say he's in California." I could hear her take a drag on her cigarette and blow out the smoke. "It's a long story. Not in front of the k-i-d."

I decided I needed my tongue twister book, and maybe one about horses, too. Then it wouldn't be so boring in the bag.

"A black T-shirt and blue jeans," my mother was saying when I got back from my bedroom. I crawled back into the bag and got comfortable. "Suede boots."

"I'm wearing my tulip skirt and my pink sweater!" I yelled from inside the bag.

"Yes, I am," said my mother. "Do you want me to take it off?"

"Are we having eggplant for dinner? I saw eggplants on the counter!"

"Uh-huh," she murmured to Syd. "Sometimes it's itchy. But not always."

"I only like it with tomato sauce!" Sometimes she chopped it up with zucchini, instead.

"Okay." I heard her giggle. "I'm free now. Are you happy?"

"What's your favorite color?" I asked the antelope. "Mine is minty green." Lopey's favorite color was yellow. All antelopes like yellow. It's just something about them. *"What's your favorite color, Debbie?"* I called.

"I gotta go, Syd. Vanessa's acting up."

I decided I needed my music box and went to the bedroom to get it. When I got back, my mother was slicing eggplant for dinner, and her bra was on the counter.

Debbie had decorated my bedroom herself with large sculpture-paintings made out of plywood and paint. She had painted my bed frame yellow, and the headboard was covered with shells she glued on after we went to the beach one summer. She was always painting things, particularly stuff in my room. But she never showed any of it to people who came over.

Right above my yellow shell bed was a long, horizontal window, like people sometimes have over their kitchen counters. Before the building was converted to apartments, Debbie said, the kitchen must have been larger, and my bedroom must have been a part of it. I liked having a view of the backyard.

That night, after our eggplant, my mother and I sat in my room working on my Halloween costume. The Cambridge Harmony PTA put on a Fright Night party every year, with a haunted house, and food tables, and games. All the moms and dads wore costumes, and the bigger kids ran booths with bake sale items and glow-in-the-dark yo-yos for charity.

I was going to be a mouse. Debbie had bought two gray sweaters from Goodwill and was sewing them into a suit. My legs were going in the arms of the bigger sweater, and she was making the tail out of gray felt.

"I want to have ears with pink inside," I told my mother.

"I can do that," she said. "I think I even have some pink felt left over from last year." The previous Halloween, when I was only a second-grader, I had been Glinda the Good Witch of the North. "Do you want to have paws, or do you want to have your hands free?"

"Paws."

"Are you sure? You might not be able to eat your candy."

"It'll look better with paws."

"I think they're going to give you trouble."

"Okay, no paws."

"Okay."

I was doing finger-knitting, a thing you did with yarn on your fingers to make a thick chain that looked really neat. Debbie bent over her sewing basket to find the pink felt. When she sat back up, though, a strange look went across her face and she drew her breath in sharply.

"Vanessa, cover your eyes," she said in a tense voice.

"What?" I said. "Why?"

"Just cover them." She got up and put her fingers over my face so I couldn't see. Her hands felt cool and bony.

"Is there a secret?" I asked.

"No, no."

"Is something wrong?"

"No. Stay like this for a second. Are your eyes shut?"

"Yes."

She took one hand away from my face and banged hard on the horizontal window above my bed.

"Why are you banging?" I said, face squinched up.

"I have a reason, sugar. Don't worry about it." She hit the glass again and put her hand back over my eyes.

We sat like that for a minute, on my yellow shell bed. Then she let me go.

"All done, sugar," she said brightly. She was breathing hard. I waited for her to explain herself, but she didn't say anything.

We sat there in silence.

"Look what I finger-knitted!" I held up my hand for her to see. I had multicolored yarn, so it looked like a rainbow.

"Wow, that's very long, Vanessa," she said, lighting a cigarette with shaking fingers. "That must have taken a lot of work."

"Um-hmm. Anu made one that was rainbow like this, but it's only like a few inches."

"Would you like some curtains for your window?" Debbie asked, ignoring what I said. "I could make you some with antelopes if you want. Or horses."

"Not really," I said.

"I'd like to make you curtains. Any kind you want."

"Okay," I said. "Antelopes with lemons."

"With lemons?" She smiled a tense smile with too many teeth.

"Yeah."

"Okay, Vanessa. Antelopes with lemons it is." We packed up our stuff and went into the living room to finish my mouse suit.

I didn't ask her what she saw through the window. But even if I had, there's no way she would have told me the truth.

4.

Two Parrots

Luke's mom, Katty, was several years older than Debbie. She got involved with the Alexian Ashram in 1968, but before that, she had been a Radcliffe girl, which I understood to mean she wore pastel bikinis and teased her hair up high. She was the only daughter of some dairy farmers in Vermont, and had been Miss Cream and Butter 1955 at the age of seventeen. Though her grades were only average, Katty had steered the prom committee, headed the cheerleading team, and been a state champion backstroker. She had also (and this was "probably the kicker," Katty used to say), won the Vermont Science Fair award by creating a three-dimensional graph of the considerations involved in breeding dairy cows. So Radcliffe let her in.

At college, her bright red hair, big titties, and tiny stature had attracted scores of "Harvard men," and one of them took her to a nightclub in New York City where Dean Martin told her she had a fine set of curves. She studied art history and generally treated the Radcliffe education as an M.R.S. degree.

Katty was a bit fast for Radcliffe's conservative set—but she "never was a hippie or anything," she'd explain as she pushed me and Luke on a cart through the supermarket. Luke would tune out and suck on the beak of his favorite rubber duck, occasionally pointing urgently at sugar cereal or cake mix, but I usually asked questions when Katty talked about her past. It was a good way to find out grown-up stuff that Debbie never wanted to get into.

Her senior year at college, Katty met Randy Sherwin. He was a New Hampshire boy studying engineering at MIT, different from the athletic future lawyers of America who carried her books across Harvard yard. So Katty "let him take me, and don't ask me what that means because you'll find out when you're older." They got married over the Christmas holidays. Right after she graduated, Luke's brother Pal was born (his real name was Randolph, after his dad). Katty was a housewife and had three more kids: Bart, Turner, and Luke. Everything went along pretty normal and happy—and then Randy had an affair with a fellow engineer who was flat as a pancake.

Katty found out and told Randy she was leaving. She took baby Luke, who was only two, and moved out of the big Boston house with the trampoline in the backyard to her duplex in Cambridge, where the Harvard men still stared at her when she walked through the square. Living on a hefty alimony check, she took pottery lessons and learned to work a loom. Katty wanted to get back to the kind of Vermont craftsmanship that she associated with her childhood. That was one of the bases of her friendship with my mother. They would spend hours in the yarn shop or the craft store buying supplies, and in October they'd both sew ornate Halloween costumes.

Randy still loved Katty, despite everything. One time she showed me a love letter he wrote to her years after she had left his house. She didn't let me read it, but I guess she was so excited she had to at least *show* it to somebody. "I'm the love of his life," she told me. He had broken up with the flat-chested engineer ages ago and was asking Katty to come back, but she didn't want to.

Katty got involved with the ashram to quit smoking. She had tried cold turkey, and tried smoking only three a day, and also smoking a million cigarettes until she puked, but nothing worked. She tried bubble gum, too, and for a while when Luke and I were five, she smelled like sticky sugar all the time.

On her first visit to the ashram she was smoking two packs a day *and* chewing gum. The adventure effected an instant fashion change, if nothing else. Whereas when Luke and I were three she wore pointy brassieres and candy colors, postashram Katty wore her red frizz "natural" and her clothes the color of the earth.

"I was starving!" she said after the first week she spent there. "The food was totally anemic. You couldn't get a slice of beef to save your life."

"That's good." My mother laughed. She and Katty never fought about vegetarianism.

"Beans, beans, and then lentils and more beans," Katty complained. "Then maybe a bit of squash for dessert."

But she went back, because the guru there was so completely charismatic. Her name was Alex, and she had a small following of people who took seminars and workshops at the ashram, which was only a couple hours' drive from Cambridge. Katty liked having a female guru. It made her feel feminist and liberated to be worshiping someone with a vagina. Not like Jesus or

God, and not like the Virgin Mary, who never seemed to have any private parts whatsoever.

My knowledge of the Alexian compound was culled from overhearing grown-up conversations, but in addition to the bean-eating, it was pretty clear that people paid their respects to Alex every morning at some kind of assembly, and would then throw whatever they wanted to get rid of into a big ceramic garbage bin called the Receptacle.

Receptacle: noun. Something that holds objects or liquids. Container.

"Did you put your cigarettes in?" my mother asked.

"Yes," Katty answered. "And I also put in all my anger at Randy and the bunions on my feet."

"How do you put anger in?"

"You channel it into an object first thing in the morning before the assembly, and then you put the object in the Receptacle. You say a prayer right before you drop it in."

"What object did you use?"

"I used my bra," said Katty. "I was ready to get rid of it anyway. I filled that bra up with Randy's infidelity, and that flat-chested engineer, and the late alimony checks, and the missed parent-teacher meetings. Let me tell you, that bra was bursting at the seams like it was carrying a pair of double Ds."

"And you're not mad about those things anymore?"

Katty lit up a menthol. "I can't *believe* he missed three parent-teacher meetings." She was almost spitting the words out. "I want to fucking kill him."

There was a silence.

"I don't think your bra was big enough," my mother said.

"It doesn't always work the first time," explained Katty, inhaling deeply.

And so she went back to the ashram every couple months for a short stay. She never stopped smoking, but she'd lose about five pounds each time from the change in diet, and she'd come back all peaceful and full of generosity toward everyone. She started making homemade yogurt in a funny machine with milk from her parents' dairy. Randy objected to the whole thing and called it a cult one day in front of me and Luke, but Katty said it was opening her up emotionally and he was benefiting from it more than he knew, so he might as well just kiss her ass.

Then at one point, maybe three months before the sleepover, something happened. Two people from the Alexian Ashram fell in love with each other. They were both heavy into Alex and her teachings and lived at the compound. The woman was a tennis pro, and the man was a journalist who had a lot of free time. They were meditating and bean-eating and putting things in the Receptacle just like everyone else, only she would pop over to his room every night so they could rip off all their clothes. After a while, they realized they were deeply in love and asked Alex to perform a marriage ceremony.

But Alex said no. They had misdirected their loyalty and were too focused on each other. The affair was distracting them from their spiritual paths. They needed to concentrate on her and her teachings, not be screwing each other when they were supposed to be doing meditative sleep.

The journalist and the tennis pro disagreed. "We're in love," they said.

"You are deluded by sex," she told them, "and it's warping

your priorities. Don't see each other anymore if you want to remain members of the Alexian Ashram."

The couple was totally devastated, left the ashram immediately, and got married. It was all in a magazine. He wrote the story himself.

After that, Katty put her bra back on and started buying peanut butter waffle cookies instead of honey carob wafers. She still went for weekend workshops every now and again, but without the same urgency she had had before. I think she liked the idea of herself as the sort of person who went to an ashram more than she liked the actual thing, anyway.

On Saturday, the Saturday my mother was thinking about sleeping with Syd Wheeler, Katty made hot dogs for dinner, which seemed to me like ambrosia from the Gods of Television, a food that normal people ate. Debbie had kissed me good-bye at five o'clock and gone off in the car, but she came back at five-thirty because we had forgotten to bring my sleeping bag.

"Where's he taking you?" Katty asked, her mouth full.

"Some freaky French movie." Debbie kissed my head again, made a quick disparaging comment about meat, and disappeared out the door.

After dinner, we drove to the ice cream parlor in Katty's station wagon. The car was great because Luke and I could get in the way back and moon the people in the vehicles behind us.

There's a place called France
Where the ladies wear no pants
And the men don't care,
'Cause they've got no underwear!

It was really funny. Even Katty thought so. Sometimes the people would wave at us, or gives us a thumbs-up sign, and sometimes they'd look really irate and shocked. We tried to predict how they'd react ahead of time, but we weren't often right.

On the way home, we lay in the back with our heads beneath the window and looked up at the sky.

"We're flying up to heaven," I said to Luke.

"Like on a carpet," he said.

"Yeah, on a carpet we can steer." My mouth tasted sweet from mint–chocolate chip aftertaste and my skin felt cold and sticky.

"Did the chicken pox make it so Anu couldn't eat?" Luke put his hands on the slanted window and made fingerprints. "The ones in her throat?"

"She got to have Jell-O," I said.

"How come?"

"You get soft things if your throat is sick. She got Jell-O and ice cream and soda and yogurt."

"But she could chew, right?"

"Yeah."

"What about Cream of Wheat?"

"I don't know."

"What about yogurt with bits of fruit in it, like strawberries?"

"I don't know."

"This is important!" Luke giggled. "I need to know in case I get chicken pox."

"You already had chicken pox!" Katty yelled back from the driver's seat.

"I did?"

"When you were four. You got them from Pal."

"I already had them," said Luke, like he was trying on a new identity.

When we got back home, Katty settled down to watch a scary movie on TV. Luke and I went up to his room, and I could hear the music coming up from downstairs, making the hallway seem like a breeding ground for bogeymen and kidnappers.

Luke's walls were papered with pictures of boats: ocean liners and tugboats, ferry boats and sailboats. The bathroom was even better. It was allover horses. I would forget to pee, touching the slightly bumpy paper that covered the walls, and naming the horses to myself until Katty tapped on the door and asked me if I needed any help in there. (The first time I went to Luke's bathroom after they put the paper up, I was dying to tell Anu. It had palominos and Thoroughbreds and baby foals lying down on piles of hay! But I hadn't said anything, because I couldn't tell her I played at Luke's house. No Boys Allowed.)

Luke had a big trunk full of dress-up clothes. I'm pretty sure he didn't dress up with Will or Malcolm—he had a bunch of water guns and action figures to play with when those guys came over. But with me, he wore sparkle fabrics and Katty's discarded lipsticks; we rummaged in her closet for high heels and purses. There were makeup crayons, too, greasepaints in all colors.

That night, Luke put on a floral bathing suit and a hat like a gangster. I drew on his face so he looked like a parrot, with lots of green and yellow around the mouth. "Squawk!" he barked. "Squawkity squawk!"

I wanted to be a princess, but Luke kept pressuring me to be another parrot, so I wore an orange bathing suit with a little skirt and let him put yellow greasepaint on my face. "Squawk!"

Then we smoked cigarettes. Luke had them back behind the books on his bookshelf, where no one would ever look. We knew not to play with fire, but this didn't count. He pushed open his second-story window and we sat right by it, feeling the chill October air. "You breathe in twice," Luke explained "I know from watching my mom." He showed me how.

Two parrots lit up menthols. There was yellow makeup on my filter where my lips touched. I tried to wipe it off to make it clean, and I coughed a lot, but by the time the cigarette was halfway burned I had the hang of it.

"My brother smokes," said Luke. "Pal has cigarettes, and he gives them to me."

"Where does he get them?"

"I don't know. Pal is a sex maniac."

"What's that?"

"He has a girlfriend and I saw them kissing in the garage. She even had her titties out. Also he has *Playboys*."

I don't know if it was the smoking, which made me feel strange, or the makeup, which made me feel special and somehow pretty, but I asked Luke if he ever played doctor.

"Sure," he said. "I play it all the time."

"Who with?

"With girls."

"What girls?"

"Just girls, okay? Some girls not from school."

"What do you do?"

"You haven't played?"

"Yes, I have." My head felt spinny so I looked at my hands.

"Well, why are you asking?"

"Because there's lots of different ways to play it, Luke."

"Like what?"

I made stuff up. "You can do like an examination, like giving each other shots."

"Okay, what else?"

"One person lies down and the other one checks all over."

"Yeah, but what else?"

"You could do it in the dark, like in a closet, and see what's going on in there."

"Doctors' offices aren't dark."

"I know, but you could do it like that anyway. Or girls could do it with girls."

"No, they couldn't."

"Yes, they could. I know it for a fact. Or boys with boys."

"Okay, the closet," said Luke. He scooted down the hallway to check on Katty. "Ma, do we have to go to bed yet?"

"Not yet, baby," she called back. "I'll come tuck you two in when the movie's over. Does Vanessa have her sleeping bag?"

"She has it!"

He came back in the room and grabbed my arm. Two parrots went into the closet and shut the door. It was dark, and Luke's boots and shoes were everywhere. His clothes didn't hang down that far, so we had room to stand, but I had always envisioned playing doctor as involving lying down, so I pushed some stuff out of the way and sat.

"Where are you?"

"I'm down here."

He sat down on what were probably some rain boots and giggled. Light traced through the crack in the door. Then he put his hands straight in front of him, and squeezed my chest like he was squeezing grapefruits. There wasn't anything to squeeze except air pockets underneath the boobs of the orange suit, but I let him do it.

"Are you the doctor?" I asked.

"Unless you want to be."

"No, that's okay. You can be it."

"I have to check everything out to make sure you're okay," said Luke. He whispered in my ear, and his breath felt hot and tingly.

"I think I might have PenooMia," I whispered.

"It's NooMonia."

"It is?"

"Yeah, Ron told me. It was from the day you missed Super Duper Spellers." Luke squeezed my ass as much as he could while I was sitting on his sneakers. "Your bottom looks very healthy!"

"I want to be the doctor," I said, suddenly worried that whatever anomaly Marie was tormenting me about would be discovered here in the closet. I couldn't afford to have my butt thoroughly examined. "Let me try."

Luke lay back against the closet wall. I checked his knees and his neck. I liked touching his arms, where the skin was smooth and warmer than I expected. Then I put my hand on his penis through the floral bathing suit, his blue jeans, and the superhero undies that always stuck out the top of his pants. It felt like a pile of fabric and a zipper. I wanted to find out what was underneath, but after squeezing the pile of material once, I stopped and touched his arm again. Playing doctor probably had etiquette I didn't know about, and if I went too far, Luke might get mad or think I was a sex maniac like Pal. Also, I didn't want him to think he was my boyfriend or anything. That would screw up things with Anu and get me labeled one of the Fuckers.

Thankfully, Luke screamed like a parrot and kicked open the door of the closet. "Squawk!" he yelled. "Loo-ky want a cracker! Loo-ky want a cracker!"

"What are you two doing up there?" Katty called from the foot of the stairs.

And that was the end of that.

Katty made us take showers, one at a time in the horse bathroom, to get all the parrot makeup off. She only gave me one towel. I was glad to wash the cigarette smell from my hands. Then she settled me in on the floor in Luke's bedroom, tucked into my minty green sleeping bag.

There was dust underneath Luke's bed, and even in the dark after Katty left, I could see a stuffed elephant and that purple grease paint crayon we hadn't been able to find. It was weird being in someone else's house. I missed the light from my horizontal window.

"Neat sleeping bag," whispered Luke, wiggling around so his head was at the foot of the bed.

"I picked it out. I could have got orange or blue or red, if I wanted."

"Can I try it?"

"You wanna get in?"

"Like we're camping. I don't have a sleeping bag."

It was big enough for two, and Luke put his wet head next to mine on the pillow. "We're staring at the stars," he said. "We're on top of a mountain."

* * *

The house smelled like bacon, and the room was sunny. Morning. Katty freaked out when she caught us in the sleeping bag together. I could see it on her face, this look of violated innocence, amusement, and disgust. All she said was, "Aren't you two precocious?" But I knew she was a little mad. I could tell she thought of it as a Sleeping Bag Incident.

"We're camping," said Luke, opening his eyes.

"What's Precocious, again?" I asked, sitting up. We had had the word in Super Duper Spelling, but I couldn't remember the definition.

"Never mind. Don't you want to get up and get dressed, Vanessa? I'm making pancakes."

"I'm in a sleeping bag!" yelled Luke, scrunching himself down so his head was inside.

Katty stood there in the doorway. "Kids, let's go! Breakfast is almost on the table."

"It's green in here!" giggled Luke.

"I know," I said. "That's the best part about it. You can't tell at night." I stuck my head inside, too.

"Vanessa, I'm taking your clean clothes into the bathroom for you to get dressed, okay?" Katty was getting my T-shirt and underpants out of my backpack and collecting my jeans from the floor. "Come on, Vanessa," she said. "Let's give Luke some privacy. You can say good morning to the horses."

I followed her out.

By the time Debbie got there, my mouth was full of salty bacon and sticky maple syrup. I tried not to look her in the eye until I finished eating, for fear she would take the bacon away.

But she didn't seem to notice. She gave me a big hug from behind the kitchen chair I was sitting in and poured herself a cup of coffee from Katty's percolator.

"So how was it?"

"I'll tell you about it later," Debbie said, tipping her head toward me.

"Did you have a good time?" Katty wanted to know.

"I don't like French movies."

Did that mean she really didn't like Syd? Or did "French movie" mean something that I was too young to understand?

Debbie had been on dates before. It wasn't like I never met any of her boyfriends. But I hadn't ever heard her say she was sleeping with anyone. A couple times one summer we had gone to Walden Pond with a sandy-haired man called Jake who bought me a rubber dinosaur. He was pretty fun to swim with, but he played shark a lot, swimming up and grabbing my legs underwater unexpectedly, which freaked me out and made me pee. I don't think Debbie liked him all that much. She kept telling him, "Stop being a shark; Vanessa is getting hysterical," but he didn't really listen. She dumped him after a couple months.

Before Jake, she did some nature stuff with a guy named Roger who worked at the zoo. He'd take her hiking or looking at birds through binoculars. But when we actually went to where he worked, and he showed us around wearing a tan uniform and knee socks, she decided it was over. The animals weren't happy in their cages, she said. The tiger was pacing, and the elephants didn't have enough room. The monkeys were shivering on the cold floor of the enclosure, picking bugs off each other and eating them. She told me we should have compassion for our fellow creatures, help them when they're in need, and we were boycotting the zoo from then on. Roger was never heard from again.

I suppose Debbie was hesitant about dating because she didn't want me to think she was replacing Jordy. But honestly, at that point he rarely crossed my mind. He didn't write, he didn't call. We had no pictures of him, and I didn't remember ever hearing his voice. Life had never been anything but Debbie and me.

"What's wrong with French movies?" I asked.

"I don't talk French," she answered. "Why don't you two kids go color in the living room?"

"I'm still eating pancakes," said Luke.

"You can have more later," pushed Katty. "Go color."

"When is Halloween?" asked Luke.

"On Wednesday. Now, go color."

"Do you want to be a parrot, Vanessa? I'm going to be a parrot."

"No," I said. "I'm going to be a mouse."

Luke sat still and took a big bite of pancake.

"Luke, don't you want to draw?" his mother said, in a warning voice.

We drew at the coffee table in the living room. Luke had coloring books. We feigned perfect absorption, like we always did when something interesting was going on in the next room. We'd stick our tongues out the sides of our mouths, choose crayons from the box, and peel the paper off the sides—all the while listening intently to conversations adults assumed we were too busy to hear.

"Did you screw?" Katty brought her voice down a register and giggled.

"We left the movie in the middle," said Debbie, "and went for a walk through Harvard Square. Then through the quad, which is all lit up at night."

"And?"

"The stars were out."

My mother poked her head around the corner into the living room. I was coloring very carefully, and Luke was lining up all the crayons in perfect rainbow order.

"Then he said something weird," Debbie continued, back in the kitchen. "He said he felt that he was expressing total openness with me, but that I was holding something back; I had a part of me closed off."

"Oh, man!"

"He said he believed in complete disclosure and honesty," Debbie continued, "but that he wasn't getting that open vibe from me. Do you think that's true?"

"You're very open," said Katty.

"Well, what kind of open did he mean? I couldn't even think of anything he said to me that was especially personal. Nothing that I'd consider complete disclosure."

"What did he tell you?

I could hear my mother striking a match for her cigarette. "He has trouble with his car; he thinks I'm pretty. He speaks good French because he was over there for a year in college; he lied last week when he told me he'd been parachuting. He said he was trying to impress me and it just popped out, but now he wanted to clear the air and be honest. Then he said, why couldn't I be open with him, too?"

"So?"

"So I took him home and slept with him." My mother laughed. "Do you think that's sleazy?"

"I think that's what he wanted in the first place," Katty answered, clanging some dishes around in the sink.

Then Katty told Debbie that at the ashram, Syd had done something even weirder than lying about parachute jumping and pushing people for deeper honesty. She had forgotten about it until now, but here it was. One week about two years earlier, when they were both staying at the ashram, there was this ritual where people got in a hot tub together, dunked themselves in the water, and showered blessings on each other's heads. Participants would go two at a time, and all the other people would be in a big circle around the tub singing and banging on power drums. For example, Katty got in the tub totally naked with this woman who traveled all the way from Arkansas, and Katty knew from GE—Group Expression—that the Arkansas lady was having trouble with her no-good alcoholic son who never even called her. So she put a blessing on this woman's head for the son to be a source of joy to her; and the woman blessed Katty with freedom from cigarettes, and they both went under the water and came out again. Everybody cheered.

Well, Syd Wheeler would not take off his clothes. He insisted that his body was private and that part of keeping it sacred was not getting naked in the hot tub. The other guy was already in the tub, naked as could be, but Syd insisted on doing the ritual in drawstring pants and a tie-dye shirt. People got all freaked out, and someone went to get Alex to find out if the blessing counted if one of the two people wasn't naked. Some felt that with Syd clothed there was a power imbalance, and it wasn't fair for Morty—the other guy—to be naked if Syd wasn't. But Morty said he really didn't mind, and he was already naked anyway, so it was okay. And other people said that nakedness wasn't the point, the blessing was the point.

Alex arrived, and there was a big group hug, and then she told them that Syd could go in with his clothes on if he wasn't yet ready to surmount the Wall of Shame. Syd said he didn't have a Wall of Shame, his body was a temple, and it was sacred; it was out of respect for himself that he wasn't getting naked. And Alex said that someday he would see it as a Wall of Shame, but she respected his current state of being. So Syd got in the hot tub, and gave Morty a blessing for a healthy heart and total openness; and Morty gave Syd one for surmounting the Wall of Shame, which pissed Syd off, and he got out of the tub and stomped away. His tie-dye shirt had bled in the tub, though, and all the water turned green. So people remembered Syd's Wall of Shame until someone drained the tub three days later.

Debbie laughed a booming laugh that made me feel like all was right with the world. "Well, he took off his clothes with me," she said.

5.

Fright Night

The morning of Halloween I wore my mouse suit to school. The two gray wool sweaters were sewn together with padding inside, and the center part closed with bows across my stomach. I had a tail that was long enough so I could drape it over my arm, but it didn't drag on the floor because Debbie put wires in it. And I had ears with pink insides. The only problem was my feet, which looked pretty nonmousy in my sneakers. I solved that, though, by convincing Debbie to let me wear my party shoes.

I still have a photograph from that morning. As we got to school Mrs. Bhaduri drove up with all her kids in the car. She had brought them so their costumes wouldn't get messed up on the walk over. Debbie took a picture of us with her camera.

In the photo, Baby is sulking because Samir has just pinched him for wearing a dwarf outfit. Baby had lederhosen and a peaked hat but he couldn't pronounce *dwarf* properly. He kept calling himself a *dorf,* and every time, Samir would pinch him and say, "You've got to learn to talk right." Samir is too cool to be wearing a Halloween costume. He's got his soccer jacket pulled up around his neck. And Ram is on the other side, dressed as a gypsy fortune-teller. He's wearing lipstick, and what looks like some old sari fabric of his mother's tied into a skirt. On his head there's a scarf, something diaphanous, tied so the fabric hangs down his back. He was absolutely the most beautiful thing I had ever seen, that day.

Anu still has some chicken pox, scabbing up across her arms and chin. She is dressed like a pumpkin, in a round orange globe with her arms sticking out through holes in the sides. She wears an orange leotard and tights, and a green hat like a stem. She and I are staring into the camera, holding hands. My mouse head is tilted toward her, and we are laughing at some secret joke. I don't remember what it was, maybe just Baby saying "dorf." Her chin is tucked in by her neck like she always had it when she was really happy, as if she needed to stop the mirth from bursting out and spilling down her chest.

Looking at that picture now makes me cry.

Luke was a parrot, and Malcolm was a superhero I had never heard of from television. Marie wore a clown suit, with a wide fake smile and rubber nose that she kept taking on and off. I wasn't too scared of her though, because Summer and Anu would titter whenever she walked by, grab one another by the arm, and tell secrets. Summer even told those Fuckers Didi and Angelique about Marie showing me her ass. I was worried that with their experience—doing whatever it was they did with boys—those girls would uncover the lie in my story. But they didn't. They just laughed and whispered about the Bottom Incident, followed by the less interesting Diorama Incident.

And so I had become, in the days after my mother slept with Sydney Wheeler, something close to popular. Anu and I still sat at our little table for lunch, but during recess, Summer and I swung on the swings singing,

Miss Lucy had a steamboat, the steamboat had a bell (toot! toot!)
Miss Lucy went to heaven and the steamboat went to . . .
HELL-o operator, give me number nine!
And if you disconnect me, I will cut off your . . .
BEHIND the 'frigerator, there was a piece of glass!
Miss Lucy sat upon it and it went right up her . . .
ASSk me no more questions, I'll tell you no more lies!
The boys are in the bathroom and they're unzipping their flies!

Angelique, who never talked to me before, pulled me aside and said she heard what a weirdo Marie was, and I shouldn't worry because everybody knew it wasn't my fault. She said that Marie drew a picture in art class of her family and it had only two people in it, her and her dad, and wasn't that weird, too? And she still wore overalls like a kindergartner.

I just shrugged. Then Angelique asked if I wanted to play jacks, so I did.

We all did our schoolwork in costume. Ron let me keep my tail on even after I knocked over a jar of poster paint with it, because, he said, I was a mouse crumpet and what was a mouse without a tail?

At Circle of Sharing, Summer sat next to me on one side, sucking her thumb. She was dressed as a cat and said she had to sit by me because I was a mouse. She sucked her thumb all the time, almost in a show-offy way, and there was even a raised red bump on her knuckle from it. It was part of her identity, somehow. Her popularity made it acceptable. "My Daddy can't quit smoking," she said, "and I can't quit sucking my thumb. We've tried everything."

"What did you try?" I asked her when she first told me about it, only the day before. She seemed excited to have a fresh audience; all her real friends knew the story already.

"When I was a baby, I tried pacifiers," said Summer, "But I always spit them out. And last year I got this bitter stuff that we put on my thumb every morning because it tasted really bad. But I got to like it!" she said. "Now I like bitter things. I even like coffee."

I wondered if she had tried putting it in a Receptacle. "What else did you do?"

"I got hypnotized. But it didn't work. The doctor had me look at this weird spinning circle, and also at his watch swinging back and forth, but it was too funny and I kept laughing. So I still suck my thumb. I like sucking it."

I stuck my thumb in my mouth for a bit right after she told me all this, but it was pretty boring. I needed my hand to write.

Marie never talked during Circle of Sharing. I often did, and so did Anu. There was just always something to say. On holidays, the braided teacher usually asked if we knew the history of the day and why we celebrated it. It seemed weird that she was asking us if we knew stuff she had never taught us. She did that a lot. She'd say, "Can anybody tell me who J. S. Bach was?" Or, "Does anybody want to tell us what a symphony is?" when we had never learned anything about symphonies, or Bach, or anything.

Some kids would raise their hands, and then when they got called on they'd guess that a symphony was something to do with being phony, or simple, maybe. Or they'd say they forgot when she called on them. Eventually, she'd tell us the right information, but always she'd go through letting all the kids tell you wrong stuff beforehand, which made it embarrassing for them and also hard to remember which was right when you got home and wanted to tell your mom what you'd learned.

Once I told Debbie that plants got their energy from bumblebees, because that's what a kid said in class, and I remembered that better than all the stuff about sunlight and water.

I only raised my hand when I was sure I knew the answer—but even so, that was pretty often because a lot of the questions in Circle of Sharing were really just about everyday stuff, like, "Do you have grandparents?" Or, "Does anyone here have a pet?" Or, "Would you like to share with us what you ate for breakfast, so we can see what food groups you're eating?" That kind of thing.

Marie never, ever, raised her hand, and the teachers never called on her. She just sat, solid and unmoving, as if she wasn't quite taking in everything around her. Sometimes she picked at her fingernails, but she didn't wiggle, or fidget, or whisper. It almost seemed like she didn't *feel* anything, like she was a lump of dough hardening into a dry, flaky sculpture of a person. I wanted to shake her, poke her, something—but her passivity frightened me, too.

Halloween, she had a curly red wig standing stiff around her ears. I clapped my fancy party shoes together in front of me and petted Summer's next-door knee with its brown striped kitty-cat tights. Marie sat staring into space, talking to no one, rubber nose pinching her nostrils—and suddenly her face ceased to seem impassive. It began instead to seem sorrowful.

"Like minestrone," Anu whispered to me from my other side, wrapping her arm around my shoulders.

Sydney Wheeler was in the car when Debbie picked me up from school. He was an ordinary-looking man: medium height, medium build, with a mustache and hair that flopped over his eyebrows. He didn't get out of the front seat when I got there, so I had to sit in the back.

"Syd's coming with us to Fright Night!" Debbie said brightly. "Say hello to Syd, Vanessa."

I said hello, although he hadn't said hello to *me*. I wanted to sit up front.

"Great mouse suit, Vanessa." I could tell he was trying to be friendly.

"Say thanks, Vanessa," Debbie prompted.

"Thank you. Is the Fright Night going to be scary?"

"Were you scared last year?"

"No."

"Then I'm sure it won't be scary. It's cupcakes and pumpkin carving, and things like that."

Actually, I was scared last year, but I didn't want to admit that to Debbie. Anu and her brothers had pulled me over to the House of Terror, which the older students had built on the stage area of the school auditorium. I didn't want to go in, but Samir promised it was really fun, and so we all stood on line in a dark entryway that was guarded by a high school boy in a rubber mask. He looked like a dead person. "Beware! Entry is not for the faint of heart. Small children and chickens should turn back now." He laughed a horrible laugh. "Six people descend to the dungeon at a time. Not all of them come back out!"

Before I knew it, Anu had gone in without me. The dead man was taking people in groups, and I got left behind when he called her and her brothers.

I was alone at the doorway to the House of Terror.

No Anu, no Debbie, no one.

The only person anywhere near me I recognized was a thirteen-year-old girl named Landis. There was something I liked about her; she had long blond curls in ringlets that looked fuzzy like a lamb. But I didn't really know her. Not even to say Hi.

The teenage dead person called the next group of six, and I was swept into the completely black entrance room, along with Landis and a bunch of other eighth-graders. I could hear the bustle of the bake sale outside, and the voice of the guy in front saying "Good-bye, suckers!"

I shut my eyes for a second to adjust them to the darkness, but it didn't help. I couldn't see. I could only feel bodies rustling.

A flashlight turned on, shining up at the ghoulish face of a decaying mummy. I backed as fast as I could into the pack of eighth-graders, tripping and clutching at their clothes. They laughed and poked each other. "It's Mickey Shiner," I heard one of them say. But it looked like a mummy to me.

"Our collection of starving rats has escaped their cages!" cried the mummy, bending down so he was eye level with me. "Watch your feet and tasty fingers! Don't let them run up your legs or down the backs of your shirts! Listen!" A squeaky sound of hungry rats filled the space. It was too dark to see if anything was really there. I stood on tiptoe, holding my Glinda the Good Witch dress down and folding my hands into fists to keep my fingers from being bitten. "We haven't fed them in weeks!" cried the mummy, and switched off the flashlight.

In complete darkness again, some of the girls screamed.

Were there rats on the floor?

What did I feel on the back of my neck? I was trying not to cry.

The mummy pushed us into the next room, where I could see a little better. Four cannibal zombies in long white robes grabbed our hands and tried to force them into buckets of decaying brains.

"I don't want to!" I pleaded. "I don't want to feel the brains!"

"You have to feel them," hissed the zombie who had hold of my wrist. "If you don't, we'll eat you for dinner and *your* brains will be lying here for other people to feel!"

"I don't want to!"

"You look like a delicious child," mused the zombie, turning to one of her friends. "Doesn't she look delicious? This girl doesn't want to feel the brains!"

"She must feel the brains," agreed her fellow cannibal. "If she doesn't feel them, we'll pull her limb from limb and roast her over the fire!" They cackled with glee, and the first zombie picked me up around the waist, crushing my Glinda skirt and spinning me around in a ritual cannibal dance.

"Feel the brains!" it chanted. "Feel the brains!"

I thought I'd be sick. I didn't know what was in the cauldron of brains, but it seemed unbearably squishy and real. The room was spinning, and the zombie had me in its clutches. Another one waved the brains bucket in the semidarkness, offering it to my flailing hand.

"Don't make her, you guys. She doesn't have to feel anything." It was Landis, stepping forward. "I see you, Lisa Richards, and you, Tom Durbin, and if you don't let that kid down, I'm going to tell Stuart." Stuart was the principal. We called him by his first name at Cambridge Harmony. "Can't you see she's really freaked out? Man, you guys."

The world stopped whirling. The zombie handed me over to Landis, telling her, "Sorry," but not saying anything to me.

Landis put me down on the floor and wiped my nose with some tissue from her pocket. "Are you okay?"

I wanted to say yes, but there were still several rooms left in the haunted house.

"Do you want me to hold your hand?" she asked.

I went through the rest of the House of Terror clinging tightly to Landis and hiding my face in her sweater. "It's not real," she kept reminding me. "That's Bob Wells from the tenth grade," or, "That's Susan Irwin from my art class." She even picked me up and carried me part of the way.

When I could finally see light at the end of the dark hallway, I jumped down and ran toward it as fast as I could, arriving in the brightness and banging my face smack into the soft fabric crotch of Stuart the principal.

"Watch it there, Vanessa," he said, bending over to squeeze my cheek in a funny way that seemed partly like a joke and partly like a punishment. Stuart was a tall man with a graying ponytail. He knew every kid's name. "What do you say?"

"Excuse me."

"That's right, excuse me. Well, I do. I excuse you." He said it like it was funny, but I didn't see why.

I wished he would let go of my cheek. Stuart was always doing things like that—things that made you think you might be punished even though he was pretending to be nice.

"Vanessa! We lost you!" Anu ran over from where she had been waiting and laughing with Ram and Samir—smiling, like it hadn't been scary at all.

Stuart let go of my cheek then. "Have a happy Halloween, Vanessa. Don't overdo it now. . . ."

"Vanessa! Syd is asking you something," Debbie remonstrated from the front of the car. I hadn't heard. I was thinking about the zombies from last year and how weird it was that principals have crotches like everybody else. "Man," my mother said to Syd Wheeler. "What a space cadet she is."

"I asked what kind of goodies you're giving out," Syd repeated.

I told him how Debbie and I had put candy corn in plastic baggies and tied each one with ribbon to make a package of treats. The year before we had baked brownies.

When we got back to the house, Syd and Debbie took me trick-or-treating. I felt very grown-up, even though it was still daylight, because the two of them walked together about fifteen paces behind me. It really looked like I was a solitary mouse out there to play tricks and collect treats.

Later, we gave out candy to the older kids who trick-or-treated in the real dark.

* * *

For Fright Night 1970, the Cambridge Harmony auditorium was decorated in black and orange streamers and filled largely with white grown-ups who worked at one or the other of the several universities near Boston. Kids in homemade costumes ran in packs past the bake sale tables, which overflowed with carrot cake and oatmeal cookies. There was a jar of jelly beans, with a prize for guessing how many were inside, and a table where someone's dad was teaching people how to make beads out of colored clay. Alyssa Bent, head of the PTA, had a face-painting booth, and a big corner of the floor was covered in plastic for carving jack-o'-lanterns. One person had brought this really humungous pumpkin that came up to my waist.

Debbie, Syd, and I got little ones and sat down to carve them. Syd kept rubbing his mustache on Debbie's neck, kissing her, but she pushed him off because she was being artistic. She even took a pencil out of her purse and sketched what she was going to do on her pumpkin beforehand, then used the knife like she was whittling something out of wood.

My own was very simple. Just a big smile and triangle eyes.

"Don't you want it to have a nose?" asked Syd.

"No." I liked it very basic, and besides, the noses were never any good because you couldn't make them stick out in front.

"How's it going to breathe?"

"It can breathe," I said.

"Maybe you could make just a little nose," Syd said, as if a little nose was almost like no nose when actually it's a totally different thing.

Ron the teacher came over wearing a top hat and complimented my mother on her pumpkin. "She's doing great with the Super Duper Spelling, Mrs. Brick. And we love having Vanessa share our classroom with us." Ron cleared his throat. "But I wanted to mention—the nurse told me that she wasn't getting enough to eat for lunch."

Debbie sighed and wiped her forehead with the back of her hand. Her jeans had a few pumpkin seeds stuck to them. "I'm giving her enough to eat, Ron," she said, trying to smile. "I think it was just that one day. Check and see for yourself. You'll let him look in your lunch box, won't you, Vanessa?"

"Oh, I believe you," said Ron and turned to me. "Do you have enough to eat at lunchtime?"

I did, and I told him so, but even if I didn't, I could never have said anything about it in the middle of carving a pumpkin and with my mother and Syd sitting right there. It was pointless to ask me. Anyway, he would *never* look at my lunch, never *had* looked at my lunch. He wasn't even the teacher who ate lunch with us. Talking about it was just a way to let my mother know he didn't think that much of her. Because we didn't pay. Or because my dad was eating fried chicken all over the state of California.

Ron disappeared when Mister Bhaduri came over, wearing fake teeth in his mouth like a vampire and holding Baby's hand.

"Good evening, Debbie."

"This is Syd Wheeler," my mother said, standing up and drying her hands on her jeans. "Syd, Jay Bhaduri."

"I'm Debbie's lover," Syd announced, staying seated on the floor.

My mother blushed. Mister Bhaduri leaned over and shook hands.

"Where's Anu?" I wanted to know.

"I'm not sure," he answered, "but we're all here somewhere. I think she ran off with a redheaded boy."

"Was it Luke Sherwin?" my mother asked, looking around the auditorium. "I haven't seen Katty here yet."

"I don't know," said Mister Bhaduri. "I didn't recognize him."

"Glinda the Good Witch of the North!" I was standing at the table with the jelly bean jar. The voice came from above me.

"I'm not Glinda." I guessed 564 jelly beans and handed my paper to the dad behind the table. "I'm a mouse."

"I know you're a mouse, Mouseling!" Landis said, grabbing my tail and giving it a friendly pull. "But you were Glinda last year. I took you through the haunted house, remember?"

I did. Landis turned to her friend, a girl named Connie with a shaggy haircut, and explained. "She got separated from her mom, I think, and I took care of her."

The friend didn't pay much attention. She was scouting the auditorium, looking for someone.

"How are you, Mouseling?" Landis squatted down to be at my eye level. "Are you going in the House of Terror again this year?"

I shook my head. "How come you're not wearing a costume?" I asked. She had some glitter dusted across her cheeks, but that was the only thing different from usual.

"I'm too big to wear a costume."

"You're still a kid."

"Yeah, but someone I like is here," Landis answered. "Do you know what I mean?"

I shook my head again.

"A guy. A guy I like is here, and I didn't want to wear a costume in case he thinks it isn't cool."

"What guy?"

She lifted me up and held me on her hip like a baby, turning around the auditorium in search of him.

"There he is," said Connie, jerking her head to one side. "By the cotton candy."

"Oh, yeah. See the one in the blue shirt? That's him. Shaun."

The boy was leaning on the door that led from the auditorium out into the parking lot, slouching back with his hips pressed out. He was watching the cotton candy twirler spin balls of fluffy sugar into waiting cones.

"What do you think, Vanessa?"

I thought he wasn't as beautiful as Ram Bhaduri, but there was something nice about his slouch. "He's not wearing a costume," I said.

"No," said Landis, "he's not."

"Does he like you back?"

Landis giggled to her friend. "Shall we tell her?"

"Landis put a note in his locker this morning," whispered Connie.

"He wrote me one first!"

"He did, he wrote her one first, but it was in English class, about the homework."

"It wasn't romantic or anything."

"Right, so then Landis wrote this note that told him that she liked him, and put it in his locker. And then . . . nothing! She hasn't seen him since!"

"I didn't exactly say I liked him," Landis explained. "I just hinted, and said I knew he liked The Beatles and maybe he'd want to come over after school someday and listen to my records."

"He didn't go to English today, though."

Just then, Syd Wheeler strolled up, wearing donkey ears on his head. "Vanessa! Want to go in the House of Terror?" he asked. "I'll take you in."

"I bet she doesn't want to." Landis laughed. "We went last year, and it wasn't fun, was it Mouseling?" I shook my head. "Is this your dad?"

"I'm not her dad." Syd smiled. "I'm her mother's lover."

Landis and her friend giggled.

"I believe in being very open about everything," Syd went on. "Even sensitive subjects. What's your name?"

Landis introduced herself, and Syd asked if she ever baby-sat, since he and Debbie had a music festival they wanted to go to over the weekend.

"Sure, I baby-sit," said Landis.

"I'm not a baby," I corrected.

"What should I say, then?" She shifted me on her hip a bit.

"Kid-sit."

"Okay, kid-sit."

"No, wait. Mouse-sit."

"I get a dollar an hour," Landis told Syd, writing her phone number on an orange Halloween napkin.

And that was how Landis Rutherford became my mouse-sitter. I would end up knowing all about orgies and heartbreak before I turned nine.

* * *

Syd was gone. Landis and her friend had run off in a fit of giggles. I couldn't see my mother anywhere—not at the bake sale, the pumpkin carving, or the PTA sign-up table. She had probably gone outside to smoke a cigarette.

I squeezed past clowns and black cats and two people dressed as a horse, found the door that led to the parking lot, and pushed. Outside, the Halloween night smelled like leaves.

But Debbie wasn't there. In fact, there was no one in the parking lot except a single dad and his crying toddler getting into a station wagon. Over to one side, the chain-link fence opened onto the Cambridge Harmony playground. I had never been in there at night, and it looked beautiful and supernatural. Someone had placed jack-o'-lanterns atop the various pieces of equipment. I could hear voices and laughs coming from underneath the main climber.

I opened the gate and went in.

My feet made a soft crunching noise on the wood chips, and I almost tripped over a wooden step, but I made my way across to where the noise came from. There, lit by the candlelight that flickered through the jack-o'-lantern grins, Anu and Luke sat huddled together. Whispering.

One pumpkin had her round shell off and her leotard pulled down to show her chicken-pocked behind. One parrot poked a chicken pock with an outstretched finger, then laid his cheek on her bottom for an instant, like a pillow. I could see Anu's skinny chest, shivering in the October chill, and she turned around to say something to Luke that made him tap her lightly on the bottom. She wiggled her ass a little and got to her feet, jumping up and down as she pulled her leotard and tights back on. One pumpkin, jumping. One parrot, watching.

"Vanessa!" Anu's voice was loud and sharp as she caught sight of me standing by the tire swing. "What are you doing out here?"

"I was looking for you," I said. "To see if you want to guess the jelly beans."

"I'm playing with Luke." Anu had got her arms through the sleeves of her leotard and was stepping into the globe of the pumpkin.

"I already had chicken pox," said Luke.

"I know," I said. "I know that already."

"Fright Fest was boring." Luke took a few steps out from under the climber.

"I said, I know."

"We can play together if we want." Anu cried defensively. "I can play with Luke."

"I know," I said again, and started to walk away.

"Vanessa, wait!" Complete in her pumpkin suit, Anu followed me back into the parking lot. She touched my arm and leaned in toward my ear. "We were playing doctor," she said, in a whisper that was a little too loud to be really a secret. "Luke wanted to see my chicken pox."

"So?"

"So, he was checking to make sure they're healed," she said. Her giggle was tense and superior.

"The pox are gross," I burst out. "I don't know why you ever show them to anyone. People think they're awful."

"No, they don't." Anu's eyes widened.

"Yes, they do. They're nasty."

"It's natural," she said, an echo of her mother's lilt in her voice. "Everybody gets chicken pox."

"I don't."

We stared at each other under the parking lot lights. A car drove past, making a gravelly sound.

"Luke said you didn't want to do it," she said, finally.

"Do what?"

"Play. You know."

"He said I didn't want to?"

"He said you went over to his house."

I was stunned. I thought she didn't know I was friends with Luke.

"My mom brought me," I said.

"Do you go there a lot?"

"Pretty much." I shrugged to try to make it seem like less.

"He said you didn't want to, and asked, did I think that was weird?"

"Weird not to play?

"Yes," she said. "Did I think it was weird not to play doctor."

"I thought we didn't do that," I answered—because really, I thought so. No Boys Allowed. Didi was a Fucker.

"But it is weird, if you were over at his house," she pushed. "Not to do anything."

"No, it's not. We smoked cigarettes. It wasn't a big deal like you're making it."

"So why were you over there all the time?"

"I told you, my mom brought me."

"It's still weird." At first I thought she meant weird not to touch each other, but suddenly it seemed like she was saying weird to go over there and play at all. Everything was switched around. I thought she had betrayed *me*, hiding under the climber, but now it seemed that I had been betraying her.

"We said No Boys Allowed." I sniffed reproachfully. "That's why I didn't tell you."

"You were keeping secrets."

"I didn't want to make you mad!"

"Why do you think I'm the boss of you?" said Anu. "I'm not the boss of you."

"I know that."

"So stop acting like I'm the boss."

"But you're mad at me!" I cried.

"Because you kept secrets," she hissed.

"You keep secrets, too."

"I do not." Anu folded her arms, and neither of us spoke for a while.

"You shouldn't have been out there, underneath the climber," I finally said.

"Don't tell me what to do, Vanessa. You're such a scaredy-cat."

"I'm not!"

"That's what Luke said."

I suddenly realized I had been lying. Luke and I *had* played doctor, *had* been two parrots together in the closet. Even though my pants never came off, and I didn't have any chicken pox for him to inspect, we had fiddled around with each other, and hid what we were doing from Katty. And, even more intimate (but somehow not under discussion at all), we had spent the night twined around each other in my sleeping bag.

I was taking a completely false position. A betrayer again. Why was I still lying to Anu? And why had Luke told her we didn't do anything?

"Vanessa!" Debbie was standing, silhouetted against the door that led back into the bustling auditorium. "Come in out of the cold, sugar."

I crumpled into tears.

6.

Another Incident

About a month before Marie showed me her ass, Debbie adopted a kitten. There was a news show on television in early September that year about a boy who walked to school every morning by himself in New York City. It was only four blocks, and his mother used to stand on the stoop and watch until he went around the corner. Then one morning, he didn't turn up in his classroom. He didn't come home, either, and nobody ever saw him again.

His name was Patrick Threep. He was only six years old. Something happened between the corner by his house and the school four blocks away, but no one will ever know exactly what. They put his picture on a milk carton and sent it all over the country. I don't think anybody had ever been on a milk carton before that. But it didn't do any good.

After a few weeks, the police said they weren't even looking for Patrick Threep anymore. They were just looking for a body.

Debbie found the kitten near the Dumpster at the natural food co-op. It was crying and covered with flea bites, and she wrapped it in her sweater and took it home. She named it Patrick Threep. Patrick Threep because *we* saw it again, *we* rescued it, *we* gave it a good home; and hopefully that's what happened to the real Patrick, she said.

Though she had to admit, probably not.

I wanted to name it Fuzzy, but Debbie said no.

Our Patrick Threep was very nervous at first. He hid in the closet and had to go to the veterinarian several times before he got rid of his worms and fleas. He figured how to use the cat box, though, and ate crunchies from a bowl, but he wouldn't if you watched him. Debbie said he had to get used to us, and spent a lot of time sitting outside the place where he was hiding, whispering encouragement.

Bit by bit the kitten responded, and soon he was sitting in her lap to be petted. By the time Halloween rolled around, he would let me scratch his underneck a little, and he was sleeping every night on Debbie's pillow. So when Syd Wheeler stayed at our house on Halloween, Patrick Threep didn't like it one bit. I could tell because when I woke up the next morning, he was curled on my floor, asleep.

I knew Syd had stayed over because Debbie had talked to me about it in a very careful way before I went to bed. I had been teary from my fight with Anu, but she assumed I was tired and cranky from all the sugar and the long day wearing the mouse suit. When I was tucked in, with my face scrubbed clean and Lopey by my side, she explained that Syd was going to sleep over, and wasn't he nice?

Truth was, he was only sort of nice, but I said Yes because I knew that's what she wanted to hear.

The sun woke me early, shining bright through my horizontal window. Debbie had tacked some fabric over it while she was working on my curtains, but I always undid the tacks that held the material closed in the middle, because waking up in the dark felt so strange to me.

Patrick Threep and I went into the living room to play with a piece of string, and before long I could hear Syd fiddling around in the kitchen. He was making coffee, and I could smell toast and melted butter. After a bit, he walked in to the living room, wearing nothing but his underpants and a thin white T-shirt.

His penis was sticking out. Really far out from the frayed cotton edge of his briefs, poking into the sunlight like a confused mole.

I had seen the Sherwin boys' dicks when we all changed to go running through the sprinkler, and once I saw Baby's when he escaped from his bath. But I had never seen a grown-up one, and I really had no desire to. I felt embarrassed for Syd, like he had had snot or chocolate sauce all over his face, or some big piece of vegetable between his teeth. Didn't it feel weird to have it wedged over to the side like that? Little boys' always poked straight out.

"Vanessa!" he said. "Good morning. Would you like some coffee?"

I knew he was making a joke, but I shook my head and tried not to stare at his crotch.

"I'm kidding, man. What do you eat for breakfast? Can I get you anything?" I usually ate oatmeal, but only Debbie knew how to make it the right way, so I didn't tell him. Syd tried to scratch Patrick Threep on the head, but the cat scooted under the sofa and wouldn't have anything to do with him, so he sat down on the butterfly chair and thumbed through a magazine.

Didn't he know it was sticking out? How could he be that unaware of his own body?

Or what if he *was* aware? A suspicion half-formed in my mind. He wasn't waggling it, or thrusting it, or doing anything particular except letting it droop—but for a guy who had to enact the hot tub blessing ritual in a full suit of clothes, it was weird that he wouldn't know what was going on with his own penis.

"It's sticking out!" I finally yelled. "Put it away!"

"What?" he looked around the room as if searching for an intruder.

"It's sticking out!" I yelled again, this time pointing my finger.

Finally, he looked down at his body. Then reached down and tucked it back in. "I'm sorry, Vanessa," he said, after a minute. "I didn't do that on purpose."

"I wish I could wear my mouse suit to school every day," I said.

Syd took a drink of his coffee and didn't react to my change of subject. After another moment of silence, he leaned forward. "You're not going to tell your mom about what just happened, are you?"

"Patrick Threep would like it if I dressed as a mouse, wouldn't you, Patrick?" I asked the kitten, looking for his stripy, furry body underneath the couch. "We could play chase."

"Vanessa, we don't need to tell Debbie, do we?"

It seemed to me like Syd was more nervous than he should be. If it was really a mistake, why should he act so guilty? What did he think Debbie was going to do to him? After all, she walked around naked after she took a shower. It wasn't that big a deal.

And what would Anu think about it? The Sydney Wheeler Incident. Maybe it was a good enough secret to make up with.

"Vanessa, we won't tell, will we?" said Syd. "About my . . . you know."

For a guy who believed in total openness, Syd was a quick liar.

"It's called a penis," I told him, "P-E-N-I-S." And I went to wake up Debbie.

7.

Girls Chase the Boys

We adopted the second cat the Thursday after I told Debbie about Syd's dick sticking out of his underpants. That afternoon, she found Fuzzy mewling under a bush outside school. Fuzzy was no kitten: She was a big, bruised-looking alley cat with one ear lopsided from scar tissue, but she purred when Debbie picked her up. Her fur had a dusty look, and her breath smelled funny, but Debbie said she would clean up nicely and be a good companion for Patrick Threep, who was more of a loner than was good for him. Besides, it was now November. Too cold for cats to be living outdoors.

Debbie had taken news of the Syd Wheeler Incident very well. I wasn't sure she would believe me. She hadn't when Luke took my Barbie doll home with him on purpose. She had told me there was no way Luke wanted a Barbie to play with. He must have stuck it in his backpack by accident. But this time, she listened closely and then asked me a couple of questions.

"Do you think he did it intentionally?"

"No," I said. "But he didn't want to me tell and tried to make me promise."

"I bet he felt embarrassed," she reflected. "You know how it feels to be embarrassed, don't you?"

"Yes."

"I think he wants to impress me."

"I never thought of it that way."

"Did it upset you?" she asked.

"I thought it was stupid that he didn't even know what was inside his pants and what was out."

"That's why he feels embarrassed, and we have to feel sorry for him," Debbie explained. Then she said that penises were normal. "It's normal for boys to have them, and it's basically normal for them not to always know what the penises are doing. So don't worry."

But she told me to be sure and tell her if it happened again.

Fuzzy made herself at home right away, and even though Patrick Threep hissed at her, she tried to lick him. Within a couple hours they were curled up together on the couch.

At school that day, Anu and I hadn't spoken very much, but we didn't fight, either. We ate lunch sitting at a big table with Summer and Angelique and some other kids. It didn't seem like a good time to tell her about Syd, so I just kept my mouth shut and ate my yogurt.

At recess we played kissing tag, girls chase the boys. It was a new invention of Didi's. Didi the Fucker. You didn't have to actually put your lips on the boy you caught. You just had to kiss your hand and then touch him with the fingers you had kissed.

Normally in kissing tag I would have kissed Luke—because he was the safest and wouldn't make fun of me—but that felt too awkward now, so I chased Malcolm and Will and a boy whose name I forget, making sure not to concentrate too much on any one person.

"Angelique's got a crush on Malcolm! Angelique's got a crush on Malcolm!" we chanted gleefully when she caught him for the third time.

"I do not!"

"Angelique's in love with Malcolm!"

Angelique turned red. "Anu's in love with Luke! That's who's got a crush!" Anu had just hit Luke's cheek with her kiss-moistened hand.

"I do not." Anu had stopped running.

"Well, why'd you kiss him, then?" asked Angelique.

"It's a game." Anu shrugged. "It's just a game."

"Anu and Luke, sitting in a tree! K-I-S-S-I-N-G!" Angelique began to chant, and Summer joined in with her.

Was the thing between Anu and Luke common knowledge, or had Angelique only responded to what she had just seen on the playground?

"First comes love, then comes marriage. . . ."

Their chant lasted only a few seconds. Luke stopped it. "Gross! Gross! Get it off me!" He was wiping Anu's kiss off his face with the tail of his shirt.

"It's not that wet," said Anu, looking at the wood chips underneath her feet. Her hair was so pretty. She was such a pretty girl.

"Yes, it is. It's all slobbery! Gross, gross, gross!" Luke ran off in the direction of the swing set.

Anu stayed where she was. I wanted to go over to her, to hook my arm through hers and tell her Luke was a stupid boy. But I didn't. She wouldn't believe it, anyway, now that she knew I played at his house. And yesterday I would have been sure she was hurt by his behavior, but now I didn't know. They had something between them that was closed off to me, and it seemed perfectly possible that his running away wasn't a rejection at all—but an invitation.

So I looked at Anu, with her black hair blowing and her ski jacket unzipped; her sad, angry, superior face. And I walked away.

I didn't go home with her that afternoon, like I usually did on Thursdays. I sat in the playground by myself until the braided teacher came out and asked me where my mother was. I said she was late to pick me up, and the teacher took me inside, gave me a cup of juice, and called Debbie at work. "Did you forget you go to the Bhaduris' on Thursday?" my mother asked, when the teacher put me on the phone.

I told her yes. "I forgot because of Halloween, yesterday," I said, and she seemed to believe me. That's when she came to school and we found Fuzzy.

Curled up next to me on the sofa, Patrick Threep didn't think I needed a best friend. Patrick Threep thought Summer was very nice and might even invite me to her house one day, and Angelique was okay, too. Besides, best friends was already taken care of by him and Fuzzy and Lopey, so who was I to go wondering and worrying?

But I did. And I still do.

If I hadn't walked away.

If I had just gone home with her like usual.

If I had recounted the Syd Wheeler Incident at lunchtime and gotten her to laugh. Would she have been all right?

8.

Peanut Butter Boys

Landis, my new mouse-sitter, was coming over. It was Saturday night, and my mother and Syd were going to the music festival. Debbie dressed up, applying makeup in the bathroom while she talked to Katty Sherwin on the telephone. The phone cord stretched all the way from the kitchen.

I was in the tub.

Debbie seemed agitated. "He's not queer, Katty," she said as she lined her eyes. "Didn't you take psychology at Radcliffe?"

I splashed a little in the water. Syd was queer, Syd was queer, Katty thought that Syd was queer.

Queer: adjective. Differing from the normal or expected.

"That doesn't mean he's a fairy," Debbie explained. "It's natural for someone like him."

Fairy. Tinkerbell. Clap your hands if you believe.

There was squeaking on the telephone, but I couldn't make out any words.

"I didn't mean that, Katty." Debbie sounded as if she were

trying to interrupt. She sat down on the toilet seat and crossed her legs tightly. "What I meant was, clothing is part of identity. What people wear reflects something about them. They experiment. Like you and your bra."

My Barbie was supposedly having a pool party with a plastic horse and the rubber dinosaur I got from Jake, but really I was listening in. Just for show, I put Barbie on the horse's back.

"Like finding yourself. Lots of men are straight who wore girl's clothes when they were little. Ram Bhaduri wore some kind of mumu for Halloween, did you see him? Prettier than a girl. . . . Uh-huh. That's what I'm talking about. It's an experiment." Debbie lit a menthol.

I told her not to smoke in the bathroom, but she just waved her hand up and down in a shushing way.

"Okay, I shouldn't have said, 'Someone like him.' " My mother's voice was tight. "I meant someone with a lot of older brothers. I really didn't mean anything bad."

It was Luke they were talking about, not Syd at all. Katty was upset about Luke dressing up in women's clothes.

"He doesn't play with girls too much. What is too much, anyway?"

There was a pause, and Debbie got me out of the bathtub and wrapped me in a towel, the phone pressed between her shoulder and her ear.

"What are you saying, Katty?" my mother said sharply. A pause. "It's not Vanessa's fault." Another pause. "I can't help the sex of my child!" She was standing up now, and her eyes were watering. "What am I going to tell her?"

I was standing right there. I don't think she could even see me.

"I can't believe you, Katty Sherwin," my mother said finally. And she stomped into the kitchen and hung up the phone.

"Hey, Mouseling, do you have Halloween candy left?" Landis wanted to know. Debbie was gone. I told Landis yes, but I wasn't allowed to eat it whenever I wanted. The bag was stored high up on top of the 'frigerator.

Landis reached up and got it down. We sat on the floor in the kitchen with the candy and spread it out all around us. I ate a whole packet of chocolate-covered raisins and four sour candies and six mini-chocolate bars. I let Landis have all the peanut butter–flavored things because I didn't like them anyway, and she really wanted the licorice so I let her have that, too.

When we finished eating, we lay back on the floor and stared at the ceiling. Patrick Threep came over and sniffed our ears. We made lists of things, like games I hated to play that everyone else seemed to like:

Monopoly
Dodgeball
Keep Away
Snowball Fight
Lava Monsters

I didn't put Doctor on, because I hadn't decided about it for sure. Landis said I was an unusual mouse. Then we made a list of our favorite bathing suits of all time, including ones we didn't fit into anymore.

Mine: minty green stretchy, cow-print bikini, red racing stripe
Landis: tie-dye bikini, padded bra purple, polka-dot frilly

They were pretty useless lists—not like the word lists for Super Dupers, which gave you a big vocabulary your classmates wouldn't understand, and not like grocery lists, or Christmas present lists—but Landis was really into them. I liked listening to her talk. She told me about her older sister who was already in college in New York City, and how she wished she had a driver's license, and how she had big tits now, but they only grew last year. She was glad to have them, she said, because she hadn't had a boyfriend yet, and all the girls she was friends with had already gone to second base.

"I've never even kissed a boy," said Landis, twirling a piece of her curly hair up in front of her eyes. "Have you?"

I had kissed boys in kissing tag, but she said that didn't count.

"I kissed a boy in a play," she said. "But I'm not counting it. He had braces, and I would brush my teeth like crazy before rehearsal even though we hardly ever even practiced it. Bruce. Who wants to kiss a boy named Bruce?"

I made a face.

"Exactly. Shaun, or Paul, or Jimmy. Not Bruce Prunicker. Can you believe it? The only guy I've kissed is Bruce Prunicker. And it was all spit. Don't let guys spit all over you, Vanessa."

I promised I wouldn't.

"Kissing a boy who spits on you is much worse than that peanut butter candy," she said, waving a Nutter Butter in my face. "Here, eat this, and you'll know what it's like!"

"No!" I scrunched up my face and laughed as she pushed the candy toward my mouth. "No!" She tickled me, and I kicked my legs shouting, "No peanut butter kissing boys! No, no, never! Never! No peanut butter boys!"

"Well, anyway," Landis said, suddenly stopping her tickle and lying back down on the floor. "That's a good name for it. For boys you kiss but don't really want to, like because of a play, or mistletoe, or something, and they get drool all over you. Peanut Butter Boys."

"Is it bad for boys to dress up in women's clothes?" I asked her. "Does it make them queer?"

"Oh, my God." Landis laughed. "Where did you hear that?"

"I don't know."

"Well . . . how old are the boys?" she asked.

"Kids like me."

She thought for a minute. "Are they doing it at school? Or just at home for fun?"

I didn't see why it mattered where they did it, but I told her they did it at home for playing dress-up. Or for Halloween.

"And you want to know if it's bad?"

I nodded.

"No, it's not bad. It might be weird if they did it all the time, like if they came to school in a dress and lipstick. Or it might be weird if they were older, but I don't think it's weird for an eight-year-old. Kids like to play dress-up, right?"

"But why is it weird if they're older?"

"I don't know," said Landis. "It just is."

"Why is it weird at school but not at home?"

"It just is!" She was laughing again. "Well, not if it's Halloween. Then you can dress up however."

"Okay." I ate one more sour candy, just because I could. "What happened with the boy from Fright Night?"

"Shaun?"

"Yeah."

"Oh, man. It's complicated. Do you really want to know?"

It turned out Landis never did talk to Shaun on Halloween, and the next day at school he didn't mention the note she wrote him at all. She saw him in English, and he said, "Hey, Landis," but he never looked at her once after that, and at the end of English, he disappeared pretty quickly. She had looked up their love match in an astrology book. It said that Shaun was a Gemini, which explained why he might like her back and still not talk to her. Gemini was the sign of the twin, so he had two different sides to his personality.

Then Landis began to wonder if he ever got the note. She should have handed it to him directly, because now she was worried she put it in the wrong locker, and oh my God, that would be really bad, because this snobby girl named Hannah had the locker next to his.

Also, she had used this pink pen, which she thought was very cute at the time, but had since decided was babyish. She wished she hadn't used it. Did I think it looked good to dot your *i*s with circles?

I did.

Friday was better. Shaun had been standing by her locker in the morning, leaning with his hand against the door of it. When she went to undo her combination, he had put his other hand on the door, too, locking her between his arms for a second.

"I'm trapping you!" he said. "I'm on a mission!"

Landis's heart beat really quick, and she stood there in amazement, but then he just put his arms back down and asked her about the homework for English. In conference later, Connie had said that a guy would never put his arms around someone that way unless he liked her. Maybe she should have done something back, like pushed him in the chest or tickled him. On the other hand, if he *had* read the note, then he knew for sure she liked him. In which case, maybe he was using her for the homework. Or maybe he liked her back but she wasn't cool enough, so he didn't want other people to know. That would be okay, said Landis, as long as he liked her.

"And to top it all off," she moaned, "I've got my period. I hate having my period."

I didn't know what that was, so she explained it to me in detail, told me Tampax was better than pads, and it was embarrassing to buy them but you had to do it, and then sent me off to brush my teeth and hair while she cleaned up the candy wrappers from the floor.

In my bedroom, moonlight streamed in my horizontal window. Debbie had shut the makeshift curtains before she left, but Landis and I had opened them again so I could see out. I got my hairbrush off the dresser and tried to pull it though my hair, but there were tangles left over from my bath, and it wasn't that easy.

As I brushed, a large white bottom appeared at the window. It was a man's bottom, fleshy and slightly pink on the lower part, round like the moon behind it. Its owner must have been standing on our woodpile, and his pants must have been down around his knees, because I could see his arms reaching down to hold them. The arms were wearing a red cotton shirt with a cigarette burn on the cuff, but I couldn't see a face or feet because the window was only about twelve inches high.

The bottom waggled back and forth, and back and forth, in a

very silly way. Then it pushed against the glass for a minute, squashing into ridiculous flat shapes. Then it waggled again, briefly, and disappeared.

Who knew my window was so perfect for that kind of project? I could do puppet shows out there, standing on the woodpile, for anyone who was in my bedroom. Or I could pop up suddenly and surprise Debbie when she was inside vacuuming. I climbed up on the bed for a second to see if I could get my own bottom up to window height, and I almost could.

What a strange and silly thing for someone to do, standing at the window like that. A performance, a game. So funny, that bottom.

It didn't occur to me to wonder whose it was.

Not only wasn't she speaking to Katty Sherwin, Debbie had a bad time on her date. I heard her telling Grin on the phone when they had their Sunday-morning chat. My mother's parents were always very excited about anyone she was dating. I guess she told them about her boyfriends because she knew they worried when she wasn't seeing anyone, and because having a man was a big achievement in their eyes—but she never seemed to like dealing with their reactions. Back when she dated Jake, for example—the one who played shark in the water at Walden Pond—Grin came down for a visit and met him briefly. Right afterward, she mentioned that she had a complete set of beautiful china that she'd give to Debbie if she got remarried.

My mother got upset. A set of china, sitting in the garage? Why hadn't she got it when she married Jordy? She couldn't think what on earth Grin was saving it for.

"I was saving it for the right time," Grin said.

"What kind of right time? Was it because Jordy wasn't a doctor or a lawyer? Because he didn't have a college degree?"

"No, of course not."

"Well, what was it?"

"It wasn't anything particular." Grin had shifted in her seat uncomfortably.

"You didn't approve of Jordy. Just admit it."

"Not even you approved of Jordy," Grin said mildly.

That was beside the point. It was like Grin and Pompey knew that Debbie and Jordy wouldn't stay married and had saved the china for a better man.

"Well, you didn't stay married. Did you?"

"Just give the china to me now," my mother snapped. "I'd love to have it. Vanessa and I are eating off this ugly chipped stuff I got at Goodwill."

But Grin balked, saying it was very difficult to pack up china and send it all the way from Chicago. It might get broken.

Debbie said we were eating off crap.

If those plates cracked, it would break her heart, Grin said, and asked what happened to the plates Debbie received from the Bricks as a wedding present.

"I threw them at the door after Jordy left," my mother answered. "Please, just give me the china."

Grin said she had been thinking about using it again herself after all these years. It was really very pretty, and difficult to pack properly for shipping.

"Are you saying No, Mother?" Debbie asked.

Grin said she wasn't saying No, it was just that she didn't know when she'd find the time to pack them up and get them to the post office, and what was Debbie in such a hurry for? That nice young man with the sandy hair could afford lots of nice plates. What was his job again? Wasn't he a dentist?

Debbie said it was ridiculous to be thinking about her marrying that man; she barely even knew him.

"I just want you to have a perfect marriage, like your father and I have," said Grin, turning on her South of France accent like she always did when she asserted superiority.

"It *was* like yours."

"What is that supposed to mean?"

Debbie sighed. "Do you want another glass of wine, Mother?"

Grin nodded, and my mother poured. "I don't know what you're talking about," Grin went on. "Pompey and I just wanted you happily married."

"It's too late for that," Debbie answered. "It's far too late."

My grandparents learned about Syd after he came to Halloween Fright Night. Pompey got all worked up because Syd worked for public television.

"How do you like the new young man?" Pompey asked when I answered the phone on Sunday morning. I said he was okay and he wore neat donkey ears on Halloween.

Did I know Syd made television shows?

Yes.

That was a very good job. Did I know that?

Kind of.

Was he tall?

Pretty tall. Medium.

Did he take my mother nice places?

I didn't know.

Then Pompey told me how he and Grin were coming for Thanksgiving, how they were going to try to get Debbie to make a turkey, even though she was a vegetarian, and how Grin made the best stuffing anybody ever ate.

Okay.

My mother took the phone then, and Grin got on the other end, and Lopey and I sat at the breakfast table while Debbie served me oatmeal with maple syrup swirled in the center. That's how I found out about what happened on the date.

Syd was an hour and a half late for the music festival, that was the main problem. Debbie had waited at the entryway for twenty minutes and eventually just bought her ticket and went in. At first she was worried, thinking he might have had an accident, but pretty soon she was just annoyed. The concert was outdoors, and there weren't any seats—just a stage and big open lawn where the audience danced around to the music. Debbie had wandered aimlessly for a little and finally sat down on the ground, over on the side, and watched the crowd. She was chilly. The whole thing was full of college students, and she felt sorry she was wearing makeup and a nice dress.

When Syd turned up, he pulled her to her feet and kissed her, said the band was out of sight and she was beautiful, and wasn't it a beautiful night? And she had trouble staying angry when faced with his outright assumption that absolutely nothing was wrong.

If he had apologized even the littlest bit, she could have gotten mad at him. But he exuded this sense of mellow righteousness, seemed to think she was really cool and open, that she couldn't be mad about a tiny thing like time. Time was for the uptight, time was for the establishment. Syd was flexible, Syd was relaxed; he wore his lateness like a virtue.

So Debbie hadn't said anything; had tried to dance to the music as if she was having a good time. Tried to relax out of her anger and let it go. But when they went out afterward to a party full of Syd's friends that she didn't even know, and he had introduced her as his lover, she had told him Fat Chance and stormed downstairs to the VW.

Grin told her that any man who called a woman his "lover" was a man better off dumped, even if he did work for public television.

Debbie said that was not the point. The point was being late and making it so that she couldn't even talk about it.

They hung up, and Debbie took a drink of coffee. Her hand was still on the telephone when it rang again. It was Mister Bhaduri, calling to say that something serious had happened to Anu. She wouldn't be in school for a while. Would it be okay if I didn't go home with them the next couple of Thursdays?

9.

Dirty Words

Button came to live with us the next weekend. He was absolutely tiny, a dun-colored cat only three weeks old. At first Debbie said she found him on the stairs. When I asked a lot of questions, though, and wanted to go out and look for the mother cat, she admitted that she got him at the pound. He was small enough so she could hold him in one hand.

Patrick Threep was a little pissed off at the new kitten, but Fuzzy took to mothering him right away. He ate crunchies that Debbie softened with warm milk, and he cried a lot at first, but soon he and the other two were wrestling on the living room rug.

Even though Anu wasn't in school on Friday or Monday, my near popularity continued. Marie didn't dare penetrate it. I even went to the park with Angelique and her baby-sitter after school. It was weird, at first, the two of us playing. We had only been friends for a little more than a week. But once we got going with this game about having horses with wings that nobody knew about, we had a pretty good time.

Angelique's baby-sitter was a Cuban woman who gave us goldfish crackers in a plastic container, and I liked her very much, but otherwise I had absolutely no curiosity about Angelique's life. I didn't ask where her mom was, or her dad, or her brothers and sisters. I didn't care where they lived, or in what kind of house, or whether she had her own room. I didn't care if she had pets. All we needed in common was something to pretend.

Angelique was indecisive, though. For example, I asked if she wanted the horses to fly only at night when nobody could see them, and she asked me a question right back: "What do you think?"

I thought maybe she wasn't answering because she wanted to say no and was scared it would make me mad. Of course, I wouldn't have suggested it if I didn't think it was a good idea, but to be nice, I told her I was happy either way. If I said that, I figured, she'd feel comfortable saying what she really thought. But then she came back and claimed she didn't care, either.

We hung upside down off the jungle gym. "I can't decide if my horse is brown or black," Angelique mused. "Which should it be?"

"Brown could be chestnut or it could be a really dark brown, or more tan. Black is just black," I said.

"I know, but which should it be?"

"What color brown, you mean?

"I'm not sure. Which one is the prettiest?"

Angelique was tall and had a hard jaw and watery eyes. Her smile was surprising, shining across her face and changing it into something warm. I liked her for that.

Landis said she thought Angelique had low self-esteem. She looked up her sign in the astrology book, and it confirmed that Angelique doubted the validity of her opinions. Or even worse, didn't know she had opinions.

"Everybody has opinions," said Landis. "Sheesh."

We got the candy down again from the top of the fridge and took it outside on the steps even though the air was brittle with November. Landis was feeling very good because she was going to a party with Shaun the next weekend. Well, not exactly *with* Shaun, but with Shaun and a bunch of other people. He probably never did get the note she put in his locker, she figured. He hadn't mentioned it, and the way he was acting he would certainly have written her back if he had. All signs were to the good. He had caught up with her in the hallway one afternoon and walked out of his way in her direction. He was wearing a "Let It Be" T-shirt and his hair was getting really long. Landis thought he was so foxy. And the day after that, he asked if she was going to Dave's party.

There was another girl, though. Hannah, who had her locker next to his. There was no way Landis could compete. Hannah was much prettier and generally groovier. Plus she had already had about a million boyfriends, whereas Landis was a novice.

Even if the party went great, Landis was worried she was a bad kisser. You weren't supposed to drool a whole lot; that she knew. And you were supposed to use your tongue. But what on earth did you do with it? It seemed weird to just wave it around in somebody's mouth, but it also seemed weird to go actively licking his teeth or the side of his lips like a cat. Also, it was more advanced to keep your eyes open, she knew, but how freaky was that if the boy had his eyes open, too—and you were both staring bug-eyed while licking each other's teeth?

Another problem was lip gloss. Landis and all the ninth-grade girls wore shiny, sticky flavors like strawberry and grape. It looked good, but would it be weird for the guy to taste a flavor if he wasn't expecting it? Maybe you should warn him subtly by saying something about how you always wore watermelon lip gloss because watermelon was your favorite fruit—so he'd be prepared. And would it be sticky? He probably wouldn't like that, but on the other hand, Landis felt she looked much more kissable with the gloss on.

Later, while I was playing with plastic horses in the living room, Landis got my mom's sex books off the very top shelf. I hadn't read them, but I knew they were up there because sometimes I'd stare systematically at every single section of the bookshelf, hoping there'd be something good for kids that I'd overlooked. One time I had found *Aesop's Fables*, but mainly it was books on how to do crafts, vegetarian cooking, the history of art.

There were only two on sex. One was a guide for women that told all about their bodies and the diseases they could get. It had a big section on having babies. The other was a how-to manual, with pictures of hairy white people doing it in all kinds of positions. I had looked at it for a couple minutes once, but it bored me because there was no *story* about the people and what they were doing in their crotchless tights and knee-high boots. They didn't have names, or jobs, or personalities, so it wasn't interesting to me what they did with their clothes off.

Landis found it interesting, though. She said she could learn a lot baby-sitting for me that would prove useful in later life.

* * *

We stopped eating eggs the week after Debbie's fight with Katty, and my mother got very particular about what I ate at school. She seemed like she wanted to protect everyone and everything from harm. Sometimes she'd quiz me about what there had been for snack, which was usually just juice and crackers with peanut butter if you wanted it, but one time had been tuna salad. We even left the pizza place near Harvard Square before our pie came one day, because the people next to us had this giant Meat-Lovers' Special, with sausage, ham, Canadian bacon, ground beef, and pepperoni. Debbie couldn't sit there, she said, looking at all those dead animals on a platter, so we left ten dollars on the table and went home for cucumber sandwiches.

Anu came back to school after only a couple days' absence, but things were strained between us. I felt as if someone had drained the energy out of me, like everything was tinged with gray. She was like that, too. I didn't know what had happened to her, or why she had been gone. And she didn't tell me. She didn't say much at all, actually, and looked at the floor when she was walking. She didn't raise her hand during Circle of Sharing, either, not even when the braided teacher asked, "What is a baby horse called?"

We hadn't had any lessons about horses, so some kids said Pony and one kid said Calf, and Summer said Gelding. But I knew the answer, and I knew that Anu knew it, too: Foal. I elbowed her in the side, but she didn't respond. Finally, I answered it myself.

The teacher went on to ask what a baby turtle was. Nobody knew, but Luke raised his hand and said a Turd.

"Didn't you know it was a Foal?" I asked Anu later, while we were all making individual choices and developing at our own personal growth pace.

"I knew." She shrugged.

"Then why didn't you raise your hand?"

"I didn't want to."

"I can't believe Summer thought it was a Gelding."

"I don't want to talk about it, Vanessa."

"Why not? It's just horses."

"I said, I don't want to talk about it."

"A Gelding is a boy that's had his balls cut off."

She didn't even crack a smile. She picked up her notebook and walked over to a different table.

After that, she and I were no longer on speaking terms. I didn't even realize it at first, but as I was hanging up my jacket in my locker that afternoon, Summer came by.

"What did you do to Anu?" she asked.

"Nothing."

"She's not talking to you."

"Yes, she is."

"No, she's not. What did you do?"

"I didn't do anything to her. She did something to me."

"What was it?"

"Just something."

"Come on, you can tell me."

"I'm not telling."

"Why not?

"None of your beeswax."

"Anu wouldn't say, either," Summer told me philosophically.

* * *

In Super Duper Spelling, a potential Incident had been building. The week following Halloween—the same Tuesday Anu came back—it started getting serious.

One day in late September, a boy had brought in the word Fornication, asking if we could all learn to spell it. He had been reading some religious literature that a door-to-door evangelist dropped off at his house, and that's how he came across it. I don't think he knew what it meant. Ron hadn't batted an eye but treated it the same as any other word. We all wrote it down and learned to spell it. Fornication: noun. Intercourse between a man and woman not married to each other. A couple weeks later, someone else brought in Estrogen, and we learned to spell that, too.

After Halloween, though, a group of mischievous fourth-graders brought in a whole collection of words they probably knew they shouldn't.

Fellate.

Gestate.

Masturbation.

Gonorrhea.

Syphilis.

Homosexual.

Ron was clearly flummoxed. He actually left the room and went all the way down to the first floor to confer with Stuart the principal. We heard about this conference later, because a note got written to our parents saying that it was the policy of Cambridge Harmony not to introduce sex into the classroom until high school biology class, but that if children proved themselves inquisitive, the teachers were not going to refuse them information. Information, after all, was the essence of schooling. A child's learning experience should not be censured or interrupted because he or she inquires about socially inappropriate things. Therefore, Cambridge Harmony's policy in such events would be as follows: to inform the child gently that subjects like these were usually best discussed with parents at home, and then to answer the child's question or point him in the direction of a research material that would do so.

This letter became the subject of a big parent-teacher meeting in which lots of adults who had long ago committed to fornication as a weekly practice—and who had been dedicated for at least half a decade to women's liberation, civil rights, and whole grains—had to confront their discomfort with certain sexual matters. These people let their kids run naked on the beaches of Martha's Vineyard; they talked openly about "relationships" and the natural state of the body when it wasn't shaved or decorated with cosmetics. None of them protested teaching young children about sex because the subject was intrinsically immoral. They had already told their kids about the sperm swimming to the egg and had earnestly explained that sex comes from love between two people. They protested because they were suddenly realizing that an open education philosophy could threaten the innocence of their children. These spelling words opened up possibilities our parents did not want to imagine for us: that we might be gay; we might get sick; we might be adulterous or engage in fellatio. Our parents did not want their third-graders knowing about syphilis and homosexuality. Not even if the third-graders *wanted* to know.

They said nothing of the kind at the meeting, of course. I

imagine it was impossible to articulate. What they did say was that certain subjects were subjects for home education. If children ask to drive a car, the school doesn't teach them, and the parents don't teach them, either, until they are old enough for a learner's permit. If children want to learn to cook, the school has no lessons for that; it's taught in the domestic sphere when the parents feel the child is old enough to operate the stove safely. Same with manners, same with swimming, although some people protested that those last two were not good examples because the school would in fact offer swimming lessons if only it had a pool, and because certain parents taught their children no manners at all.

The teachers countered, saying they could not deny children an education when they were asking for it. Anyway, they weren't holding lessons on fellatio; they were just responding to an inquiry by pointing the child toward a dictionary.

Some parents got upset at the apparently flip and intentionally humorous reference to lessons in fellatio and objected to being forced to imagine a bunch of third-graders being instructed in that practice.

One divorced dad said he thought such lessons would probably benefit a lot of the uptight people at the meeting.

The end result was essentially nothing; a parent committee was formed to draft a letter suggesting an alternate policy for the school to take. Then they would have to figure out whether to have people vote on it, or sign a petition, or what.

Debbie went to the meeting. She sent me outside to play with the other kids in the playground, and I said Okay, but really I crept inside and watched the whole thing from the back of the room. My mother spent most of her time talking to the man sitting next to her—a hugely tall person with gray-blond hair. His name was Win. He was old, about forty, and had introduced himself when he squeezed in beside her on the bench. Debbie asked him what sort of name Win was, and he said it was short for Winston.

"My daughter is in that spelling group," my mother confided. "Last week she spelled Fornicate, and this week she's spelling Syphilis."

"Syphilis? That's what all this uproar is about?"

"They learned to spell Pneumonia, too. I don't really see that it's all that different."

"I suppose not," the man said. He was tweedy and thin, despite his height.

"Gonorrhea, Tendonitis, Halitosis. I don't think any one is worse than the other for a kid to learn to spell," Debbie went on.

"What about Fornicate?" the man asked.

"My kid is so far from having a sex life at this point," my mother said. "It's just information to her. She takes it in, this material, but only about a quarter inch deep, you know? She doesn't really consider people screwing outside of marriage; she doesn't picture it, or wonder about it. She thinks about the word and tries to remember what it means for the next time she has a test."

"My daughter's not a speller," the man said, almost as if he hadn't been listening. "She's more of a mathematics type. She was very slow to read."

"I really don't care if she can spell it, so long as she doesn't practice it, or catch it, or do anything else with it at the fragile age of eight."

Win scratched his graying sideburns. "I know what you mean."

"Spelling is spelling," said Debbie. "I looked up all kinds of things in the encyclopedia when I was a child."

"So did I."

"I looked at naked people in the *National Geographic,* too, and I don't think that did me any harm. In fact, I could have used a little more information in general. I might not have ended up pregnant at age fourteen."

I was leaning against the wall about four seats away from them.

"I didn't even know how babies were made, exactly. Much less how you got rid of one you didn't want to have."

Whatever it was, Debbie had done it. She had done it, and she had never told till now.

Why tell this man, this tweedy, tall man so much older than she was?

Fourteen was Landis's age. Landis hadn't even kissed anybody except Bruce Prunicker.

I stood still.

Debbie and Win were silent for a minute. We all listened to Ron stand up and tell about how Super Duper Spelling was a resonant learning experience for all the children involved. My mother's face was hot and pink.

"I'm so sorry," Debbie finally muttered, wiping her eye. "I don't even know you. I can't believe I just told you something like that. Please forget it."

"Okay," the man said, and he flashed a kind smile that made his eyes crinkle up. "It's forgotten."

"Just like that?" Debbie seemed surprised. Syd would have pressed for total openness.

"Just like that. Do you think there will be milk and cookies when all this is over?"

"I hope so." Debbie smiled, shaking her head. "I fornicatin' hope so."

10.

In Which I Volunteer

The bottom returned to my window on two subsequent nights, waggling in the light of the moon. Always, its arms were wearing the red cotton shirt with the cigarette burn, and always, it did nothing more than swish side to side with a certain amount of plump pride, then press itself to the glass and disappear.

It inevitably arrived when I was already in bed; Debbie would read me a story, tuck the stuffed animals in alongside me, and close the curtains if they were open. She had finished them pretty quickly, and they were decorated with brown felt antelopes and sun-colored lemons. Then she'd kiss me good night and go back to her cup of tea in the living room, or head to the kitchen and clunk around doing supper dishes. I would always open the curtains right away after she left, at first because I liked the sunlight in the morning, but now because I knew the bottom might appear, like a fat, fleshy puppet on the woodpile, dancing back and forth like the world was all just fine, like there was nothing to worry about except shakin' it.

The third time it visited, I applauded, and Debbie came back from the kitchen saying, "Vanessa? Why are you clapping?"

"I just am," I said. The bottom had cleverly disappeared.

"Well, now is not the time for music," she said. "Go to sleep, sugar."

She closed the curtains again, not seeming to remember that she had shut them fifteen minutes ago. I let them stay, since the bottom wasn't coming back again the same night.

At school, we quietly continued learning the dirty words. Syphilis: noun. A chronic infectious venereal disease. Gestate: verb. To carry unborn young in the uterus for a period following conception. Or, to develop in the mind. I only understood the definitions in the vaguest way, but I liked spelling the words because they were big ones that people didn't use every day. Special words. I liked the *y* in syphilis, because *y*s don't get used that way very often, and also the *ph*.

To dissipate the furor over our vocabulary lists, however, Ron announced that the Super Duper Spellers were going to put on a play. We would perform it for parents and the other children in the lower school. I think he was hoping that a demonstration of the spelling group's constructive influence on the Cambridge Harmony community would fix its flailing reputation—and it wasn't a bad idea, really, in spite of how things turned out.

Using our spelling words—and not, he was careful to emphasize, the words we brought in ourselves, but the words that he had chosen to be on our weekly lists—we would decide on scenes that could be acted by two or three people. The scenes would illustrate our understanding of particular words we had spelled. For instance, he said, we could have a scene where a baby is a genius and knows how to do times tables, demonstrating that the baby is Precocious. Or we could show someone pretending to walk on a tightrope, which is very Precarious.

We all raised our hands and said ideas for what kinds of scenes might go in the play. I had an idea for Collection that showed a collection of cats, and someone else had an idea that showed people taking up a Collection to buy a sick kid a teddy bear. Luke kept coming up with ideas for Ridiculous, but none of them made any sense. "That's the point!" He kept laughing. "It's ridiculous!"

"But people aren't going to know that, Luke." It was the first time Anu had spoken. "They aren't going to know it's ridiculous. They're going to be confused."

"I wouldn't be confused," said Luke, and stuck out his tongue.

After we had "brainstormed" for most of the spelling lesson, Ron asked if somebody wanted to volunteer to write a first draft of the play. That person would use some of the different ideas people had generated to write a series of scenes. He or she would give the characters names and personalities, and write their dialogue. Then later, we could all work together to edit the manuscript and get it ready to perform.

The classroom was silent for a minute. No one's hand came off the desk.

"Doesn't anyone want to be an author?"

No one moved.

"It's a chance to express yourself," Ron coaxed, "to make yourself heard. You can show everybody how you see the world."

Again, no one moved.

How you see the world.

"Anyone?" Ron folded his arms and tried to look stern.

Express yourself.

"I hope I don't have to pick someone."

Make yourself heard.

I put my arm in the air.

Spelling over, we trooped downstairs. No one ever talked much on our way back to the second floor. Our brains were tired. Today, though, Luke called my name.

"Vanessa, wait up!" he said. "I have something for you."

"What is it?" I was suspicious. We had hardly spoken since Halloween night, but that wasn't too unusual, since we didn't hang out together at school. I was angry at him though, and my mother was angry at Katty, and there was something of a wall between us.

"It's an eraser," he said.

I climbed back up a couple steps to where he was standing. "What kind of eraser?"

"It's a green one that fits on the end of your pencil. You like green, right?"

It's true, I did.

"Here, give that to me," Luke said. I handed over my pencil, and he squished the eraser onto the end and gave it back. Minty green like a waxy candy.

"Thank you," I said. "It's neat."

"I just thought you'd like it." Luke scuffed the banister with his sneaker. "It doesn't mean anything." And he ran down the stairs.

The eraser suddenly made me feel warm and wrong, like I'd been unfair to Anu. After all, I hadn't told her about me and Luke, and I had lied and said "No Boys Allowed" when I didn't mean it. I missed her, and looked down the stairwell to see if her brown hand and her fuzzy, blue-sweatered arm were visible on the handrail. I could see Luke's freckly paw, jerking forward as he jumped down two stairs at a time, but no Anu. Maybe she was still upstairs.

I climbed back up to the top floor. Anu wasn't an apologizer, that I knew. I would have to say "sorry" and not expect her to say anything back. I remembered from when we had a fight about her using her plastic horse to boss mine around. She made him go swimming in the toilet when he really didn't want to, and made him dress up in plastic panties from her Baby Alive doll. I had been upset, and cried, and she had simply sneered at me. "Man, Vanessa, what's your problem?"

So I had taken my horse, ripped off his plastic panties, and stormed downstairs to watch cartoons with Baby and Ram until Debbie came to pick me up. The next day, Anu had been mad at me for hanging out with her brothers when I was supposed to be there to play with her. She wouldn't speak to me until I told her I was sorry. Then she said okay, but never said anything about what she did to my horse, or the mean way she had asked me, "Vanessa, what's your problem?" She just acted like it never happened, like I went downstairs and watched cartoons for no reason at all.

I figured I would catch her coming out of the top-floor classroom and say I was sorry I yelled at her, and I wouldn't keep secrets anymore, and could we please be friends? I had a long piece of rainbow yarn finger-knitting in my jeans pocket, and I planned on giving it to her if she seemed resistant.

The door to our classroom was open, and I stopped for a second. Ron and Anu were still in there, sure enough. But they weren't talking about spelling, nor were they talking about the play.

"I heard about what happened from your dad," Ron was saying, leaning in across the table.

Anu looked at her hands.

"I'm very sorry to hear about it. It's not your fault. Do you know that?"

Anu nodded.

"It's not your fault at all." Ron said. "And if you ever want to talk to me, you can say the word, okay?"

Anu just sat there. Were her parents getting a divorce? I wondered. Or had some kind of accident happened to Baby that Anu was responsible for? I hadn't seen him at school lately, although that didn't mean he wasn't there. The little kids had their classrooms in the basement. "This is very hard, I'm sure," Ron said. "And sometimes it helps to talk about these things." There was a pause. "It's okay if you were aroused," he continued. "And it's okay to express that, you know?"

"I wasn't." Anu's voice sounded small.

"It can be very hard to admit that sort of thing," Ron said.

"I wasn't." She sounded firmer. They were sitting in the gray of the classroom with the overhead light turned off, and Ron had already put most of his teaching books in a tote bag. Sunshine came in the window and made squares on the scarred wooden table. Ron put his pencils and the last of his books into the bag.

"Do you know what I mean by arousal?" he said.

"Yes," said Anu. "I know."

"Well, it's a natural response in a situation like that. You wouldn't need to feel ashamed."

"I don't," said Anu. "I didn't feel that way you said."

"I hear you," Ron said, and again they were silent. "Sometimes, though, feelings get buried that we don't feel comfortable with. I just want you to know that if you have those feelings, you shouldn't be afraid to talk to someone about them. You could talk to your mom, for example."

"I didn't feel the way you said." Anu sounded something like her own self now, standing up to Ron.

"Well, any feelings you have are legitimate and valid," said Ron.

Anu kicked her feet against the legs of her chair. "Can I go, now?"

"I hope you feel comfortable talking with me," Ron said. "I won't judge anything about how you feel."

"Can I go?" she asked again.

"I'm not keeping you, Anu. You're free to leave at any time."

I bolted down the stairs before she could come out of the classroom. By the time she got to the second floor, I was already working on my diorama.

11.

Where the Sour Clover Grows

Even though he was a pushy late guy who called himself her lover and couldn't even tell whether his dick was inside his underwear or not, Debbie kept dating Syd. He came over a couple times after I went to bed and stayed the night, and once he came early and we all watched a movie on TV. It seemed pretty clear she'd forgiven him for what happened the night of the music festival. In the mornings they were lovey-dovey in front of me, Syd cooking breakfast, the two of them kissing with their tongues in the kitchen.

It turned out that following his tie-dye blessing experience in the hot tub at the Alexian Ashram, Syd had surmounted his Wall of Shame and become a total nudist. At our house he was very conservative—the aftermath of the Incident—but at home, Debbie said, he did everything in the nude. He hammered things in the nude, did push-ups in the nude, read novels, listened to the record player. He was nude at any Alexian event where nudity was appropriate. He was completely free and open with his body, now that he had processed his shame. He had even been to one of those nudist camps, where he had gotten an all-over tan and played naked volleyball. Debbie told me all this so I'd understand that he hadn't really meant to show his penis. He was so used to having it out that he simply didn't notice.

Though I had given the idea some consideration, I hadn't told anyone about the bottom. It was still appearing—not every night, but fairly regularly, about twenty minutes or so after my bedtime. I kept track of it in a diary Landis had given me. It was a real official one that came with a lock and key. She had also given me a minty green pen, and the first time I wrote in the diary, I wrote something about the bottom: "It is never embarrassed," my diary says. "Even though it is not very pretty."

I figured that if I told, Debbie would freak out, do something to stop my seeing it. Nail the curtains shut or something. Maybe she'd even call the police. And Landis would be grossed out, or might feel frightened while she was baby-sitting, even though I was pretty sure there was nothing to be frightened about. In my mind, the bottom really wasn't connected to any kind of human being; there was no man outside on the woodpile, no person who might come into our house through a window. There was just a body part out there on its own in search of adventure.

I looked up all the words for it in the dictionary: Ass, Bum, Behind, Rear, Rear End, Butt, Buttocks, Rump, Posterior, Seat. Also Hindquarters, but I wasn't sure if that really counted for people. It counted for horses.

I began writing the play for Super Duper Spelling immediately, making notes in my green pen and writing scenes in my best cursive with a sharp number-two pencil. The characters all had names based on my research in the dictionary: Mister Posterior, Allowishus Rump, Susannah T. Bum, and Mrs. Ingrid Hindquarters. They used each other's names a great deal when conversing.

"I have a collection of cats, Mister Posterior," one of them said.

"How many cats is that, Mrs. Hindquarters?"

"Three. I have three cats. Their names are Syphilis, Gestate, and Homosexual."

"Three cats is not enough for a collection, Mrs. Hindquarters."

"Homosexual is the cutest. She is all white, with long fur. Do you like cats, Mister Posterior?"

"I'm telling you, you don't have a collection. Collection is a noun: a group of objects kept or studied together."

"Three is a group," said Mrs. Hindquarters.

"I agree," interjected Allowishus Rump. "Two is not a group, but three is a group."

"You do have a collection," put in Susannah T. Bum. "I agree with Allowishus Rump."

"Do you study your cats together?" Mister Posterior asked Mrs. Hindquarters. "That's part of having a collection."

"No, I just keep them."

"Well," said Mister Posterior, "don't bring them near me. I'm afraid of cats!"

Then three more students came onstage, crawling on their knees to portray Syphilis, Gestate, and Homosexual. They meowed loudly and purred, and Mister Posterior ran off in terror. That was the end of the skit.

I was pretty proud of how the play was progressing, although I wished my handwriting was neater. The next one I wrote was for the word Precocious. Two kids were in a sleeping bag together. One of them was a genius. First the genius kid, Louisa Tushi, spouted a whole lot of brilliant definitions, proving that she was extremely Precocious. The other child, Biff W. Hiney, commented on her precocity, and then a mom came in, Mamma Hiney. She said that it was very Precocious of Louisa and Biff to be in the sleeping bag together, because after all, they were only eight years old! And Biff, who kept saying "Mamma Hiney" every time he addressed his mother (for added comic effect), asked how could Precocious mean Louisa was a genius and also mean being in a sleeping bag with a boy? And Louisa—because, after all, she was a genius—explained that Precocious didn't mean extra smart and it didn't mean you studied a lot, and it didn't mean you were naughty, either. It meant you were advanced for your age, and it was an adjective.

I worked lying on my tummy on the floor of my bedroom after school. Debbie asked what I was up to, and I told her it was a spelling project, but I didn't tell her any more than that, except when I asked her how to spell Posterior.

On Saturday, the end of the week I volunteered to write the play, my mother and Syd and I were sitting around in the living room playing Parcheesi. I was winning, and the rain was making noise outside the window. Button curled up on my lap and Fuzzy, her coat no longer dusty and her sores healed up, was washing Patrick Threep, who lay like a sultan receiving his due. Debbie kept getting up to check the lasagna she was baking, and Syd was annoying me by not counting how many spaces he moved one at a time, just eyeballing it and leaping his pieces ahead, but we were having fun anyway, until Mister Bhaduri knocked on the door.

He was wet from the rain. Even though he was dressed in a

bright yellow slicker, he hadn't worn the hood up or zipped the zipper closed. He looked smaller in his weekend clothes than he did when he came back from Harvard on Thursdays: his blue jeans showed how thin he was, and his mustache looked a little jagged at the edges, whereas usually it was neatly trimmed.

"Debbie," he said, standing on our steps, "I'm so sorry to bother you, but I wonder if I could have a minute of your time?"

"Sure, sure," my mother answered, stepping back to invite him inside. "Have you met Syd Wheeler?"

"Yes, at Halloween. I'm Debbie's lover." Syd smiled and held out his hand for Mister Bhaduri to shake.

Debbie said something about how long it had been since Anu had last come over. "I guess the girls usually play at your house, don't they? It's so much bigger. I don't think you've been here since last June."

Mister Bhaduri shook his head apologetically. "Yes, Anu was here to play in the splashy pool."

"That's right."

"The rubber pool in the yard."

"Yes," Debbie said. "Do you remember, Vanessa?"

I said I did, and Debbie offered Mister Bhaduri a cup of tea. "It's cold out, isn't it? We're really getting some winter weather." She was prattling and putting honey into mugs while the water boiled. "I think today is the first day it really smells like winter. There's a winter smell, a snow smell, don't you think?"

"Oh . . . yes." He sat himself down at the kitchen table, rubbing the skin on the back of his hand with his thumbnail and making white marks on his deep brown skin. I started to wonder if Anu had told him about our fight. Maybe he was here to tell my mother that I couldn't play with Anu anymore since I had lied about playing with Luke; or maybe Anu had told him I was mean and made fun of her chicken pox and that she wasn't speaking to me anymore. He was probably going to tell Debbie what a bad girl I was, and how he thought she should know about it and send me to prison, or to the psychologist, or down into a dungeon for bad kids who don't know how to play nice.

I wondered if I could defend myself. Would I tell on Anu about showing her chicken pox butt? Would I describe how she had said "No Boys Allowed" when she never meant it, and how she didn't speak to me at school? Could I explain the problem at all, the problem with Luke, and what she'd said about me, and what he might have said?

Debbie finished making the tea and led Mister Bhaduri into the living room.

"I'm sorry to intrude," he repeated, perching himself on our secondhand couch. "I have something to talk to you about that I don't think Vanessa should hear."

Was that good or bad? Did it mean it was something that had nothing to do with me, something about the PTA? Or did it mean that what I had done was so incredibly horrible he didn't even want me present while he talked about it?

"Vanessa, sugar, will you go play in your room, please? You can take Button with you." Debbie picked up the mewling kitten and handed him over. I left the living room as Syd settled into the butterfly chair and Debbie poured tea from the pot.

I didn't go to my room, though. I stopped and sat down on the kitchen floor in front of the stove, leaning my back against the warm metal and smelling the lasagna smell. Listening.

Mister Bhaduri wasn't there to talk about me at all. He was there to tell Debbie what had happened to Anu. He just wanted

Debbie to know why things would be different from now on. Really, he said, he needed to tell someone. They didn't have many friends that they could talk to, only professional colleagues and horse trainers. The only people who knew about Anu right now were a couple of the teachers at Cambridge Harmony, although he supposed it would all come out pretty soon. It should come out, he said, so that other little kids could be protected. But still he felt embarrassed about it.

Syd said Mister Bhaduri should feel comfortable being totally open.

Mister Bhaduri cleared his throat.

On the Friday after Halloween, Anu and her brothers had been walking home from school. The boys were roughhousing, as they often did, having sword fights with sticks. Even Baby. Anu wasn't really interested, and had stepped into this clearing she knew about to pick sour clover. There was a gap in a hedge; she liked to squeeze through it into a small corner of a park, he said, back behind some trees and a bench. It was like a hideaway, though none of his children had ever told him about it until now. Samir was supposed to watch out for the younger ones. He was twelve and old enough to take responsibility, but he never watched Anu when she was in the clearing. He just kept walking and waited for her at the corner. It was understandable, Mister Bhaduri supposed. It certainly wasn't Samir's fault. It wasn't anybody's fault.

Anu had slipped into the hideaway to pick some clover, and there was a man in there. Expecting her. He had a ski mask over his head and face. He was white, and of medium height, but she hadn't been able to say anything else about how he looked. Anu had been startled, had turned to push her way back through the gap in the hedge, but the man had said, "Wait," in an authoritative way, and so she had waited.

There was no one in the park that she could see, no one sitting on the bench or playing with a dog.

The man in the ski mask had turned around, unzipped his pants, and pulled them down. He had exposed his bare ass to Anu, waving it around like a sexual threat, bending his knees so it protruded toward her. She had never seen a naked grown-up. Mister and Mrs. Bhaduri were very private about their bodies.

At first she was struck silent. And then she began to scream.

"It was so heartbreaking," Mister Bhaduri told my mother. "She was still screaming and crying when she walked in the front door of our house. The whole walk home, her brothers couldn't get her to talk." Samir had asked her repeatedly what was wrong, but she wouldn't—or couldn't—answer.

Mister Bhaduri had wrapped her up in the afghan from the couch and patted her head; Samir had made her a cup of warm milk. But it wasn't until her mother came home that Anu would tell anyone what happened.

"Did you call the police?" Debbie asked.

"Yes, we called them, and they came and took a description of the crime. But they said that unless the same man assaults other children, they probably won't be able to find him. They don't have enough to go on. He could be anybody, really," Mister Bhaduri said, looking at Syd. "Any Caucasian man of medium height."

"Is it a crime, what the man did?"

"Oh, yes. Indecent exposure."

"And if you find him, can you prosecute?"

"Yes," answered Mister Bhaduri. "But really, the reason I came to talk to you was about Anu. She is very upset by all of this. She doesn't want anyone to know, even though she understands she needs to tell so that we can find the bad man who did it."

There was a clinking of mugs as Debbie poured some more tea.

"We don't let the children walk home from school anymore," he went on. "We pick them up in the car and drive them eight blocks. I don't want to take any chances, and it is the only way we can even get Anu to go to school at all. We are all the time driving back and forth, my wife and I."

"Is there anything I can do to help?"

"Not really. I just wanted you to know why Anu doesn't want to play with anybody after school right now." He sounded like he was about to weep. "She wants to sit in her bedroom and read, she says. She doesn't eat very much. She carries that afghan with her everywhere in the house, and she has nightmares. Wakes up crying. I just don't think we can have Vanessa over on Thursdays, and I didn't want you to take it personally."

It was silent for a moment. Mister Bhaduri was sobbing. "She's not the same little girl," he said. "I cannot believe this has happened to us."

"Children are resilient creatures," my mother said. "Anu is a very strong person. I'm sure she'll pull through."

"I know it could be so much worse," he said. "I know that. My wife keeps telling me. You've read about Patrick Threep? They never found him. Never found him, can you imagine? If my daughter disappeared, I'd want to kill myself." Mister Bhaduri's voice rose higher. "But in a way this is almost as bad, because I have to see her suffer."

"I'm sure she'll recover," Debbie said. "I'm sure she will."

"And think!" he went on, as if he hadn't heard her. "Think what that man could have done to her, isolated there in that hideaway. He could have shown her more parts of his horrible body; he could have raped her, or hurt her, or taken her away."

I had never seen a grown-up so upset; he was crying like a kid. I peeked around the corner to get a look: his elbows were on his knees, fingers clasped, his head bowed toward the floor. The tears dropped onto the carpet in irregular rhythm. He had a tissue in his hands, but he didn't use it.

"I'm thinking of taking her to see a psychiatrist," he said. "A child psychiatrist, someone who knows what to do for this kind of trauma. Do you know of anyone who might be good?"

"No," Debbie said. "I don't know anybody."

"Thank you, anyway." Mister Bhaduri started moving in his seat as if he was getting ready to go. "It seems strange to send a little girl to psychiatry, to have her analyzed, doesn't it?"

"Not if you think it will help. Half the people we know spend their lives on the couch, right?"

I didn't know anybody who spent her life on a couch.

"Sure, sure. But I can't get it into my head to send a child there. My wife wants to do it."

He was referring to Anu without saying her name. "A little girl." "A child."

"It helps a lot of people," my mother said neutrally.

"I know. I know." He got to his feet. "I'm so sorry to impose on you like this, I hope you understand."

"Please, Jay." Debbie had on her hostess voice. "Think nothing of it."

And then Anu's father was gone. I hid in my room while he walked through the kitchen.

* * *

"Can I share an insight?" Syd was saying to my mother when I reentered the living room.

"Yes." Debbie looked weary and was lighting a cigarette.

"That girl, nothing really happened to her," Syd said. "At the ashram, people share their nudity all the time. They go nude in the hot tub, or sunbathing, and the children there see naked bodies, totally open and without censure. They're not traumatized. Nothing bad happens to them."

"I think that's different, Syd."

"Why is it different? A behind is a behind. It's all natural. The girl is overreacting because she needs attention," Syd went on. "If she stopped and considered it, she'd see that a body is a body, and it doesn't matter so much whether it's naked or clothed. You can just notice it, and move on."

"There's such a thing as privacy," Debbie said, exhaling. "You know I think that."

"It's not a matter of privacy. The girl didn't have to get undressed. She just witnessed someone else undressed. That's the way we all come into the world. It shouldn't be traumatic just to see a naked body."

"It shouldn't be, maybe, but it is," Debbie said. "The Bhaduris don't run around the house naked. They're book people, they live in the world of books."

"The naked body is the subject of art. It's a beautiful thing. They're making a trauma out of nothing."

"Didn't you see that man?" Debbie pointed to the door as if Mister Bhaduri was still standing behind it. "That man was crying. I don't even know him, I pick my kid up at his house once a week. And he was here, crying, because he didn't have anyone else to talk to about what happened to his daughter!"

"Yes, I saw that." Syd's voice was artificially calm. "I was sitting in the butterfly chair."

"So what are you saying?" Debbie asked.

"I'm saying that the Bhaduris perceive the incident as traumatic because of their limited view of the world. They're deciding to be traumatized."

"Bullshit, Syd." Debbie covered her mouth involuntarily, the way she always did when she swore. "Anu didn't decide to be traumatized. She reacted to what happened to her."

"I think her parents are encouraging her to see it as a trauma," Syd said.

"How are they encouraging her?"

"They're distraught. They called the police. They took her out of school."

"What were they supposed to do?"

Syd was silent for a minute. "Laugh, I guess. Or talk to the child about how everyone has a bottom and there's not any part of anybody's body that's particularly scary. It's like showing the kid that the bogey man isn't hiding in the closet. You open the closet, no bogey. The child isn't afraid anymore."

"You obviously don't have kids," my mother said.

"What is that supposed to mean?"

"The child is *still scared* after you look in the closet. The reality of there being nothing in there doesn't erase the fear. She thinks of the closet like a scary place—when it's dark, and she's alone, turning on the light and looking in there doesn't solve the problem."

"Debbie," Syd interrupted.

"Anu Bhaduri knows she has a bottom, Sydney. She knows she has one, she knows everybody else has one. This is a confident kid. The thing is, her own bottom at home, her brothers' bottoms—they're not the same as some strange man's ass when she's all by herself. In that situation . . . You just see the thing differently if you're somewhere unfamiliar and isolated."

"The parents are freaking out," Syd said. "You have to grant me that. They're not even letting the kids walk to school anymore or play with their friends."

"She's allowed to play with her friends. She doesn't want to."

"What about the walking? They're overreacting."

"I don't think so," Debbie said. "You have no idea how it must feel. You don't even have a pet, for God's sake."

"What?"

"You're not responsible to anything smaller than you, besides a couple of jade plants."

"Debbie," Syd's voice was condescending. "What does this have to do with some streaker in the park? Whether or not I have a pet?"

"You're not responsible for anyone but yourself. You don't know what that man might do. And he's not a streaker. Streakers are college kids running naked through the square to get a kick. That man is a flasher. He's showing himself to defenseless children to get a reaction. To satisfy some sick urge to exhibit himself."

"So?" said Syd. "That's doesn't mean he's causing any harm. He's only causing harm if people choose to see it as a criminal activity. At the ashram we have a concept called 'showing.' There's no truth to an event. There's just each individual's reaction to it. There's only a problem if the guy shows up to the child as frightening. Anu—is that her name?—If Anu could see it from another perspective, it would show up to her as benign."

"It is not benign," my mother said. "Who knows what this guy might do next? He could be lurking around the school planning to kidnap someone. He could be a complete—" she stopped to search for the word.

"Pedophile," Syd prompted.

"Pedophile."

"And what does this have to do with me not having a pet?" Syd smiled. I could tell he was trying to coax my mother out of her anger by making her feel silly.

"You don't have children. You don't know how your heart would break if they got hurt, so don't even begin to judge the Bhaduris. I would do exactly what they're doing if the same thing happened to Vanessa."

"You'd send her to a shrink because she saw somebody's behind?"

"Yes, I would."

"And drive her to school every day?"

"Yes."

"And let her wrap herself up in an old blanket and hide in her bedroom?"

"Yes, if that was what she wanted," Debbie said.

"You're being ridiculous."

"I don't think so."

They stood, staring at each other across the room. The burned smell of lasagna suddenly filled the air, and Debbie went to the oven to turn it off. Then she faced Syd Wheeler and asked him to leave. "I don't want you in my house anymore."

Syd didn't say a word. Just walked out and slammed the door behind him.

"I'm sorry, sugar," my mother said to me, as soon as he was gone. "You shouldn't have to watch grown-ups fight."

We put our coats on and got in the car to go to the pound.

The new cat was called Dirigible.

12.

A Disturbance

That same day, when I was in the bathtub, Debbie called the police about what she had seen outside my bedroom window three weeks earlier, the night when she decided to make the antelope curtains. I heard her on the telephone explaining, could hear her all the way down the hall.

A red shirt with long sleeves, she said. Blue jeans, maybe.

No, no more of him than just his butt.

No, he hadn't been there again. "I hung curtains in my child's bedroom after that," she explained.

No, she wouldn't let Vanessa play outside by herself, Officer. She was always watching her. Always.

That last part wasn't true, actually. I used to walk to the candy store with twenty-one cents in my pocket to buy sour candies and caramels at three cents apiece. There was only one big street to cross between me and the candy, and Debbie told me to ask a grown-up to help me cross it. I did that sometimes, and the people I asked were always nice, but most of the time I just waited and crossed by myself, walking right behind a grown-up who seemed to know what he was doing. I didn't like holding hands with strangers. It felt too intimate.

Right before she called the police, Debbie asked me very seriously if I had seen anything scary outside my bedroom window, or outside any of the windows in our house. I thought about the bottom, and considered telling her since she seemed to think it was a big deal, but the truth was, I didn't want her to ruin it. It was private, and funny, and seemed to exist only in my imagination, like a joke I was telling myself. Once, I had even flashed it back, standing on my bed to get my ass up to the right height. Though I don't think it noticed.

It didn't seem to resemble the bottom Anu had seen at all.

My mother told me the curtains were there to keep me safe and cozy in my bed, and she knew I sometimes liked to open them for the sunshine, but I should keep them closed so I was warm and private in my room, okay?

I said okay, because that was what she wanted to hear, and told her that I hadn't seen anything scary out the window. Because really, I hadn't.

But there were no more solo trips to the candy store after my mother learned about Anu Bhaduri and her flasher. Debbie didn't say I couldn't go, exactly. Each time I asked, she made up a reason why it wasn't a very good time right then. "It's getting dark," she'd say, or, "We're going to the food co-op in ten minutes." Landis would take me on the days she baby-sat. My mother hired her on as a regular baby-sitter a couple afternoons a week. That way, Debbie could earn extra money at the real estate office.

Landis and I would walk to the store and get sour candy for

me and licorice for her, and then she'd tell me everything that was going on in her life. She had just been cast in the school musical, playing a prostitute who got to sing three big numbers. I didn't know what a prostitute was. Noun. One who offers himself for sexual hire. That much I discovered pretty easily, but it didn't mean anything, really.

Landis wouldn't explain it any further. Just walked around our living room belting,

I won't betray his trust
Though people say I must.

"It's called *Oliver*, and in it my boyfriend beats me and ignores me," she explained happily. "But I love him anyway, because I've got nothing else in my life." Landis had the kind of voice that makes it sound like all the notes are easy to sing. There wasn't any wobble to it.

More importantly, Shaun had kissed her at Dave's party, in this room where everybody put their coats. It didn't turn out to be that difficult, after all. "It's pretty easy when you're not kissing a Peanut Butter Boy," Landis told me. "Everything happens naturally." He had held her hand in front of that popular girl, Hannah, so everything was official.

"What happened with the lip gloss?" I wanted to know.

"Huh?" Landis didn't seem to remember.

"The watermelon lip gloss."

"You know, Vanessa," she said, with the air of an experienced woman. "It turned out not to matter. I didn't know he was going to kiss me in the coat room when he did, so I didn't have any chance to explain or anything, and I actually thought about saying 'Watermelon' in the middle of the kiss just to explain the flavor, but somehow I didn't, and he didn't seem to mind. Besides, everybody wears lip gloss, and I bet he's kissed about a million girls before me."

Landis soon developed bona fide status as Shaun's girlfriend. He would walk with her to classes, and kiss her up against the lockers in front of other people, and when they were alone, he squeezed her breasts with both hands.

Weird. She'd always imagined it would be one hand at a time.

She spent weekends hanging out with him at Dave's house, where they listened to Jimi Hendrix and the boys played guitar in the basement. It was cool, but also a little boring. Maybe a lot. Landis and this other girl would sit on the couch and look at the covers of record albums while the boys made noise. It was too loud to talk. One Sunday, though, Shaun came over to her house when her parents were out playing golf. Landis had got up her nerve to telephone him, which made her anxious even though they had been going steady. Well, she figured they were going steady, even though he had never formally asked her. Everyone at school knew they were boyfriend and girlfriend.

They had rolled around on the shaggy rug of her room near her record player and taken their shirts off. "I think I have really good titties, Vanessa," Landis said. "I mean, I was a little worried that they were too big, or a funny shape, but let me tell you, Mouseling," and she pointed her finger at me like a schoolmarm, "that boy really seemed to like them." She burst into laughter.

She told me it felt really freaky to have skin against skin in places where you're not used to it. She had me pull up my shirt and rubbed my belly with the inside of her forearm. It felt slippery and unfamiliar. "That's what it's like, basically," she said. "Only more."

I had been working hard on my play about Louisa Tushi the genius child, and I showed it to Landis. Ron had asked me to bring dittos of it to Super Duper Spellers next week. In one new scene, illustrating the word Precarious, Allowishus Rump comes in with a giant pillow strapped to his bottom. He endeavors to walk a tightrope, with great encouragement from Mister Posterior and Susannah T. Bum. Susannah is very confident because she already knows how to walk a tightrope. She demonstrates for Allowishus, saying, "Allowishus Rump, you have to keep your balance and look toward the far end of the rope you are walking on. Do not think about how Precarious it is."

"But it *is* Precarious, Susannah T. Bum!" Allowishus complains.

"Yes, it is. But you must not think about it," counsels Susannah.

Allowishus finally gets his courage up, but just as he is in the middle of the tightrope (which we would mime, walking along a straight line on the floor), the mischievous Mister Posterior distracts him by doing a silly dance.

Allowishus falls, landing squarely on the pillow strapped to his behind, and says, "It certainly was Precarious, but at least I was prepared!" Then Louisa Tushi comes on and briefly explains that Pre is also used as a prefix.

Landis read my play and asked me, her mouth quivering, if it was meant to be funny. I nodded, and she broke into a big smile. "That's good, Mouseling. You have a big imagination, do you know that?"

Yes, I did.

"A big imagination in a tiny body," she said, hugging me around the shoulders.

The Tuesday before Thanksgiving holiday was our last day of school before the vacation. We had Wednesday off for parent-teacher conferences. And like any day before vacation, everything was topsy-turvy. For instance, we had all our American Indian dioramas on display in the hallway, and parents were supposed to come by whenever was convenient and admire them. The hallway was a bad place though, because the littler kids or the rowdy boys would grab the clay creatures and poke the construction paper buildings.

I raised my hand and said I thought we should put the dioramas up in the Super Duper Spelling room and charge admission like a museum, with a guard to prevent people from messing with them.

The braided teacher said, "Thank you for sharing that idea with us, Vanessa."

Then I suggested that maybe we should get plastic wrap and stretch it all around the dioramas so people could look at them, but not touch.

And the teacher said, "My, Vanessa, you sure do have a lot of ideas. Those are very creative ideas."

My diorama was ruined by eleven o'clock. The little cook got stolen, and several of the paper trees met a sorry fate.

However, *Mister Posterior and the Genius Child* was finished. I had even made a special title page with drawings in magic marker. Ron sent me downstairs to the main office where the ditto machine was, and told me to make copies for all the Super Duper Spellers.

They had a big bowl of peppermints in the main office, and I got to eat one. Stuart the principal gave it to me. Actually, he came up behind me and rubbed my shoulders like I was an athlete while I was waiting by the ditto machine. I thought Stuart was neat because of his long gray ponytail, but he made me nervous because he wielded so much authority over the kids and their families. He seemed to know everything about all of us: where we lived, what pets we had, who took ballet lessons or went to soccer practice. Who had to have time-outs during recess. Who paid, and who did not pay.

I was kind of surprised that he touched me. He hadn't ever touched me before, except that one time when he grabbed my cheek at Fright Night. Then he gave me the peppermint.

When I got back upstairs with my dittos, it turned out that we weren't having Super Duper Spelling after all, that day. Somebody's mom was coming in to teach us different things you can do with maize, the American Indian word for corn. She set up all these tables, and a hot plate, and helped us make corn on the cob and cornmeal tortillas that tasted like sawdust. The best was corn pudding, which she said pilgrims used to eat, which was basically corn chopped up with cream and sugar and egg. She took it away to the school kitchen to bake it, and then passed it around Circle of Sharing so everyone could get a taste.

Anu wouldn't taste anything. She shook her head and said, "I don't like it," even when it was just corn on the cob. She seemed like one of those little glass statues of a camel or a poodle that you see sometimes in jewelry stores: brittle, marked Handle With Care. When I first found out what happened, I had tried to be extra nice to her. But she wouldn't speak to me, no matter what I did. Even when I asked her a direct question. So after a bit, I gave up.

She ate lunch with Summer, now, and I with Angelique, who had adopted me in a propitiatory way, hooking her arm through mine in the playground and saying "we" a lot about things I didn't really want to be connected with. She'd say, "We like Monopoly, right?" And I'd feel like I had to say yes, because I knew she liked it. Or, "We're getting on the swings, okay?" And I'd say yes, and get on the swings, though I felt bad about the way she hogged them sometimes.

I was grateful, though, for Angelique's waxen, awkward friendship, and for her giving me access to the solid, bland world she lived in. She assumed I was like her, assumed I had a dad at home who read the paper and took me to dance practice on weekends, even asked me what my dog's name was, as if everybody had a dog. She lived a sheltered life, Angelique, and ate SpaghettiOs from a can after school for snack. I knew, because I went to her house three times, and met her rowdy black Labrador, and saw both her baby-sitter and her mom in the kitchen together, one spooning out noodles from a can and the other wearing panty hose and talking on the telephone. She had an older brother whose room smelled like incense, and a sister who was a senior who was never home, and we played Monopoly and paper dolls on the big white rug in the living room, our bellies full of SpaghettiOs.

As Angelique's friend, I even played with Didi the Fucker, who got chocolate milk in her Thermos every day and tried to befriend me by saying she liked my hair and wished we could trade. Then at recess we'd play kissing tag, girls chase the boys, and Anu and Summer played with us, too. Summer was still my friend; she gave me red licorice when she had some and cuddled up to me when it was cold on the playground, but she made it clear that the strain between me and Anu was nothing she wanted any part of. If there was a situation where she had to acknowledge it, where I said something to Anu and Anu didn't answer, for example, Summer simply walked away as if something interested her on the other side of the room.

Sometimes I wonder whether we would have been friends again, Anu and I, if only the bottom hadn't flashed her. It seemed like she transferred her rage from him to me, as if I were responsible for the fear she felt. Maybe if our friendship had been intact, she'd have laughed and pointed at the man, called her brothers in to look at him, told the story loudly to a cluster of friends on the playground. Maybe she only reacted to him the way she had because our fight had ruptured the bubble of peace and safety she'd always had around her.

But I could be wrong about that. I might simply have never meant that much to her. I was disposable, expendable, and she had been leaving me for the preadolescent world of boys and kisses, anyway. She had changed the rules of No Boys Allowed; she coaxed a section of Luke's heart away; she believed what lies he told her—or else she made them up herself. Even now, I am not sure I have forgiven the disdain she emanated toward me after our argument, the way she pulled her arm away if I accidentally touched her, the way she got up to move if I sat near her at Circle of Sharing and refused to answer if I addressed her. Every day this tension was palpable. Each hour it seemed to get more concentrated: sour and dense.

The longer it went on, the longer I felt like a martyr, and the less I was ready to leave it all behind—although I felt nonetheless that I needed to be in a constant state of readiness in case she decided one day that we were friends after all. I even planned out what to say. Sometimes it was haughty: "Oh, you can see and hear me again, can you?" And sometimes it was warm: "Let's play horses. Angelique doesn't play nearly as good as you." But as the days went by, the muck between us got denser and more sour, and I became more and more determined to ignore her when the gesture of friendship came.

Only it never did.

After the corn pudding, we all held hands and sang "This World Is Ours to Share":

This world is ours to share
Let's show the world we care
The treasure of the mountains high
The beauty of the evening sky

Run free (free! free!)
Children are free (free! free!)
Let's all take hands together
Go down to the sea (sea! sea!)

This world is ours to share
Breathe in the ocean air
The treasure of a child's bright eyes
The beauty of a baby's thighs

Run free (free! free!)
Children are free (free! free!)
Let's all take hands together
Go down to the sea (sea! sea!)

As soon as we were done, I raised my hand.

"Vanessa," said the braided teacher. "Do you have something to say?"

Since we didn't have Super Duper Spelling today, I wanted to hand out the dittos of my play to the kids in the group. The teacher said all right, so I gave copies to Luke and Anu, then went out to deliver them to the kids in other classes. When I got back, the teachers were dismissing people for Thanksgiving break, reminding us to think about the American Indians, and to have a happy holiday.

Mister Posterior and the Genius Child went home in kids' folders over the vacation. Nobody had a chance to read it first.

Grin and Pompey arrived on Wednesday morning from Chicago, and we all went shopping for Thanksgiving dinner. At the supermarket, Grin got two tins of oysters for the stuffing.

"No oysters, Mother. I don't eat oysters," Debbie said.

"Theodore, she doesn't eat oysters!" Grin called to Pompey, who was down the aisle evaluating bread crumbs.

"Doesn't like oysters? Debbie, you love oysters," he said mildly.

"I don't eat them, Dad," Debbie said.

"All right, but you used to eat them. You used to love them."

Then Pompey put two big boxes of cut bacon in the cart. "It's for breakfast tomorrow," he explained, smiling. "We thought we'd come over in the morning from the hotel and cook up a nice big egg-and-bacon mess to start off the day."

Debbie let it sit there for a couple minutes, but when he wasn't looking, she took the bacon out. "Dad," she said, "how about if

I make you two breakfast? I'll make something nice, some zucchini bread."

"Huh?" Pompey's mind was elsewhere. "Okay."

But later he said, "Where's the bacon?"

"I put it back, Dad. We don't have bacon in my house."

"No bacon? What are we having with the eggs?"

"We don't eat eggs, either. I'm cooking for you, remember? If you want bacon, you can eat at the hotel."

"No, no, that's okay." Pompey said. "We'll come to you."

Meanwhile, Grin got a pound and a half of Italian sausage for the stuffing. "Remember the stuffing I used to make that had chestnuts and sausage?" she asked. "I'll make that instead of the oyster kind. I found chestnuts in the bakery aisle."

"Mother."

"Oh!" Grin laughed a tense laugh. "But it's such a nice stuffing! You loved it when you were a girl."

"You can't cook it in my house, Mother."

"Debbie! It's just a little sausage. The pig is already dead."

"No. I really can't have it."

Grin took the sausage out, but before long, she had hold of some chicken broth. "This is important for the moisture of the stuffing," she said to me. I was riding in the cart. "You mix it with some wine and pour it all over. Mmmm. You'll like that, won't you?"

"Mother, you have to get the vegetable broth," Debbie reminded her.

"Oh, Debbie, broth doesn't count. There's hardly any chicken in here at all!" Grin clicked her tongue.

"There's chicken in there."

"Not very much. What does it matter?"

"What does it matter to you? Just get the vegetable."

Grin pouted. "Vegetable doesn't taste as good, does it, Vanessa? It's not as good." But she headed down the aisle to exchange the broth.

Both Grin and Pompey insisted on going to my parent-teacher conference later that day. "She doesn't have a father," Grin said, "So I don't see why not."

"She has a father," Debbie said, sitting in the backseat of the big blue rent-a-car. "Everybody has a father, Vanessa, you remember that."

"Jordy," I said, to show I knew.

"That's right, Jordy," said Debbie. "Jordan Benjamin Brick."

"She doesn't have a father to go to the conference," Grin said, turning around to look at us from the front seat. "Don't you think it would be good for her teachers to meet some more of the family? I went to all your teacher conferences when you were little, Debbie. I know how to act."

"I can be a parent on my own."

"Of course you can. Pompey and I just want to show our support. We're interested in Vanessa's education."

I yawned. The heat of the car was thick, and we had eaten a big lunch at Grin and Pompey's hotel.

"Yawning?" Grin looked at me inquisitively. "You had a good sleep last night. Debbie tells me you didn't wake up until nine-thirty this morning."

"She can yawn, Mother. She can yawn if she likes."

"I'm just saying, I'm surprised."

"She's a little kid."

"Sleeping so late, and yawning in the afternoon," Grin went on. "You want to take a nap, Vanessa?"

"No," I said.

"You can take a nap right here in the car while we go in to the teacher conference."

"I'm not leaving her in the car by herself," Debbie snapped. "You or Dad will have to stay with her if she does that."

"I'll stay in the car." Pompey waved his cigar around with one hand, driving with the other. The smoke trailed out a crack in his window. "I've got the sports pages here somewhere."

"How's that, Vanessa?" Debbie asked. "You can have a nap while Pompey reads the sports pages."

"I'm not sleepy," I said.

"Not sleepy?" Grin raised her eyebrows. "I thought you said you wanted to take a rest." She sighed. "Children are so changeable, aren't they?"

"Whatever you want, Vanessa." Debbie sounded irritated. "You want to go in the playground with the other kids?"

I told her yes.

"You had a good sleep last night, didn't you?" Grin asked me. "Didn't you?"

I nodded.

"I thought so," she said, and leaned into Pompey in the front seat, lowering her voice. "I don't know why she's so tired. It must be the vegetarian diet."

"I can hear you," Debbie said, as the car stopped in the school parking lot.

Pompey tried to stay in the car anyway with the sports pages, but Grin said, "Why would you want to do that?" so he had to go inside.

I wasn't at the conference, of course. I hung out in the playground with some older kids whose parents were likewise at meetings, and swung on the tire swing by myself since nobody else wanted to get on. But I know what happened. The braided teacher told Debbie that *Mister Posterior and the Genius Child* was seriously inappropriate material for a eight-year-old to be writing.

Debbie said I'd be nine in February.

The braided teacher said that it didn't matter. (Debbie called the braided teacher Joyce. That was her name. It was the first time I learned it.) Joyce said that Vanessa had been socializing well with the other girls, expanding her social circle, and that was wonderful to see. She said that Vanessa was eager to participate in class discussions and gave 200 percent to anything she was really interested in. Vanessa had some trouble understanding multiplication, but that was nothing to worry about, and she was also completely tone deaf—but there at Cambridge Harmony they didn't like to discourage anybody from the experience of music and all the joy it can bring. Vanessa was timid at sports, Vanessa was fidgety in lines, Vanessa was a strong reader and an excellent speller. Had Debbie considered sending her to a psychologist? Just for evaluation. The obsession with, well, we at Cambridge Harmony like to be very open about these things. The obsession with sex at such a young age. It warranted some examination, in the opinion of Joyce the braided teacher.

At this point, Grin and Pompey interrupted. They insisted on knowing what this *Mister Posterior* was that was supposedly so inappropriate, and how dare the braided teacher make recommendations of this sort. Was she an expert on child development?

Joyce said yes, she had a master's degree, and it was certainly unusual for a child to express such prolonged and provocative interest in sexual matters. She was concerned about the well-being of the child, she said to Debbie. "It's not Vanessa's fault. It seems possible there's some disturbance there," she said. "And we really can't have this kind of material circulating around the classroom," she added. "I'm sure you understand that."

"What's the material?" asked Debbie.

"Really, how bad can it be?" Grin interrupted. "She's just a little girl."

So the teacher read aloud my very favorite scene from *Mister Posterior*, in which Louisa Tushi the genius child explains to the title character that his bottom is not a Receptacle and he must not treat it like one. "You put things in a Receptacle," explains Louisa. "Like flowers in a vase, or coins in a piggy bank. But things come out of your bottom. Poo comes out. It is not a good idea to put anything in."

Mister Posterior says he understands, and asks, "What about my nose? Is my nose a Receptacle?"

"It is not," says Louisa. "You must not put anything up your nose, either. No beans, no peanuts, no paper clips." Mister Posterior feels he has learned an important lesson.

I was really very pleased with myself. Receptacle was one of the hardest words to find a scene for. But the grown-ups were grossed out.

"Debbie, where is she getting these ideas?" Grin demanded.

"I don't know," my mother replied. "I don't know."

"Have you been having your boyfriends sleep over?" Grin asked, as if Joyce the teacher wasn't even there.

Debbie turned to explain. "I'm a single parent," she said. "My ex-husband is in California."

"She manages very well," Grin said to the teacher, trying to cover up her slip. Debbie bareface lied and said she never had her boyfriends sleep over. I know because later she told me not to mention it in case Joyce or Ron asked me. She said they just didn't like the idea, even though they were so freakin' liberal, and she worried she might get in trouble if they knew. Did I mind having her boyfriends sleep over? After all, it was really only Syd, and he probably wouldn't sleep over ever again, anyway. I told her no, I didn't mind, because it was the truth—and promised to keep my mouth shut, because that's what she wanted to hear.

Debbie told the teacher she had no idea where Vanessa would be getting ideas like that, but wasn't it healthy she was expressing them openly rather than keeping everything under wraps?

Joyce said of course it was good to express yourself, but there was such a thing as expressing yourself in the appropriate context. School was not the appropriate context for the wide distribution of jokes about inserting things into the anus.

Pompey, lawyering, reminded her that the scene was about *not* inserting things into the anus, which was really an important message for kids to have.

Debbie told him to please be quiet, though she knew he meant well, and asked what the teacher meant by wide distribution.

Joyce explained that these dittos had gone home with all the Super Duper Spellers, and that one of the parents had come in to his conference that morning and complained about the material.

Pompey said wasn't that the fault of the teachers, if the material went home?

And Joyce said that didn't change the fact that Vanessa was very likely having some sort of disturbance.

On the way home, the grown-ups talked about me like I wasn't there. I pretended to fall asleep on my mother's lap in the backseat of the car. Pompey said it was all no big deal and little kids were curious. Lord knows what he had been up to at the age of eight. Debbie said I just had a vivid imagination and she couldn't believe anything was really wrong with me. And Grin seemed really worried that I could even conceive of putting anything up anyone's bottom. Maybe it was a good idea about the psychiatrist.

"Think how you will kick yourself if you don't send her," Grin said.

"Why will I kick myself? She's a happy kid."

"There is some disturbance there, like the teacher said. I think you have to acknowledge that, Debbie."

"There's no money to send her, anyway."

"We can put something toward it," Grin said, looking at Pompey for a nod of the head. "We can pay the bills if it turns out to be necessary."

"Do you think she needs to go?" Debbie lit a cigarette and rolled down the window.

"I don't really know." Grin sighed heavily. "I think it's worth considering."

That night, long after her parents had gone back to their hotel to drink scotches in the piano bar, I heard Debbie talking on the telephone to someone. She had on her animated voice, like when she talked to a boyfriend, only I knew it couldn't be Syd because she talked about how the guy she used to go around with was in the Alexian Ashram. She told about Grin coming from the South of France.

"My father is a lawyer," she said to whomever it was, "and he thinks he knows everything. But he can't even see me, anymore." She paused and took a drag off her menthol. "He has no idea who I am."

13.

"Oh My Mysterious Lady"

Around five o'clock on Thanksgiving day, Katty Sherwin showed up with an enormous chocolate cake. It was from a bakery, she didn't make it herself, but it was very big and she looked nervous, standing there on our doorstep. Debbie had invited her weeks ago, before they had the fight about me turning Luke into a transvestite. We had assumed she wasn't coming. The table was set already.

Luke was jumping up and down on the porch, and when we opened the door, he ran inside, yelling, "Vanessa! I ate one Thanksgiving already! I ate one already!"

I was in the kitchen, working on the apple pie. Grin had made the crust, and I had helped peel the apples with a vegetable peeler. Now we were putting them in with sprinkles of cinnamon, sugar, and nutmeg.

"Who is this?" Grin asked me, when Luke came yelling into our kitchen wearing a gravy-stained sweater.

"That's Luke," I told her.

"Well, how do you do, Luke?" Grin wiped her hands off on her apron and extended one for Luke to shake. He shook it, but shrank back a bit at the unfamiliar face, leaning himself against the stove.

I was glad to see him—his slobby, eager self—acting as if nothing had ever gone wrong between us. We were both so used to stampeding past our mutual coldness at school into friendship in one another's homes that this moment was really not so different from many others we had had.

"I'm making pie," I said. "Do you want to help?"

He nodded.

"He wants to help?" Grin asked me.

"Umm-hmm."

"You want to help, Luke?"

He nodded again.

"A boy in the kitchen! That's something you never saw in my day," Grin said. It wasn't clear if she was praising Luke or calling him a sissy, but she lifted him up to wash his hands in the kitchen sink. He sat by me and started putting sliced apple into the piecrust.

"I had Thanksgiving already today," he said. "I had it at my dad's. We had punkin pie, and a big giant turkey, and mashed potato."

"Are you hungry?" I said.

"Yah. I have two stomachs. One for breakfast and one for lunch. No, wait. Three stomachs. One for breakfast, one for lunch, and one for dinner."

"But this is two dinners."

"I know." He thought for a minute. "I put the first one in the breakfast stomach," he said, "because I knew we were coming here."

Debbie and Katty were sitting in the living room with Pompey, smoking. Katty was wearing a tight cocktail dress and high heels, as if she had dressed up to conciliate Debbie. She crossed her legs, and I could see her freckles through her panty hose. My mother wore the navy blue dress she put on whenever we went out to dinner with Grin and Pompey. It was a very conservative outfit, and she had a string of beads at her throat. Pompey sat in the easy chair and buried himself in the paper.

Katty said that her ex-husband, Randy, had had his housekeeper in to make Thanksgiving dinner for the boys. "Do you think it even counts as Thanksgiving if a housekeeper makes it?" she asked. "That's what's wrong with Randy. Why can't he buy a recipe book and cook it himself?"

"At least he did something," Debbie said. "Gave the boys a holiday. A sense of tradition."

"A tradition of women waiting table and slaving in front of a hot oven while the men sit back and eat!" Katty shot Pompey a look. Grin was still in the kitchen.

Debbie chuckled and held her hands up as if to say, *What can I do?*

I could tell she and Katty were friends again.

Katty said Joyce the braided teacher thought Luke was hyperactive. Not hyper in the clinical sense, but hyper like he couldn't calm down when he was supposed to. "That woman has got to wake up," she complained. "Little boys are frisky. It's natural to them. What's not natural is waiting in lines and doing silent reading time at the end of the day when they really need to get outside and play."

"Did Luke do something during silent reading?"

"Oh, allegedly he did headstands and threw paper airplanes and drew a picture on the wall with magic marker. Allegedly. He only does things like that when he's bored. I told her, 'You're boring my son. Give him something more to do.' "

"You don't like her?"

"I don't like any of them. These people, they sum up your children in one half-hour meeting, sitting on those dinky chairs. Why can't they give us a normal-size chair? I'm sure they could bring some in from somewhere, from the auditorium. They get you in there, scrunch you down in the miniature chair, and then analyze your kid with this superior attitude. Honestly. I want to hit them right on their piggy noses every time I have a parent-teacher conference." Katty sighed and leaned back for a minute. "How was yours?"

Pompey grunted from behind the newspaper.

"It was all right," Debbie said evasively. "But I think Joyce evaluates the kids personally, decides whether she likes them, and then thinks up things to say about their development and their socialization. I can take care of my own child's personality, thank you very much. I just want to know why Vanessa's having trouble with math."

After dinner, there was apple pie and Katty's chocolate cake. In classic fashion, Grin made a big deal about Luke and me getting big slices of both.

"You children will want your goodies, won't you?" she said. "Someone like me has to watch her figure, someone old like me, but you little ones, you eat up as much as you like." She turned to Debbie. "Vanessa eats very well."

"Thank you."

"She really consumes a lot of food for such a little person!" Grin said. "When I was young, I didn't eat nearly so much. Watch that she doesn't make herself sick."

"She won't make herself sick."

"All right." Grin waved her fork daintily over her own slice of apple pie, but the idea of my overindulging was eventually too much for her. She looked seriously at the two big slices of dessert that she herself had cut for me, and said, "Don't eat the whole thing, now, Vanessa! It's very rich! Too much will make your tummy hurt."

"Okay," I answered. This behavior was typical of Grin: to set herself up as envying my youth, and segue into remarking on some virtue of mine, shortly to be transformed into a vice that she herself had never been guilty of when she was my age.

She'd go through this same sequence of twisted logic when commenting on my activity level, my reading skills, my long hair, or my collection of stuffed animals. I had so many stuffed animals. What fun, what fun! She wished she had had a collection like that when she was my age. What did I do with so many stuffed animals? How could I play with them all at once? When she was young she had only one teddy bear and one dolly, and she loved them more than anything in the world. But could I love them all when there were nearly twenty of them? Wasn't it really a waste? It really was too much, some of them must have cost ten dollars. She didn't know how I played with them.

Luke and I went to my room while the grown-ups drank tea. We put the *Peter Pan* album on the children's record player. The perfect day for a frenzy.

"I can fly!" I yelled, getting up on the bed and bouncing up and down. "I'm Peter Pan!"

"I can fly, too! I'm John and Michael!" Luke cried, clambering onto the bed. We bounced higher and higher.

Our favorite song was coming up. That was when Peter and Hook sang this wild number called "Oh My Mysterious Lady." In it, Mary Martin, dressed up as a boy to play Peter, dressed up as a girl in order to trick Captain Hook into thinking he was in love.

It was a very exciting scene, and that day Luke and I felt we needed the appropriate costuming. We rummaged in my dresser drawers. For Peter, I put on all my green clothes, and then wrapped a long scarf of my mother's around my head to be the veil, so Hook wouldn't recognize me. Luke was to be Hook, and I gave him a purple dress I wore for parties, and a red sweater, and a piratical hat. We snuck into the kitchen and got a soup spoon for the hook.

The needle hit the proper groove, and Hook and Peter were alone, somewhere dark and mysterious: Skull Rock.

Hook believes a spirit is nearby.

"Have you another . . . name?" he asks.

Peter, pretending, answers yes.

"Vegetable?"

"No."

"Mineral?"

"No."

(Dramatic pause.) "Animal?"

"Yes!" I jumped up and down on the bed, and Luke bit his soup spoon with the thrill of it.

"Have you another . . . voice?" asks Hook.

"Yes!"

Peter trills like an opera singer—seductively, musically. Hook gets progressively more excited, begging for the mysterious lady to take off her veil and let him look at her. He rumbles and speaks Italian-sounding things while she trills and trills up to the high notes.

Tell me your secret,
Let me see your face!
Why hide your beauty
Beneath a veil of lace!

By this point, we were both back on the bed, jumping up and down in our costumes, high on chocolate cake, apple pie, and the excitement of a holiday. Luke was holding the soup spoon between his teeth, and my veil kept falling off, but overall it was an excellent dramatization of this most intriguing musical number—until Katty came in the door.

She didn't even knock.

And when she saw Luke in the purple dress, her face fell.

"I'm Captain Hook!" Luke cried, sensing her dismay. "Captain Hook wears purple!"

"I'm Peter Pan being the mysterious lady!" I explained, pointing at the record player where Hook and Peter were still trilling and teasing one another.

Luke held out the soup spoon. "This is my hook! See? It's not really dangerous."

"That's very nice, Luke," Katty said distractedly and shut the record player off. "That's a good choice for a hook. Now, can you tell me, whose idea was it to wear these costumes?"

"I'm allowed to play with the clothes in my closet," I said, which was true.

"I'm sure you are, sweetie," Katty replied. "But whose idea was it? Can you tell me?"

"It was both of ours," I said. And that was true, too. "It was Peter Pan."

"It was Peter Pan's idea?" she said, with a note of annoyance in her voice.

"Kind of," Luke answered. "It all just happened. Are we in trouble?"

"It's time to go home," Katty said. "It's very late."

My mother appeared behind Katty in the doorway. "What's going on? Did they get into a frenzy?"

"Yes!" Luke and I both cried, anxious to return to that familiar definition of what we had been doing, back to that time when there was nothing wrong with it.

"Look at Luke, Debbie." Katty had a note of accusation in her voice.

My mother looked.

"Take off the dress." Katty was firm.

"But I want to stay and play with Vanessa."

"You look like a girl," she said.

"No, I don't. I look like Captain Hook."

"Luke, it's time to go home. Will you please get changed?"

"But I don't want to!"

"Luke Michael Sherwin. What did I say?"

Luke sulked and looked at the floor. "Will I please get changed."

"That's right. Will you please get changed?"

"Okay."

"They had too much sugar, Katty," my mother said apologetically. "It makes them really hyper."

Luke pulled the dress over his head, and with a bustle of coats and not so much as a good-bye to my mother, they were gone.

The spoon lay on the floor in my room. Nobody bothered to pick it up.

14.

At the Window

On Friday, against Debbie's objections, Grin and Pompey took me to the zoo. We saw seals, and walruses, and a tiger who showed her teeth. No antelopes at all. There was a bird habitat where parrots flew around under a big skylight, and vampire bats that sucked blood and hung upside down. Before we went over to the polar bear section, we stopped to order hot dogs from a vendor with a cart.

Grin went to powder her nose in the bathroom, and Pompey and I sat together at a wooden picnic table, eating and waiting for Grin to come back. We hadn't been alone together in a long time. Maybe not ever.

"When I was young, I saw a walrus in the pond near my house," Pompey said in a quiet voice. We had just come from the walrus tank.

"With big tusks?"

"Yes indeed."

"But walruses live in cold places," I told him.

"Smart girl, Vanessa. Yes, they do. But I saw one just the same, in a pond in Connecticut."

"But they live in the sea."

"This one was in a pond."

"What was it doing there?"

"Sunning itself. I was about your age, I think, maybe a little bit older, and I used to go down to this pond near my house and skip stones across the water. I walked down, one hot summer afternoon, and there—lying with its body half in and half out of the pond—was a walrus. The thing must have weighed nearly four hundred pounds. It had big long tusks like this"—Pompey showed me with his hands—"and it was lolling on its side like it wanted to get the sun on its belly. I was scared of it at first, but I inched my way forward till I was maybe eight feet away, and it sat up on its flippers and looked at me for the longest time. Then it made a kind of barking noise. I don't know if it was saying hello or trying to scare me off, but I jumped back in surprise. And I think my movement must have startled it, because it slid back into the water with a splash."

"Then what happened?"

"That was it. I didn't see it again. I ran home to tell my parents that there was a walrus in the pond, but they said that was nonsense. There was no way it could have been a walrus."

"But it was, right?"

"It was," said Pompey. "My father even came down to the water with me, and showed me a big hollow log that I could have mistaken for a walrus. He wanted me to tell my mother that it was only a log, and that I had been either fibbing or imagining things, because she was worried about my telling tales." Pompey finished his hot dog and wiped his hands on a paper napkin. "I was something of a fabulist in my youth, before I became a lawyer. I was always getting in trouble for it."

"Did you?"

"Tell her it was a fib? No, I didn't. And I got a spanking for my insurrection, too. But it didn't matter. I was true to what I saw, not what they saw."

"Uh-huh."

"I was the one who knew what had happened to me. They couldn't possibly know."

"Yeah."

"It was my experience, I'm the only one who had it. No one can change that by saying it was a fib or a mistake. They don't know." He put his arm around me and we waited for Grin in silence.

That night I wrote in my diary with my mint-green pen. I made a list of my six favorite flavors.

sour apple candy
chocolate-covered raisin flavor
lemon
pizza
licorice
chicken slices

Then a list of my friends. Luke was first. Then Anu, Angelique, Summer, and Didi. I took Didi off, and then put her back on. There were only five on the list anyhow. After some deliberation, I forced myself to cross Anu out. I knew she couldn't really be counted anymore. Then I added Landis. She was my friend, too, I thought, even if Debbie paid her to hang out with me.

Luke
~~*Anu*~~
Angelique
~~*Didi*~~
Summer
Didi
Landis

It was very late. I was supposed to be asleep two hours ago, but I had my flashlight on, and the curtains open, in case the bottom appeared—although it came less and less as the weather got colder. I was about to lock my diary and tuck it under my bed for safety when there was a tap at the window. I was startled, because the bottom never made any noise at all, and looked up.

There was a face there, a grinning face with a brown mustache. A leering, tipsy face.

Syd Wheeler.

He tapped at the window again. "Hi, Vanessa!"

"Hello."

"Vanessa! It's me, Syd."

"I know."

"Will you let me in?"

"How come?"

"I want to share something with your mom."

"What?"

"I said, I want to share something with your mom. I knocked on her window, but she didn't wake up."

"I meant, what do you want to share?"

He paused. "I want to be open with her, you know? We had an argument, and I want to apologize. But I couldn't get her to wake up."

We looked at each other. I could see his breath, foggy in the cold. Could I possibly turn over and go to sleep? Pretend like he wasn't there, like I had never seen him?

No, he would never go for that.

He looked drunk. Could I go out of my room into the body of the house and wait for him to leave? Maybe he would get bored and wander off somewhere.

He tapped on the window again. "Vanessa! I need to talk to Debbie. Are you going to wake her up for me?"

"Stop tapping," I said, to see if he would.

"This is important, Kiddo," he said, tucking his hands inside his sleeves to protect them from the cold. He had never called me Kiddo before. "Let me in. I just want to talk with her, share some insights."

"She doesn't like to be woken up," I told him.

"It's important."

"She doesn't like it."

"Vanessa!" Suddenly, he was starting to look angry. "What did I ask you to do?"

"You asked me to get Debbie."

"That's right, I did. Are you going to do it?" He banged his jacketed fist against the glass, making it rumble. Like he wanted to hit me. "Are you?"

"Yes."

I grabbed Lopey and scooted out through the dark kitchen and down the hall to Debbie's room, scared almost that Syd was right behind me, although I knew he couldn't get in.

My mother's door was slightly open. She was asleep, dressed in a white flannel nightgown with little red roses on it that made her look awfully young. Her gnarled feet were cuddled up in a big pair of wool socks. She lay facedown, the covers kicked off onto the floor, hair spread wild around the pillow.

"Debbie," I whispered, tugging at her arm.

Syd's face appeared at her window.

"Debbie."

"Did you have a bad dream, sugar?" she asked, without opening her eyes.

"No."

"What happened? Do you want to get in here with me? You can get in if you want." She didn't move.

"Syd is here." I shook her shoulder.

Her eyes opened. "Syd is where?"

"Out the window," I said. "He wants me to get you up."

Still lying on her belly, she lifted her head and turned it slowly. Syd was standing on the other side of the glass, shivering in the cold, a beatific smile on his face like she should be glad to see him. "Can I come in?" he asked, grinning and spreading his palms open in supplication.

Debbie sighed and stood up slowly. "Don't wake my kid up in the middle of the night," she said. "What are you thinking?"

"She doesn't have school tomorrow."

"It's ten-thirty, Syd. We all want to be asleep."

"It's so cold out here, Debbie. I'm freezing."

She looked down at the floor like she didn't know what to say.

"Please let me in. It really is cold. And I have something I want to share with you." A pause. "I threw pebbles at your window for twenty minutes, but you didn't wake up. Just let me talk to you. It's like ice out here, Debbie."

My mother didn't answer, but she turned and went down the hall to open the front door. Syd was there, rubbing his hands together and making a big show of how chilled he was, as if our house was the only place he could get warm in all of Cambridge. He came into the kitchen, and Debbie made some chamomile tea.

"Shouldn't Vanessa be going back to bed?" he asked.

"You woke her up, Syd. And now she's up." My mother sounded irritated. "I don't want you waiting around here while I read her a story all over again and sing lullabies. It could take half an hour. Say what you've got to say."

Syd, weaving a bit in his chair and smelling like beer, winked at me conspiratorially, as if to imply that he and I knew his intentions were good and it was just a matter of getting Debbie to come around. I squeezed Lopey into positions unnatural for an antelope and waited for my tea to get cool enough to drink.

"Debbie," he began, smiling his broad smile. "I feel a deep connection to you. I thought about the argument we had, and I realized that I wasn't practicing empathy. It's true, what you said. I don't know how it would feel to be a parent."

"No. I don't think you do," said Debbie sharply.

"I can see how it would appear to you that there was danger to that girl, how it would show that way to you."

Debbie touched my shoulder. "We're talking about how Anu got scared and had to stay out of school at the start of the month," she explained. "There is nothing to worry about."

"I think we have a special vibe together, Debbie," Syd went on. "And I realized that you'd understand where I was coming from if you visited the ashram with me for a weekend."

"The ashram?"

"Right now, you think in facts and truths. You don't think

about subjectivity, which is how Alex teaches us to view the world."

Debbie said she didn't object to the ashram in principle, but she didn't think there *was* a special vibe between her and Syd anymore. The relationship wasn't going to work out. "I need someone who understands where I'm at with my kid. Not someone who wants me to come around to his position."

"Debbie, you're misunderstanding," said Syd, leaning toward her. "I have no position. I have no point of view. I have an approach to talking about things that's based in acknowledging that certain situations appear to certain people in certain ways—but those ways are not based in fact. They're subjective. It's the *opposite* of a point of view, because once you see that perception is subjective, you have the power to change what the world means to you."

"Syd, that girl was assaulted," said my mother. "That is an objective fact." She lit a cigarette and rubbed one foot on top of the other like she was cold.

"Debbie, Debbie." Syd stood up and crossed toward her. "Now you're sounding hostile. I didn't come over here to be hostile. Let's have a hug." He opened his arms.

Debbie met his embrace with a slight grimace and patted him on the shoulder.

"That's not a real, deep hug, Debbie," Syd said as he let her go. "That's not a deep, open hug you just gave me. Let's have a real, honest, connecting hug, because even if we're not together, I want to share myself with you."

"Syd—"

"Really, Debbie, let yourself be open to it. You'll feel better, I promise."

They hugged again.

"Syd, I'm really not in the mood for this," my mother muttered, in the middle of the embrace. He squeezed her tighter. "Syd," she said. "I don't want to be hugged right now. I want my personal space. Will you please let me go?"

He stepped back, a look of annoyance on his face. "It's that new guy, isn't it?"

"What new guy?

"You're seeing a new guy. A father from Vanessa's school."

"How did you know that?"

"Katty Sherwin told me. I ran into her this morning."

"It's just starting. We've been out together twice."

"Were you seeing him when you were with me?"

"No," Debbie looked nervous. "No. I had met him, but I didn't spend any time with him until after you and I broke it off."

"Some conservative older guy."

"He's older than you, yes."

"You think someone like him is going to solve all your problems, give you a nice stable existence. Don't you, Debbie?"

"That has nothing to do with it."

"You want some guy who doesn't challenge you, some guy who doesn't force you to confront your prejudices and open up."

"Syd, please."

"Some guy who says 'Okay' when you don't want to talk about things, right? Some guy who doesn't push past those boundaries you've set up for yourself."

"Well, yes," said Debbie. "That is what I want."

There was a pause.

"You're missing out, Debbie," he said.

"Then I'll just miss out," she said. "You can feel sorry for me."

He reached a hand out and stroked her face. "You had so much potential," he said. "So much potential."

Then he grabbed his coat and walked out the door.

15.

The Genius Child Causes Trouble

To Button, Patrick Threep, Fuzzy, and Dirigible, we added two more kitties the day after Syd appeared at the window. Debbie got them from the upstairs neighbor, Terry Mandible, the guy who was always sitting in the front yard and commenting on my appearance.

Terry must have inherited the cats from an aunt who died or something, because he certainly wasn't a cat lover. He'd only had them for a couple weeks—beautiful animals, with long, silky hair and squished-in faces like the cats in calendar photos. We felt sorry for them. On cold days, they'd meow pitifully at his door for hours, huddling together for warmth. Terry would never let them in, even when we knew he was home.

Every time they saw us, the cats would follow us down the driveway, crying and crying. Debbie put food on our back steps for them to eat, and they got very friendly. We were starting to wonder what would happen to them when it snowed, and then one day Debbie witnessed Terry actually kicking the gray cat out of the way as he was taking off for a carpentry job. That was it. She marched right over that minute and offered to adopt them.

No, Terry said. They were purebred cats. She couldn't have them.

Debbie offered him twenty dollars.

He said No way, man. Those cats were worth a lot of money.

She offered him thirty.

He said he wanted thirty per cat.

She gave it to him.

It was our Christmas money. We named them Pompadour and Deluxe.

The Tuesday after Thanksgiving, after the parent-teacher meetings, we had Super Duper Spellers.

"I trust you all have Vanessa's play in your folders?" said Ron, smiling a stretched sort of smile.

Some people did. Others had left it at home or downstairs in their lockers.

"I wasn't allowed to read it," said a fourth-grade boy. "My mom was looking over my homework, and she took it away."

"I wasn't, either. My father said I wouldn't like it." Anu's husky voice surprised me.

"It was funny! Like when Allowishus Rump falls down on his butt!" Luke was too loud. He never seemed to perceive exactly what noise level was appropriate. But everyone in class giggled.

After what had happened at the parent-teacher conference, I was expecting Ron to say that we had to throw the play in the garbage, that it was dirty and I should be sent to a psychiatrist. Instead, he just cleared his throat, handed out some extra dittos, and announced, "Lets all say thank you to Vanessa for doing that hard work to write a play for our group. Vanessa, you're really an author."

"Thank you, Vanessa!" said Luke loudly, and a number of other kids said it, too.

Then we read through *Mister Posterior and the Genius Child*, each taking different parts. Even Anu and the boy whose mother didn't like it participated, and Ron was Mrs. Hindquarters when everybody else already had a part to read. He read it in a high, squeaky voice. Everybody laughed in some places—the tightrope-walking scene in particular—but they stayed silent and somewhat perplexed in others. Precocious (the part with the two children in a sleeping bag) did not go over nearly so well as Collection (the part with the cats who frighten Mister Posterior).

As it progressed, I breathed more easily. It all seemed so normal. Maybe Joyce's suggestion that I see a psychiatrist wasn't a true reflection of what people thought about me.

Nonetheless, the next day another family sent in a complaint about *Mister Posterior*: the Bhaduris. Apparently Mister Bhaduri stopped in after school and told Ron and Joyce that he didn't blame me, I was a very nice child, but clearly there was an atmosphere of sexual provocation at Cambridge Harmony that was overwhelming to young kids. Especially after what happened to Anu, he couldn't tolerate her performing in a play all about bottoms when it was none other than a bottom that had traumatized her. He followed up by announcing at the next PTA meeting that the issue of dirty words and the Super Duper Spelling group had not been adequately resolved, making a movement to revisit it. Then he stood in front of the entire community and read the dirtiest excerpts from *Mister Posterior and the Genius Child*, giving great emphasis to the part about learning not to use your ass as a receptacle.

Debbie didn't have a baby-sitter because Landis had an *Oliver* rehearsal, so I was there, lurking in the back of the room. When everyone took a break for coffee and butter cookies, my mother ran outside to chain-smoke. She didn't even say anything to me, just started pulling a menthol out of the package before the announcement about refreshments was finished, and slunk out the side door with a hunted look.

I crawled quietly under the buffet table, ate Lorna Doones, and listened.

"She dittoed it herself and gave it out, I hear."

"Don't Joyce and Ron keep an eye on those things?"

"You'd think they'd read every ditto they send home."

"It's a natural expression of preadolescent sexuality."

"Preadolescents don't have a sexuality."

"Haven't you read Freud?"

"If they do, it shouldn't be encouraged at school."

"It's just curiosity."

"It's bathroom humor."

"A healthy child should not be writing things like that."

"It's a cry for help."

"Do you think she's neurotic?"

"Everyone's neurotic. Haven't you read Freud?"

"How can a child be thinking about sticking objects up there? She shouldn't even know about that kind of thing."

"She needs our sympathy."

"She needs treatment. It's not the school's fault."

"What are they doing to help her?"

"I don't know that they're doing anything."

"There's no 'they.' It's only a single mother."

"Oh. Well."

After the coffee, Mister Bhaduri took the floor again. Cambridge is a city, he said. There are bad men in dark alleys looking to take your children's lunch money or do something worse to them. We pay to send our children to Cambridge Harmony because we know it's a good school. And part of knowing it is a good school is not just programs like art, music, and the study of American Indians. It's knowing, for example, that the playground is safe. We have wood chips on the ground, strong, solid equipment, and a big fence. It's knowing that the building is safe, that there are fire drills and air-raid drills where the children hide under the tables. It's also knowing that our kids are learning to love one another. That they will learn to treat people's bodies respectfully—not to hit, or pinch, or even tease. It's knowing that the children will be taught reverence for every living thing. Cambridge Harmony doesn't tolerate racism or sexism.

Vanessa Brick, he said, is a very nice girl. But for whatever reason—her emotional problems, a broken home maybe—she has lost track of that respect and kindness. Her play encouraged laughing at other people's incompetencies and misfortunes. It made jokes out of serious venereal diseases by naming cats after them. It made fun of people for their large bottoms and for their unusual names. It mocked Mister Posterior's fear of cats, instead of taking a sympathetic view. This play displayed disrespect for the feelings of others, and because of its sexually explicit nature, it also transformed the protective environment of Cambridge Harmony into a threatening one. Children could be—and had been—hurt by reading this play.

Mister Bhaduri did not blame Vanessa Brick. She was just

expressing herself, expressing herself artistically as best as she knew how and with whatever problems she may be experiencing in her personal life. He blamed the teachers for not better encouraging Vanessa to recognize that certain words and behaviors are inappropriate in certain contexts. He blamed them for not taking the play as an opportunity to help Vanessa work on her empathy skills, and to discuss with her how sad it made other people to be ridiculed. And last, he blamed them for allowing the distribution of *Mister Posterior and the Genius Child.*

No teacher would assign a textbook he hadn't read. No teacher would show a filmstrip he had never seen. Why, then, would a teacher send home a play that he had never bothered to read, especially after the Super Duper Spelling group was already deemed in need of monitoring by a large percentage of the PTA? That teacher, Ron Trafalgar, was being irresponsible.

Childhood, said Mister Bhaduri, is an innocent time. Children are unself-conscious. They are sometimes rude, sometimes silly, but they are open and honest, and they know how to live in the moment. These are all qualities that adults need to embrace themselves (nods from the parents in the auditorium) and they are qualities that we must treasure and foster in our children.

Thunderous applause, followed by a group sing-along of "This World Is Ours to Share."

Most of the PTA members signed a petition to have Super Duper Spelling disbanded until the following year. We would miss the Boston-area spelling bee that happened in March, and we would not perform *Mister Posterior and the Genius Child.* Not now. Not ever. Once the issues could be sorted out, the petition implied, once we could all come together and establish what was in the best interests of the students, the group might re-form in the fall. Possibly, Ron Trafalgar would cede leadership of it to another teacher.

After that, the PTA happily discussed the Holiday Ice Party, which happened on a pond in Arlington that froze solid every winter. People signed up to run hot chocolate stands and contribute to the bake sale. Someone said she would bring a pot of chili on a Bunsen burner. There would be a pine tree there to decorate, and everyone was supposed to bring an ornament.

Sitting on my mother's lap in a back corner of the auditorium, shadowed by a stack of folding chairs piled one on top of the other and feeling her knee jiggle with nervous energy underneath me, I wondered about the ice on the pond.

Was it thin in places? Could a person fall through?

16.

In Which There Is Heartbreak

The next day Debbie asked if I wanted to meet Win Gifford, the person she talked to at the earlier PTA meeting, the tall blond man in the sweater vest who was probably forty. The person Syd Wheeler was jealous of. She told me she had been out to lunch with him two times now, and to the movies once, one night when Landis baby-sat. Today, he was going to come and meet me. She hadn't been to meet *his* family yet because his wife had died in an accident only a year ago. It didn't seem right to barge into his house after only three dates.

Win had lots of dogs.

"How many?"

"He has beagles," Debbie said, "or some kind of hunting dog. I think he has four."

"What are their names?" I asked him, when he came to our house. He was too tall for our living room, looked awkward sitting on the couch in a big ski parka.

"You heard about the dogs, huh?"

"Yes." Win put his hands around the cup of tea that Debbie made him, but he didn't drink any. She was wearing her favorite sweater and had put her hair up in a bun, fancy.

"They're called Fred, Robert, Sandra, and Allison."

"Those aren't dog names!"

"Vanessa, sugar. Be nice," Debbie said.

"But they're not! Dog names are like Fido and Spot."

"Like Fido and Spot, huh?" Win asked.

"Yes. Like Fuzzy and Button."

"What about Patrick Threep? I know you have a cat named Patrick Threep."

"She didn't get to name that one," Debbie interjected. "I named Patrick."

"I named my dogs after people I loved," Win explained. "That's why they don't have dog names. Fred was my brother, who died from leukemia when I was pretty young. Sandra was my great-grandmother, who used to knit booties for me when I was a baby." He paused. "Is it okay for me to tell her this?"

Debbie nodded.

"Robert was a friend of mine who passed away four years ago from heart trouble, and Allison was a friend from college who swam out to sea and never came back."

"Did you name one for your wife?" I asked.

A spasm crossed Win's face, and he put his teacup on the table.

"I don't need help remembering her," he said.

"Who swam out to sea and never came back?"

"Allison."

"What happened?"

"Nobody knows."

"Do you think she met a walrus?"

"A walrus?"

"Yes."

"I would like to think so." Win laughed. "She met a big, friendly walrus, and he took her away to see the wonderful undersea places where walruses live."

"Yeah," I said. "Do you wanna see my sleeping bag?"

"Why do you want to show him that, Vanessa?" my mother asked.

I didn't know. It would have made more sense to show him my room, or some cats he hadn't met, or Lopey, but the sleeping bag was what popped into my head. He looked old. I guess I thought he wasn't that familiar with sleeping bags. And he knew so many dead people. I thought it might cheer him up. It was a very good-looking bag.

Debbie said it was time to go, they were going to miss their reservation, and we all got into Win's station wagon and drove to pick up Landis. Her house was big, and had lots of lights on, and Landis was standing on the porch steps waiting for us. Shaun was there, too, looking up at her, making snowballs and throwing them high in the air and only sometimes catching them. He had on big snow boots but no coat. Only a long-sleeved cotton shirt.

Debbie leaned out the window of Win's car and waved. Landis trotted down the lawn, wrapping her scarf around her neck. (My mother had already given Landis a little talking to about my supposed preoccupation with sexual matters. I had heard them on the phone earlier that afternoon. Was there anything Landis had noticed? Debbie asked. Because Joyce the teacher thought something might be wrong with me, and the PTA was all in a tizzy about some spelling project I did. . . . Okay. . . . Well, that was reassuring. . . . Good. . . . But just in case, would Landis make a point to say affirming things to me? Like about what a smart, adorable kid I was? Because it might be a self-esteem problem.)

"Mrs. Brick," Landis cried, peering in the window of the unfamiliar car. "I didn't know it was you in there." She looked in the backseat. "Hey Vanessa! How's the greatest kid in the world?"

My mother smiled at her encouragingly, and Landis looked over her shoulder at Shaun, who was still messing about in the snow: "Listen, Mrs. Brick. My boyfriend is here. He just came over, came and surprised me, and I was wondering if he could come along tonight."

My mother paused for a second and turned to me. "What do you think, Vanessa?"

I shrugged.

"I guess it's okay," Debbie said.

Landis went up to fetch Shaun, and Debbie looked at Win. "I didn't know she even had a boyfriend! Did you know she had a boyfriend, sugar?"

"Yes," I said. "I know all about him."

After Debbie and Win went off to dinner, Landis and I gave Shaun a tour of the house. When I showed him the cats, Shaun liked Fuzzy the best because of her lopsided ear. He kept saying, "Fuzzy rules the world!" and holding her high up in the air. I wasn't sure she liked it, but I didn't say anything.

We played Parcheesi, and then I got out all my stuffed animals, which was something I usually did with Landis, but the two of them wanted to watch TV instead, so we looked at a program about policemen who had problems that I didn't really understand, and at a car race where the cars kept crashing into the walls on the side of the track. Shaun put his arm around Landis as they watched, and she looked at me and wiggled her eyebrows as if to say, "See? He's real!"

Shaun didn't seem all that interested in mouse-sitting. He didn't want to help me brush my teeth or get a drink of water. He wasn't curious about my pajamas or which particular cats usually slept with me. When Landis read me bedtime stories, he listened to the first one, but then he went back to the living room where the TV was.

"He's cute, right?" Landis asked when he left.

"Yeah," I said, and it was true. Despite his lack of interest in certain obviously interesting things, Shaun had a shine to his shaggy hair and a curve of his lower lip that made me want to look at him a lot. Something about his thin white wrists coming out of his shirt cuffs.

He was only in the chorus of the musical, and that was a little weird, Landis said. She had one of the main parts, and he got jealous of the guy who played her abusive boyfriend, Bill Sykes. Bill Sykes was a senior, and he owned a car. On Thursday, he had driven her home from rehearsal, and on Friday, yesterday, Landis and Shaun had had their first real fight.

"This play is so square," Shaun had said, as they smoked cigarettes together in the parking lot.

"It is not."

"The people are square. Bill Sykes is an asshole."

"He's sweet."

"If you like that kind of thing. He sure doesn't sing on key."

"What?"

"He sings like a buffalo."

"I can't believe you, Shaun."

"I can't believe you, making cow eyes at him all the time."

"I'm not making cow eyes."

"He's a big buffalo, and you're making cow eyes at him."

"It's my character. I'm supposed to be his girlfriend."

"Well, he's an asshole buffalo, and this whole play is square. I'm thinking about quitting."

At this point, Landis realized Shaun was jealous and tried to pacify him.

She told him she was sorry. She told him she didn't even like Bill Sykes. She said Shaun was her boyfriend and that was all that mattered.

Nothing seemed to work.

He wouldn't look her in the eye. Still claimed *Oliver* was stupid kid stuff, and he didn't know why she was so interested in it in the first place.

"But then, Mouseling, I had a flash of brilliance," Landis confided Saturday night as she tucked me into bed. "I said it was old-fashioned for him to be worried about me and Bill Sykes. He needed to let loose. Couldn't be tying me down like I was some old lady. If he loved something, he had to set it free, not be all possessive. Just relax, I said. I laid that whole trip on him, and walked away to my Friday rehearsal without even kissing him good-bye."

That's why Shaun had been over at her house when we came to collect her for baby-sitting. He had come to make up to her, had taken the bus all the way across town in the cold weather and knocked on her family's door at six o'clock on Saturday. He was sorry, he didn't know what he had been thinking. He had just freaked, but he was mellow now. They had kissed on the porch.

"So it's a happy ending, Vanessa," Landis said to me before turning out the light.

A week later—this was the start of December, now—there was an orgy. I know because Landis told me a little about it when Debbie and Win went on another date, and mainly because she talked on the phone with a friend of hers long after she thought I was asleep. I listened with my ear against the bedroom door.

One night after rehearsal, the teacher who was directing the show made sure that all the kids had rides, gave the key to a responsible senior, and went home. People hung around the auditorium, laughing and drinking sodas from the machine. Landis and Shaun had been cuddling on this pile of old mattresses that were part of the set, and Connie with the shaggy haircut had come and laid her head in Landis's lap. Then Hannah, the popular girl, had come over and cuddled up next to Shaun, saying "Looks cozy here, can I join?" Landis hadn't wanted her to, thought it wasn't at all the same for Hannah to wrap her arms around Shaun as for Connie to rest her head, but she hadn't said anything because Shaun had started kissing her neck just at that moment, so she felt like everything was okay. Then Hannah asked Shaun for a back rub, saying her shoulders were really tense, and Shaun had said sure, so Landis had to sit there and watch her boyfriend rub some other girl's body. She couldn't really object, because she had told him he was uptight for being jealous about Bill Sykes, had set a standard of openness that now she had to live up to. So when Shaun's friend Dave came by, Landis had called out, "Dave, do you want a back rub? My hands are free."

Dave sat down and took off his shirt. Landis had to rub his bare skin, which she hadn't been expecting, but she felt like she couldn't say anything since she had initiated the massage. Pretty soon Dave pulled her hand down across his chest, and Shaun kissed her on the neck again, and Hannah's hand was on Shaun's inner thigh. Connie kissed Dave, and somebody got up and turned the stage lights off. Shaun never kissed Hannah, Landis didn't think, but he definitely grabbed her titty and squeezed it like he liked it, even though it wasn't anywhere near as big as Landis's were.

Dave tried to kiss Landis, but she didn't let him. She kissed Shaun and let Dave rub her on the outside of her pants. Hannah started making moaning noises that Landis thought were really absurd and kind of creepy, and after she did that a couple times, Landis decided she didn't like what was going on and stood up.

"I have to go," she had called into the darkness of the auditorium. "I have a curfew."

"Don't go, Landie," Shaun had said, reaching his hand up and rubbing it around on her butt. "Don't go."

Hannah made another moaning noise, and Landis couldn't really see whether it was Shaun or Dave or even Connie who was touching her, or whether she was just moaning because she thought it was a sexy thing to do.

"What time is it?" Landis had asked.

"It's not late," Shaun muttered.

"Dave." Landis nudged him with her knee. "You said you'd drive me home. I really have to go, or my mom will have fits."

Dave had a driver's license. He got to his feet in the dark, put his jacket on over his bare chest, and jumped off the edge of the stage without a word. When the light from the parking lot streamed in the doorway after he opened it, Landis followed him. Outside, a bunch of juniors and seniors were smoking and horsing around. A girl was riding piggyback on a boy's narrow hips. Someone had a bottle of wine, and people were taking sips out of it.

Dave drove Landis home without saying anything.

The next day, Shaun wouldn't look Landis in the eye. He said "Hey" when he saw her in the hall and did a kind of military-style salute at her, possibly to say hello in a playful way, like a GI would salute a pretty woman on the street, or possibly to indicate that she was the uptight one after all. She wasn't sure.

She put her arm around him on line in the lunchroom, and he whispered, "Not here in front of people," as if they had never made out in the hallways where everybody could see. Still, after school he had promised to call her that night at baby-sitting, and that cheered Landis up. She jumped into Debbie's car that evening with a big smile.

"How's the play going?" Debbie said.

"Pretty cool," Landis answered. "Pretty cool. The performances aren't till February, but we got fitted for our costumes this afternoon. I think the kids on the costume crew are overdoing it a bit. My boyfriend has to wear a leather vest. Isn't that weird? Like an orphan pickpocket would have a leather vest." She giggled.

"What are you wearing?"

"Something low cut. I'm a little nervous about Shaun's parents seeing me in it. My character is a prostitute."

"I'm sure they know you're not your character," Debbie said.

"Yeah, they probably do."

Debbie left to go to the movies with Win, and Landis put me to bed. Later, when I was supposed be fast asleep but was really waiting to see if the bottom showed up at my window, I overheard her on the phone with a friend.

"I have to go now." Landis finally sighed, after telling the whole orgy story in gross detail. "He's supposed to call me here around nine. I don't want him to get a busy signal." After she hung up, I listened a while longer and heard her turn on the television set. I got back in bed.

I couldn't sleep.

Lopey's round plastic eyes looked very alert in the moonlight.

The bed felt cold and wouldn't warm up.

So I grabbed my antelope and went into the living room. Landis was on the phone again. "Shaun," she was saying. "Was it something I did?" The cords of her neck stood out and her nose was running. I went over and sat next to her.

"Aren't you going to give any reason at all?" Her voice was tight. "I think I deserve an explanation."

There was silence on the other end of the line.

"Well," she whispered. "Vanessa just woke up and I have to go."

He answered something, and she hung up. Her lips were quivering, and her fingers twisted into each other. She looked incredibly sad.

"Are you going to cry?" I asked.

"Yes." Landis's face melted and she reached for a tissue. "He broke up with me, Vanessa," she said, tears dripping down her soft red cheeks. "He didn't even call when he said he would, I had to wait, and wait, and finally call him, and when I did, he acted like he never even said he was going to, like I was being silly to think he meant it when he said he would."

I didn't know what to do. I sat Lopey on her knee.

"Come on, Mouseling." Landis wiped her face. "Let's get you back in bed. It's too late for you." She picked me up, she was a strong girl, and carried me back to my room. I got under the covers, and she lay next to me on top of them, holding a big handful of tissues. Her voice was high and choked. "Today at school he seemed kind of weird. But only a week ago he took the bus all the way across town to get to my house, remember?" She stopped talking to blow her nose. "Connie thinks he's jealous, jealous of the Bill Sykes guy and Dave. But I would have never touched Dave if he hadn't been touching Hannah. I was just trying to act like I didn't care!" She burst into tears again. "How can you break up over the telephone when only last night you were French kissing? God, Vanessa, two days ago he brought me a flower!"

"What kind?"

"Carnation. I should have known then, probably. A carnation is the cheapest kind of flower you can buy."

We looked at the ceiling. The moonlight made patterns.

"Maybe he thought he couldn't get someone as pretty and popular as Hannah, so he dated me just because I was there. Because I put that note in his locker! Then yesterday he realized he *could* get Hannah, and now he wants to be rid of me so he can go out with her instead!"

She turned her face away. "This never would have happened if I had played hard to get. Boys like that, you know, Vanessa? When you pretend not to like them back."

"He's dumb," I said.

She paused. "No, no, I bet it was the dance. There's this holiday dance in two weeks, you know, the Cambridge Harmony Winter Groove, where everyone dresses up. Shaun didn't want to go, he thought it was corny, but I really wanted to. Connie is going with a senior, and everyone else is going, but Shaun said, Why should we do what everyone else is doing? Aren't we individuals? And I said, Sure we are, but I still wanted to go to the dance!"

She sniffled. "Now he'll go off with some girl who's more of an individual than me, someone who thinks just like he does. And he'll take her to the dance, because she's so cool that she doesn't want to go. God, Vanessa, I wish I had never let him take my shirt off!"

"I thought you liked it."

"I did, I did," she said, "but now I feel like he got something off me."

"What did he get?"

She didn't know. "I wish he hadn't done things I liked," she finally said. "I wish he was a Peanut Butter Boy, that's what I wish. Him with his stupid Beatles T-shirt and his stupid hair and his never writing me notes. Did you know that, Vanessa?"

"What?" I was starting to feel sleepy.

"I wrote him notes, cute things like with a horoscope for the day or a lyric from a song. And he never once wrote me back. One little note would have made me so happy, one thing addressed to me in his handwriting. But he said he wasn't the writing type." She paused. "I don't think there's anything inside his head at all. It's like he's a robot," she said. Her lips were trembling. "I just don't understand why he doesn't want me anymore."

Then, in the cold early December moonlight, the bottom appeared. I don't think it could have realized that Landis was with me. It never showed itself when Debbie was tucking me into bed. On its arms, it wore its usual long-sleeved red cotton shirt, despite the icy weather. On its bottomly self, of course, it wore nothing at all. It waggled atop the woodpile with quite a lot of *joie de vivre,* swishing from side to side like a cabaret dancer and then pressing itself foolishly against the cold glass of my window. I often imagined it singing one of the songs Anu and I used to repeat over and over when we spun on the tire swing:

Ta Ra Ra Boom-dee-ay,
I'll take your pants away,
And while you're standing there,
I'll take your underwear!

I looked at Landis to see if it was cheering her up, but her face was contorted. "Oh, my God, Vanessa." She was whispering. "Don't be scared. Don't be scared, sweetheart. All the doors are locked. There's no way he can get inside. I promise."

The bottom disappeared, and Landis jumped up to shut the curtains. "What a complete and total freak that guy was! Are you okay?"

I nodded.

"Oh, man," she said again, raising her eyes to the ceiling. "I can't believe somebody just flashed us! That is so gross!"

"It's only the bottom," I said. "I'm used to it."

"What?"

"I'm used to it. It comes all the time. It's not hurting anybody."

"What do you mean, it comes all the time?"

"I don't know."

"How often?"

"Every week, I think. Maybe more."

"Since when?"

"Halloween."

"Did you tell Debbie?"

"No."

"Why not?"

"It's just a bottom," I answered. "Everybody has one."

"Oh, Mouseling," Landis said, touching my face with her fingertips. "It's not just a bottom. It's really not."

She said we had to tell.

I said, no we didn't.

"No one's going to be mad at you, Mouseling," Landis explained. "It is absolutely not your fault that some freaked-out lunatic is flashing you."

"Why is he a lunatic?" I wanted to know.

"For showing you his butt! You don't want to be looking at the rear end of somebody you don't even know, do you?"

I shrugged. "I don't mind."

"Well, he shouldn't want to show it to you. It's gross. It's like what happened to Anu."

"Is not."

"Do you even know what happened to Anu?"

I hesitated. "Only kind of."

"It was a lot like this," said Landis. "Your mother told me. Oh my God! I bet it's even the same guy. The exact same guy, running around showing his rear end to little girls! What a freak. I wonder if we should call the police."

I didn't have anything to say.

Landis told Debbie as soon as we heard her key in the door.

17.

A Real Doctor

Debbie was nearly hysterical when Landis told her about the bottom. She said she had seen something like that out the window once, long before Halloween, had sewn curtains to protect Vanessa, would never want to expose her daughter to anything harmful. She cried. She said she should have known because of my play, should have known because the teachers were suggesting psychotherapy, should have known because it was happening practically in her own home.

Could it be Syd? He had showed up at that same window, that very same window not so long ago and had behaved very inappropriately. That man had no sense of boundaries, had no sense of what kind of trauma this sort of thing inflicted on little kids. He had even argued that Anu Bhaduri hadn't really been hurt when she was assaulted in the park! He didn't seem to think actions had particular moral meanings; he thought it was all open to interpretation. And oh, God, she had totally forgotten, oh, God, this clinched it, he had actually shown Vanessa his penis. It had looked like a mistake, looked like it was hanging out there by accident, but now that she thought about it, it fit right in with his hugging people when they didn't want to be hugged, his nudist philosophy, his knocking on the window, and his saying he was "Debbie's lover" to people when it wasn't any of their business to know. He was a deliberate penis-exposing freak, that's what he was.

The police took Syd Wheeler's name down as a possible suspect. They asked me very nicely about the bottom's characteristics, established that it had white skin and wore a red long-sleeved shirt with a cigarette burn on one cuff. They seemed to think it likely that the perpetrator was indeed the same person who had flashed Anu Bhaduri while wearing a ski mask.

Had I seen a ski mask?

No. I had never seen anyone's head.

Only the area below the waist?

Yeah.

Had I seen the front side of the perpetrator?

No.

Just the backside?

Just the backside.

Had the perpetrator tried to enter the home at any point?

No, he hadn't.

Had I noticed him coming on a schedule, such as Saturday nights?

At night.

Every night?

No.

Any particular nights?

No.

Just some nights?

Yeah.

After dark?

Yeah.

Did he carry a weapon of any sort?

No.

No knife, no gun?

No.

Did I know it was against the law to show your backside to someone who hadn't asked to see it?

I didn't know that till now. Now I knew.

Did I know it was not my fault?

Yes.

Did I know it was a good girl for telling, that I was a big help to the police?

Yes, I did. Thank you.

Debbie boarded up the window in my bedroom. For the first few nights, she just made sure the curtains were tightly shut, but finally she said she couldn't sleep and tacked up a bunch of plywood, blocking all the sunlight.

She had to wake me up every morning, after that. With the room dark, I always overslept.

The idea of the psychologist was presented to me very carefully. It wasn't that I had done anything bad, my mother said. It wasn't that anything was wrong with me. It was just that I had been going through this trauma with the bottom for almost two months. Maybe that was why I didn't play with other kids very much, and why I was having trouble with math, and why I wrote the play. Debbie said Doctor Eng would help me understand my feelings better. The office would be a safe place. Doctor Eng was there to be my friend and help me be the happiest person I could be.

"Do you want to go, Vanessa?"

"Okay," I said. It was what she wanted to hear.

"But do you *want* to?"

"I don't mind."

"It's going to help you feel better. I really believe that."

I shrugged.

"It's just talking to a nice doctor lady."

"Patrick Threep likes the snow," I said. "Did you see him outside on the porch? He was eating it."

"Good enough." Debbie sighed, and made the appointment.

I started going twice a week to a little office in a big corporate building. Debbie would take me on Tuesdays, and Landis took me on Thursdays, when my mother had to work. When I used to go to Anu's.

The first time I went, Debbie stayed with me and told Doctor Eng all about the bottom appearing in the window by moonlight. She explained about Anu getting flashed, and the play that included things about sticking things up your behind—

"*Not* sticking things," I interrupted.

"Okay, not sticking things, but it had lots to do with the behind, all kinds of jokes, a real preoccupation. The teachers are concerned."

Doctor Eng had gone to Boston University and had a Ph.D. in clinical psychology. I know because there was a plaque on her wall. She kept her long black hair parted in the middle—not like a doctor at all—and she didn't wear a white coat. She wore a turtleneck. The room was set up like a playroom, with art supplies and stuffed animals, a dollhouse, and a lot of toy soldiers. After listening to Debbie talk for a while, Doctor Eng smiled briefly and asked if Vanessa could go in the waiting room for a minute. The grown-ups needed to talk privately.

The waiting room was all right. There was a receptionist there who didn't pay any attention to me, and grown-up copies of fashion magazines and the daily newspaper. There was also a shelf of children's books. One of them was called *It's Okay to Feel Angry,* and another one was called *Where Did Grandpa Go?* I picked one that had an antelope on the cover.

When Debbie came out, I went in to see Doctor Eng by myself. She said I could play with the soldiers and art supplies any way I wanted, or we could sit and talk if I preferred. She also said I could call her Julie, but I liked calling her Doctor Eng.

It felt a little weird to start playing right off the bat with a real live doctor looking at me, but I also didn't know what to say. There didn't seem to be anything she *wanted* me to say. So we sat there, in silence.

"I see you picked an alphabet book," she said after a while.

"Yeah." I was still holding it.

"Your mom tells me you're a good reader."

"Yes."

"Do you want to read to me?"

"Okay." I held the book up so the pictures faced her, the way teachers do in class. "A is for Antelope. B is for bear. C is for cat. D is for dinosaur." I read right through to the end.

"Thank you, Vanessa. You are a very strong reader."

"Uh-huh."

"Would you like to tell me why you chose that book?"

"I like antelopes."

"Is that an antelope on the cover?"

Sheesh. Didn't she know an antelope when she saw one? "Yeah."

"It's an easy book to read, mmh?"

"It's okay."

"It's a good book for very young kids. Kids who are just learning the alphabet."

"I know."

"Sometimes its nice to pretend to be a baby, someone so little she can't read."

"Oh."

"It can feel good to play at being someone who doesn't even know her alphabet yet."

"I like antelopes."

Doctor Eng paused. "I see. What do you like about them?"

"I have an antelope at home. His name is Lopey."

"You do?"

"Yeah."

"Is he a stuffed antelope?"

"Yeah. He likes yellow."

"Can you tell me some more things about Lopey?"

I had to think for a minute. "He's always awake whenever I am. And he likes to play."

"Anything else?"

"He's stretchy."

"Is there anything special about him being an antelope?"

"He has long legs. And he matches the curtains. Debbie made me antelope curtains. Antelopes and lemons."

"On the curtains in the bedroom?"

"Yeah."

"Where the flasher was?"

"Uh-huh."

"I see. Will you tell me some things about antelopes in general? Things that you know about them."

I thought. Truth was, I didn't really know anything about antelopes. I liked Lopey. He had been given to me when I was too young to remember, and he was soft and had a goofy, happy look in his plastic eyes. His felt tongue sticking out made him look a little bit stupid, but he radiated good humor. That's what I liked.

"Do you like the horns?" Doctor Eng asked me, when I hadn't answered her.

"They're okay."

"You mentioned long legs. Do you like how they run? They can run away fast."

I didn't know.

"They can run away fast whenever there's danger," she said.

We were silent for a minute.

"They're vegetarians," I said at last.

"Are you a vegetarian?"

"Sort of," I said. "I eat meat."

"Antelopes don't eat meat at all."

"No."

"But you do?"

"Yeah."

"Like what? What meat do you eat?"

"Chicken slices. And bacon."

"I see."

"Don't tell Debbie."

Doctor Eng looked interested. "You don't want me to tell your mother you eat meat."

"She's a real vegetarian. My father is eating fried chicken across the state of California and might explode."

Well, that was it. All she wanted to talk about after that was Jordy. I went back three times before we talked about anything else, even though she ostensibly let me drive the course of the conversation.

One thing we did a lot was play a game where Doctor Eng drew a squiggle on a piece of paper, and I made it into a drawing of something—whatever I wanted. She was always seeing something about Jordy in my pictures. If I drew a bird, it was a fried chicken. If I drew a person, it looked like a dad. If I drew a woman, the dad was absent. If I drew the sun, it was exploding.

Why did I think Jordy might explode?

What did exploding mean to me?

Why was it fried chicken?

Had I ever eaten fried chicken?

Did other kids tease me about not having a father?

Did I remember anything about him?

It was strange to spend so much time thinking about Jordy. At first I thought I had no memory of him. That's what I told Doctor Eng. No memory. We had no photographs, no clothes of his, no books with his name inscribed inside. No record albums, no address in the address book. He didn't send cards for holidays, or presents on my birthday, and he had no relatives still living. His parents had died in a car accident about five months after my mother threw the plates at the door.

It was like he never existed.

I did remember something, though, a small something, a glimmer. A grin with wide square teeth and a smell of red wine. A laugh so big it made people giggle just to hear it. Made me giggle. But I couldn't figure out how to articulate that glimmer to Doctor Eng. It was like a flash of light. It wouldn't form into sentences.

In the Laundromat, mid-December, Debbie and I saw a handwritten sign on a bulletin board: "Pretty kitty, very friendly, needs a new owner. Moving soon. Save her from the pound!"

We got right in the car and drove to the address on the flyer. Our laundry wasn't even folded yet. Thank goodness, Pretty Kitty was still available, though she was actually somewhat scrawny and only an ordinary stripy cat. We drove home with her purring on top of the wrinkled clothes.

She entered our household without a single hiss. Everyone loved her right away. Patrick Threep, who scratched every new cat that came home with us, only sniffed her and went back to sleep. She curled up in the living room chair that always belonged to Fuzzy, and Fuzzy didn't object, just climbed up there and curled around her like a sweater. She was number seven, and we knew our neighbors had started talking. Terry Mandible from upstairs called me the Cat Kid. "Hey, Cat Kid," he'd say in a teasing voice, waving a can of beer at me as I helped Debbie get the groceries out of our car.

Our landlord had come by right after Thanksgiving, checking to see if everything was sanitary. Debbie vacuumed for an hour before he got there, suctioning fur balls from dusty corners, lifting matted bits of fuzz from the pillows on the couch, from the rug, from the linen closet. She burned incense that smelled like faraway places and scrubbed the kitchen floor with bleach. When he arrived, we showed him our litter boxes, cleaned every day; showed him the back lawn that was neater than Terry's ratty front one; and told him that the mouse problem he had never solved had now totally disappeared.

Were we planning on adopting any more? the landlord wanted to know.

We had no plans for that, no.

Six is really the limit, the landlord said. If we adopted any more, he would terminate our lease.

We wouldn't be adopting any more. And as he could see, everything was in order.

"This is not an animal shelter," the landlord reminded Debbie. "This is a respectable building."

"I know it is," she said.

"I could get someone in here who'd pay more than you do."

"I know, I know."

"No more cats," the landlord said. "One more and you're out." And he drove off in his station wagon.

We adopted Pretty Kitty, anyway. She needed us, and Debbie said he'd never be able to count how many we had. It wasn't like they were going to line up for him. They didn't even like him.

18.

SQUIRREL OF THE UNIVERSE

It was almost Christmas vacation, almost the Holiday Ice Party, when Marie attacked again.

I had remained relatively popular. Although my status was still insecure, Summer, Didi, and Angelique counted me in their clique of friends. Since kindergarten, I had been paired with Anu and they with one another. Now, I was suddenly the fourth member of their group, with Anu as an alternate fourth. If she, in one of her few sociable moments, decided to dominate a game or discussion with her old sense of entitlement, I was clearly expected to slink away and be on my own. But most of the time Anu kept to herself or played with Summer in a twosome, leaving me to swing on the tire swing with Angelique and Didi, to raise our hands aggressively in Circle of Sharing, to chase the boys with warm wet kisses sizzling on our fingertips. We would stand in one corner of the playground on days that it snowed, playing clapping games with mittened hands.

Oh, jolly enemy,
Come out and fight with me!
And bring your devils three,
Climb up my poison tree,
Slide down my razor blade,
Into my dungeon door,
And we'll be jolly enemies
Forevermore,
More, more, more, more!

Angelique almost always tucked her arm through mine at recess, and she shared her stickers with me, but I hadn't been invited to her house since the last PTA meeting. She couldn't come to mine because of allergies, though she went to Didi's house, and Didi had two cats at home.

Summer, wet thumb moistening the colored pencils as we made holiday calendars, said her parents had stopped letting her walk to the park by herself. They always had to come with her wherever she went. The pet store, the neighbor's house, everywhere. "And they sat me down and told me that if I heard any dirty talk I should come right home and tell them," she said, erasing part of her drawing with a big pink eraser. "Do you know any?"

"No," I answered. "Why do your parents want to know dirty talk?"

"I don't know. They just do."

"Like what?"

"Like jokes, I guess. I don't know. I don't think I ever heard a dirty joke."

"What makes it dirty?" I asked.

"Like dirty words and stuff."

"Like what?"

"Titties, Poo. Like Fart. Do you know any?"

"Jokes?"

"Yeah. Do you know any dirty jokes?"

"I bet Malcolm knows some." I didn't want to answer her directly. She didn't seem to understand that her parents weren't looking for entertainment. They were looking for information on kids like me.

"Malcolm's mind is so dirty, he should wash it." Summer giggled.

Two days later, I was struggling out of my snowsuit in the hallway, and Didi came over. "Hey, Vanessa. How come my mom keeps asking me about you?"

"I don't know."

"She wants to know everything. Like who your mom is, and what kind of car you drive."

"We have a Beetle."

"I know. She wanted to know other stuff, too, like what kinds of games you like to play."

"What did you tell her?"

"I told her jacks, and swinging on the swings. And what kind of books you read."

"Any kind of book," I said. "Horse books."

"I said that to her!" Didi slammed her locker shut. "My mom is such a weirdo. She never asks about Summer or Angelique. It's just Vanessa, Vanessa, Vanessa."

"Tell her I'm a nice girl," I said.

"She asked me that."

"What?"

"If you were a nice girl."

"I am," I said, scrunching the snowsuit into my locker.

"That's what I told her, but she didn't seem like she believed me," said Didi. "She asked me like three times."

At recess that day, we lay on the ground making snow angels. Me, Angelique, and Didi, shouting,

James James
Morrison Morrison
Weatherby George Dupree
Took great
Care of his Mother,
Though he was only three.
James James
Said to his Mother,
"Mother," he said, said he:
"You must never go down to the end of the town, if you don't go down with me."

I was staring into the sky, watching the puffy flakes swirl like they were chasing each other, when a large snowball thwacked me on the forehead. My skin stung and my eyes watered with the surprise.

I hated snowball fights. I sat up, looking around for the boy who'd done it, ready to run and tell the teacher as soon as I spotted the culprit. But the boys were all at the other end of the play yard, pelting each other with missiles of ice, and Marie stood there instead, about eight feet away, packing another snowball in her red-mittened hands.

"You hit me in the eye," I said.

"So?"

"It was in my face."

"So?"

"So, it hurt."

Marie scooped up a little more snow and added it to her ball. She hadn't bothered me since I made friends with Angelique, except to say, "Hello, Vanessa," in this extra loud voice that sounded like she was teasing me, like she was pretending to be someone else, a snooty sort, typical of the people I was friends with. She'd say this Hello, usually once a day, and it would totally unsettle me. I had no idea how to respond to it.

"It didn't hurt," Marie said, tossing her snowball in the air and catching it again.

"It did, too!"

Didi and Angelique got up and ran away toward the climber before Marie threw the next one. It hit me square in the chest, splattering white down my front.

Was she going to beat me up?

I knew I deserved it. I had ostracized her and let rumors circulate that I could have stopped had I chosen. I had whispered "Minestrone" to Summer and Anu, and wielded my social power against her. Thanks to my efforts, Marie was a friendless girl who scuffed her feet by the fence during recess, who got picked last for kickball, who never had a partner when we teamed up for science projects. People said she had cooties. They wouldn't trade lunches with her. They walked by like she wasn't there.

Marie was bent over, collecting another snowball. Could I run? She might take that as an invitation to chase me, which would be even worse. Then she could knock me down, grab me, and clutch me against her big, cruel body. Should I just sit there and let her pelt me until I cried? Maybe then she'd feel done and leave me alone.

Running through my terror, like a thread of gold in stone, was the slight possibility that Marie was unconscious of the wrongs I had done her. By throwing the snowballs she was inviting me to play, and had been saying that strange, intimidating Hello to me as a way of being funny or charming. If that were the case, I might do something friendly, like offer to build a snowman with her. Avoid the fight.

But I didn't want to build a snowman with someone who frightened me. Nor, truthfully, with someone who would threaten my precarious popularity.

I could run away. I could sit still and take it. I could make an insincere gesture of friendship. Or I could fight back.

I picked up a blob of snow as another of Marie's missiles hit me across the cheek. It stung, and I packed my ball into a solid sphere and hurled it at her. It only hit her knee—I didn't get enough arc in it—but it felt good to throw it hard through the air. I scooped up some more snow, packed it together.

Marie came forward, closer than someone usually comes for a snowball fight, and threw her next one at me. I ducked, though, and it hit the ground, and then my own ball hit her on the ear. She was almost within arm's reach now, and I scooped a fistful of snow and threw it at her neck. "I like cucumber," I shouted. "Why do you even care?"

The snow seeped under Marie's collar and into her snowsuit. She roared. "No fair! You can't put it down my neck."

"Yes, I can," I spat back. "You don't make the rules."

Scooping up more, I tried to get it down her neck again. But Marie was fast; she pulled my arm and my snow drifted to the ground.

"Don't grab me," I yelled. "It's a snowball fight."

"I am grabbing you. You don't make the rules, either."

Before I knew it, we were rolling in the snow near the chain-link fence. I was screaming and trying to get handfuls down the front of Marie's coat. She was squeezing my arms and pushing snow in my face. We were lying on it, got it in our ears, soaked our hair. Snow went up the wrists of my too-small snowsuit. One of my rubber boots came off, and I remember seeing it lying on the ground and wondering how it got there.

Some kids had circled around us. "Eat the snow," I yelled at Marie, and tried to get some of it in her mouth.

"No, you eat it!" Marie cried, taking some in each hand and rubbing it on my cheeks. It was a funny move, like a grandma squeezing my face. The snow was so cold it made my skin smart, and I looked at Marie for a minute, her mouth dribbling icy water, her hair white with clumps of snow. Funny.

We were pummeling each other in our soft padded snowsuits when Joyce separated us. She gave us both time-outs on the side of the playground. We sat in wooden chairs watching the other children who knew how to play nicely.

"Can you sit by each other without fighting?" Joyce asked.

"I don't think so," I answered, so she put us about ten feet apart, facing in different directions.

I had never had a time-out at school before, had never done anything the teachers thought was quite bad enough to warrant it. Sometimes, long ago, Ron used to say, "Anu and Vanessa, if you keep wiggling and giggling on line, I am going to have to give you a time-out," but that was the closest I had ever come. The threat of time-out had always been enough to keep me quiet and in my place. I had imagined it an immense humiliation, other kids looking at you and knowing that you couldn't control your impulses. Kids who got time-outs were naughty kids, and I didn't want to be one of them. But the nice kid I used to be—she was Anu's friend. *That* kid worried about what the teachers thought of her, told people what they wanted to hear, never hogged the swings, and cried when anyone looked at her funny.

She was gone now, replaced by a person with a disturbance. I was a pervert, a Cat Kid, a psychology patient. Not a nice girl at all. I might as well sit on a time-out chair in front of everyone.

After a few minutes, Joyce came over.

"Were you having a fight with Marie?" she asked.

"I don't know," I said. And it was the truth.

"Did you feel angry?"

"I threw a lot of snowballs."

"Do you know there are appropriate and inappropriate ways to play with the snow?"

"Yes."

"What is appropriate?"

"Throwing from far away when the person you're going to hit says it's okay." The teachers had drilled this idea into us at the start of the snowy season.

"Is that what happened with Marie?" Joyce asked.

"I don't know," I said.

"Were you far away?"

"No."

"Then was it appropriate?"

"No." I didn't want to look her in the eye, but I wasn't sorry.

"Do you know that we don't hit people at Cambridge Harmony?"

"Uh-huh."

"I've never seen you hit anybody before. Do you have a special reason for hitting, Vanessa, that you would like to share?"

"She threw one at me."

"She threw one at you? Marie says you started it."

I was silent.

"She says you started it. Is that true?"

"Yes," I said. "It is."

Of course, Joyce told Debbie that I had started a fistfight on the playground. Debbie told Doctor Eng, and Grin, and Pompey. Everybody was very interested in analyzing this new development, seeing the fight as further evidence of my acting out the misery caused by my trauma with the bottom.

Doctor Eng and I talked a lot about it. It was the only thing that got her off the subject of Jordy.

"Were you having an argument about something?" she asked.

I thought for a second. "No."

"Were you angry?"

"In the beginning."

"And after that?"

I wasn't sure.

"Do you know the name of the emotion you felt? Any emotion is okay for anybody to feel."

I didn't know the name of what I felt.

Then she asked me to list adjectives I knew that described Marie. I said Mean, Quiet, and Bigger Than Me.

Oh, and Lonely.

We talked a lot about how it was okay for me to be angry about stuff. Doctor Eng was saying things like, "Vanessa, everybody feels angry sometimes. It's a human feeling, and it is okay for you to express it." She gave me different verbal solutions to whatever it was that made me want to hit somebody. I could say "I'm very angry," for example, or "Don't do that. I don't like it," instead of hitting. We weren't really getting anywhere.

Then I thought of getting out a stuffed squirrel and a stuffed penguin that Doctor Eng had in her office. I was the squirrel. Marie was the penguin. The squirrel was in prime form, yip-yip-yipping and beating up on the penguin. Then the penguin fought back, beating up on the squirrel, and they kept butting their fuzzy stuffed animal tummies up against each other, yelling "Take that, you weirdo!"

Doctor Eng watched for quite a while.

"I'm going to sit on your head and squash you! I'm going to pulverize you in a coffee grinder!"

Doctor Eng was silent.

"I'm going to crash into you with my enormous tummy. Tip you over and you'll fall on your face, you big weirdo."

Doctor Eng continued watching. Finally she asked me:

"Are they having fun?"

"Yes," I answered, surprised.

"They're having fun," she repeated.

"The squirrel is Super Squirrel! He's the Squirrel of the Universe!"

"He's a confident squirrel."

"Squirrel of the Universe!"

Doctor Eng sat for a minute while the squirrel jumped up and down on the penguin's submissive belly.

"Congratulations, Vanessa," she said to me. "You won your first snowball fight."

"I don't know who won. The teacher interrupted us."

"You won," said Doctor Eng. "You definitely won."

19.

A Family of Meat-Eaters

Landis was heartbroken over Shaun. She lost weight and looked tragic, her eyes always slightly swollen, her hair curling wild around her shoulders. When she took me to Doctor Eng she never made jokes or did silly things. She was sober and affectionate, and treated me with a gravity that I found boring and unwarranted. While I was in there drawing chickens and staging ornate dramas with the stuffed animals and toy soldiers, Landis was supposedly doing her geometry homework. But really she drew pictures of Shaun's profile in the margins of her notebooks and doodled his name over and over in different styles of handwriting.

He was going around with Hannah, pointedly not seeing Landis when he passed her in the halls, muttering a casual "Hey" if he happened to stand next to her in the lunch line. Rumor had it Hannah screwed him in her parents' bedroom after only two weeks of dating, but lots of people didn't believe that could be true. Landis didn't understand how anything could go that far that fast. Shaun had never even tried to pull down her pants, and they had gone together more than a month.

The Cambridge Harmony Winter Groove came and went. Landis stayed home and watched a movie on TV. Her mom was really angry at Shaun, tried to get Landis to go "stag" or with another boy, a neighbor from down the street. But Landis wouldn't. She wanted to go with a real live boyfriend, to get a corsage, to know she had a partner for the slow dance numbers. She wanted someone to kiss her good night on her doorstep. She didn't want to go just to be there.

At one point, Shaun came up to her in the parking lot after school and said, "I hope we can be friends. You're not mad at me, are you?"

"Sure. Sure we're friends. Why would I be mad at you?" Landis responded, because that had seemed like the most dignified answer at the time.

But later, she was pissed at herself. Now Shaun didn't have to feel guilty for what he did; he could think it was fine to do this to girls, could think they didn't really mind, would be his friend afterward. He wouldn't have to feel awkward in the hall or on line in the lunchroom. He wouldn't have to say sorry, or feel embarrassed. He would never come to the realization, six months or maybe a year later, that he had been a horrible cheater, an insensitive lout, a liar, a deceiver, and besides that a manipulator who never wrote notes or telephoned his girlfriend, who always acted too cool for almost everything and thereby cut himself off from Landis, the most wonderful person in the world. He would never realize any of that, because she had told him she wasn't mad. Had even told him they were friends.

And still, he didn't want her. He held hands with Hannah in the hall, touched her flat miniature titties when he thought nobody was looking, sat posing with his arm around her when kids hung out in the parking lot.

Landis and I ate candy together, and I let her have all the licorice.

For the Christmas holiday, Debbie and I went to see Grin and Pompey in Chicago. They had insisted, but there had been a big battle over it because Debbie hadn't wanted to leave the cats. "They won't be able to go outside for a whole week," she told Grin. "They'll be lonely."

Grin said they'd have each other. There were seven of them now, for God's sake.

"What if something happens to them?"

Nothing would happen to them.

"I'm responsible for them, Mother. I don't know if I can find someone to feed them. To vacuum the house, and clean the litter boxes. Who will want to do that over Christmas?"

Terry Mandible was out of the question. She didn't want him anywhere near the cats after he kicked poor Pompadour. Eventually, though, the next-door neighbors were nice enough to do it, even though they thought my mother was an oddball. She took me with her when we went over to ask, and they smiled a tense kind of smile, and she said she'd do their plants sometime if they ever needed it, and they looked at me and sighed, and said yes.

Debbie picked each cat up and talked to it, explaining that we were going away for a short time, and the Andersons from next door would make sure there was lots of food and water. The cats looked at her mysteriously, some of them purring and some of them wiggling to get down and go off on important feline business. When she had talked to every single one, Debbie packed our bags, wrapped the presents, put on the blue dress that Grin found irreproachable, and drove us to the airport.

Grin and Pompey both related to my new status as a disturbed child by making almost incessant inquiries. Would I like pot roast or meat loaf for dinner? Would I like mashed potatoes? Would I like a glass of ginger ale? Or maybe I liked cola better, would I like a glass of cola?

Grin noticed I was reading at the kitchen table. I had brought a book with me all about a family that had five children. She tucked my hair behind my ears for me. Didn't I want to play a game? Didn't I want to play outside? Wouldn't I like some fresh air? That would be nice for me, wouldn't it?

Grin and Pompey's yard was flat and snowy. There were no cats to frolic with or dogs to throw sticks for, no climbing structures or tire swings. It was simply icy, Chicago in December, bitter wind and drifts of snow accumulating against the sides of houses. No, I didn't want to go outside.

It would probably have made Grin relax just to see me doing something, anything, that she could easily define as play. If I was playing, I must be happy, must be well-adjusted. I knew she'd like me to go outside, or flip her bridge cards around on the living room rug. I knew it would set her mind at ease. But I didn't want to.

"Do you want to visit with the little girl next door?" Grin asked me. "There's a little girl there. I think she's four years old. You could play with her. We could go over there this afternoon and tell her hello." Grin turned to Debbie and Pompey as if I couldn't hear. "It's good, I think, for Vanessa to interact with other children. She must be so much alone."

"She goes to school," Debbie said. "She plays with other children all the time."

"Well." Grin sighed, sliding the raw roast into a marinade. "I thought it would be nice for her, that's all. Shall we go see that other little girl, Vanessa?"

I wanted to read, to go shopping with Grin to buy a present for Debbie, to eat Christmas cookies hot from the oven. I didn't want to perform normalcy for other people's peace of mind. "No," I told Grin, to everything she asked me.

"Say, 'No, *thank you,*' Vanessa," Debbie prompted.

"No, thank you," I said. "I like to read."

We ate loads of meat that holiday season. Debbie had piles of mashed potatoes and broccoli, big glasses of grapefruit juice, bowls of oatmeal, peanut butter sandwiches. Grin and Pompey and I ate eggs and bacon and sausage in flat patties. There was liver pâté, which smelled like barf, and a big roast turkey, which tasted amazing. Debbie didn't exactly give me permission to eat any of it, but she didn't say no, and after the first dinner, when Grin put a huge piece of steak on my plate and cut it up for me with a sharp knife, after she did that and Debbie didn't say a thing, I figured I could eat whatever I liked. I wonder now, if Doctor Eng had said something to her, like Let Vanessa make her own choices, or Children need to develop autonomy. But back then, I didn't think about it. I just ate as much as my stomach would hold.

"You'll get so thin, Debbie, eating like that," Pompey ventured, his mouth full of meat loaf.

"I always eat like this, Dad. It's not any sort of problem."

"She never liked my cooking," Grin said. "I don't know why, but she never liked it. I try and try."

"I do like it, Mother. You make things that I don't eat."

"If you really liked it, I think you would." Grin looked down at her hands.

"I'm eating. I'm eating mashed potatoes. The mashed potatoes are very good."

"Does it need more salt, Theodore? Is that the problem?"

"No, no," Pompey said. "It's fantastic meat loaf."

"What if I made it without the pork? How would that be, Debbie? I bet you'd like it without the pork."

"I'm sure your meat loaf is lovely, Mother. I just don't eat it, with or without the pork."

"I have never been able to make a truly special meat loaf," Grin moaned. "I've tried recipe after recipe."

"It's delicious," said Pompey. "Look, Vanessa's eating it all up."

"Do you like it with onions, Debbie? I have a recipe that uses lots of Spanish onions, chopped very fine."

Pompey had a new idea. "We could get oysters for you," he said. "You always used to love oysters."

"That's very sweet of you, but no."

"They're not meat, you know."

"Yes, they are."

"They don't have any kind of consciousness. They don't ambulate."

"They don't need to ambulate to be animals."

"Oysters are like plants," Pompey persisted. "It's a technicality to call them animals. They don't swim, they don't do anything, they don't live a life that anybody would envy. Now, a crawdad. That I can see is an animal. Ugly as all hell, but definitely an animal. Your crawdad swims around, meets other crawdads, pinches things with its claws, eats a meal. That's a life. Really," he continued, "I think you could eat quite a lot of oysters and not feel any guilt about it whatsoever. You'd be putting them out of their misery. They wouldn't even notice it."

"Those are two different things, Dad, putting them out of their misery and them not noticing it."

"What I'm saying is that the oyster doesn't count. You might enjoy them, Debbie. You loved them when you were a girl."

"She's not going to eat them, Theodore," Grin interrupted. "When Debbie gets her heart set on one of her fads, you know she's not going to change her mind until she's good and ready."

"It's not a fad, Mother. I've been eating this way for years."

"I sometimes blame myself, do you know that? I wonder if it's all because of my cooking. I was always making new things when you were a girl. Once I made this blood sausage, a Polish recipe, and you didn't like it. I will wonder until the day I die whether that sausage scarred you for life. And a kidney dish I made one year at Christmas. You seemed very upset about that. You wouldn't eat a single bite, not even when I sent you to bed early."

"What are you saying? It's a fad, or I'm scarred for life?" Debbie's voice was bitter. "It can't be both."

Grin paid no attention. "Theodore, do you remember when Debbie decided she was only going to wear pink? She wore nothing but pink for half the school year. I had to wash her three pink blouses over and over, and she was always sneaking to borrow that pink cashmere cardigan of mine with the embroidery on it."

Pompey nodded his head. "It's true, Debbie, you know it is." He patted her on the arm. "It's the same with all those cats you have."

"No, it's not."

"Sure. You get one cat, you like it, and it becomes a fad. Cat after cat after cat. You take it to excess."

"The cats need me. I take care of them. There's a relationship."

"But so many? Why not just one or two?"

"There are lots of animals that need homes," Debbie said. "The humane society kills dogs and cats every single day."

"I remember when you got it into your head to paint your entire bedroom black in 1962," said Grin. "That first summer she came home from Wheaton. No one could stop her."

"But she painted it white again before September," Pompey put in. "She changed her mind."

"I was eighteen years old! You can't hold that against me," Debbie protested.

"It was the same when you married Jordy," Grin said.

Pompey grunted in a disapproving way.

"I'm just saying," Grin went on, "that there were certain objective reasons to be wary of Jordy. Other people knew—we knew—that there were problems with that boy. That is all I'm saying. But Debbie got her heart set on him, and once she does that, she has to have her own way."

"Mother . . ."

"I'm only stating a fact," said Grin. "It's a fact. I'm not passing any judgments. I would never have dreamed of telling you what to do."

"He was a meat-eater," I said, and my voice sounded clear and loud in the formal dining room. "Jordy was a meat-eater."

Pompey snorted, and Grin poured herself another glass of wine. Debbie looked at her plate very carefully. We finished the meal in silence.

20.

The Saturday Panties

Stuart, the principal of Cambridge Harmony, sent my mother a letter. It was waiting for us when we came back from Chicago. He regretted it intensely, the letter said, but the scholarship money for the spring semester was greatly reduced because the call-around fund-raiser hadn't been as successful as in previous years. Vanessa's usual financial aid package would not be available, and so she wouldn't be able to return to school on January 15. He was truly sorry about this situation, as he knew it would cause our family unexpected difficulty, and if any funds did surface, we would be notified immediately.

I read the letter because Debbie left it on the coffee table. We went to visit the local public school the day after we received it, even though I wouldn't start for a couple of weeks. It was nice there, my mother told me. A school where every child got to have her own desk and you called the teachers Mister and Miss. Very grown up. I would like that, wouldn't I?

Shortly after she got the letter, Debbie started calling the police up with new ideas about the identity of my flasher. It could have been Roger, for example, the ex-boyfriend who worked at the zoo. "He was always carrying binoculars," she told the detective on the phone. "He used to take me on nature hikes and look at birds through them. There's something very creepy about binoculars." She said Roger didn't ever really relate to Vanessa, he didn't seem to know how to talk to little kids. That could be a cover-up for some kind of perverted attraction, couldn't it? Plus, he worked at the zoo, spending all his time with animals kept in cages like prisoners. That would give a person a warped idea of relationships, if you spent all day telling yourself creatures were happy to see you, when really you were nothing but their jailer.

She also suspected the sandy-haired Jake, dentist and object of Grin's fantasies about a second marriage. He was too interested in Vanessa, she said. He had brought a rubber dinosaur on only his first visit to the house, and at the beach he had thrown Vanessa up in the air so she made a big splash when she hit the water. And he had actually called up not four weeks ago, asking Debbie how she'd been, seeing if she wanted to go to dinner. Ugh.

Doctor Eng wanted to talk about the bottom, too. Our conversations went something like this:

"It would come to the window and wiggle itself around."

"It wiggled around."

"Yah, and then it liked to press itself up against the glass."

"It liked to press up."

"Yeah. I think the glass was cold, though."

Pause.

"What are some adjectives you would use to describe the flasher's bottom?"

"Round. A little bit hairy. Silly."

"Silly?"

"Ta Ra Ra Boom-dee-ay. I'll take your pants away!"

"It wanted to steal your pants."

"And while you're standing there, I'll take your underwear!"

Another pause. "It might be frightening for some people, seeing a strange bottom at the window."

"Nah."

A slight sigh from Doctor Eng. "What made you think of that song, 'Ta Ra Ra Boom-dee-ay'?"

"That's the bottom song. What it would sing if it could sing."

"You like to imagine the bottom singing a song."

"Yeah. It was a dancing bottom."

"The bottom danced."

"The wiggling was a dance."

I could tell Doctor Eng thought I was avoiding something, that I should have been afraid the way Anu was. Or that I probably had been afraid and was hiding it. I would have rather drawn some more, or continued dramatizing the adventures of the Squirrel of the Universe, but she pushed forward with the current subject. How did I feel when I saw that Landis was scared of the bottom? And when I saw that Debbie called the police? "It's okay if you felt scared, Vanessa."

"I didn't."

"Children don't have to protect adults."

"Of course not!"

"Why not?"

"The Squirrel of the Universe will protect them."

Doctor Eng paused for a moment. "He can, but he doesn't have to. That's what I'm saying."

"What?"

"It's okay for you to be afraid if that's how you felt. I know your mother is alone, but she is a big grown-up and she can handle it if you got scared."

"Uh-huh."

Doctor Eng wore dark lipstick and looked like she never got dirty, and her sleek, black hair shone almost blue, like Anu's. "Do you think the bottom had a man attached to it, Vanessa?" she asked me.

I didn't really. It seemed like an isolated bottom. But I knew the answer to Doctor Eng's question was Yes. The bottom must really be a man. And when I forced myself to think about him, and how I didn't know who he really was, and how he had traveled over to my house in his car or on foot and climbed up on the woodpile and pulled down his pants to wave his naked ass at me, and how he had probably planned to do it and worn his red cotton shirt and no underwear on purpose, and how he had watched our house until he knew that neither Debbie nor Landis was in my room reading me a story—then I started to think maybe I had been wrong. Maybe it wasn't a benign bottom, after all; maybe it was a nefarious bottom.

Had it been amusing, or had something really bad happened? People kept seeing me as a damaged child. They felt I needed help, that I had been through an almost unspeakable trauma. Grin thought it. She was paying for my therapy. Landis thought it, and she thought almost everything was funny. Debbie thought it, and cried with cats sitting all around her on the living room couch. Joyce and Ron. Stuart the principal. Mister Bhaduri. They were all looking for the man in the red cotton shirt, the man who had caused me and Anu this possibly irreparable harm.

I began to wonder if the bottom might be Jordy. That would explain why I hadn't felt traumatized. Because if the bottom was Jordy, it was something I had a private connection with, something that couldn't be understood by anyone else. Its display could be a way for my father to contact me without my mother knowing.

Jordy knew how to amuse me, wanted to share a private part of himself with me, wanted me to think of him before I went to sleep. He had come back from California and tried to flash me in the place where the sour clover grew, but had flashed Anu by mistake instead. He felt very bad about that part, I was sure. He would never have flashed a stranger on purpose.

Then he discovered my woodpile and my special horizontal window, and that allowed him to visit me in secret. Although we didn't know each other, he got to hear me laugh every once in a while.

Doctor Eng and I talked about this idea a lot.

Meanwhile, the police said they were doing everything in their power to find the flasher. When pressed, they admitted "everything" meant that they had posted a description of the man around town. Debbie was furious. Hadn't they interrogated those suspects she told them about? She could think of several more to give them, too. Couldn't they give us a patrol man on our corner? Couldn't they come down and have German shepherds sniff our woodpile? Couldn't they compare the description I gave them with every known child pervert on the books?

They said No they couldn't, No they wouldn't, and nearly every child pervert was a Caucasian male aged twenty to sixty. Did Mrs.

Brick think the Cambridge PD was her own personal guard service? They had murderers and shoplifters to chase down, too. A case of indecent exposure wasn't their number-one priority.

Debbie was obsessed, though, so she got Win to promise he'd bring his beagles over to our house to sniff the woodpile. Fred, Robert, Sandra, and Allison. I was excited they were coming.

When Win arrived, I could hear the dogs barking outside our front door. "Vanessa, will you open it?" Debbie called from the bathroom. She was putting on makeup.

I answered the door feeling grown-up and hostessy.

Marie was on the porch.

On *our* porch, in a snowsuit and red mittens. Looking enormous, all bundled up, hair sticking to her face.

"This is your house, huh?" she said. The beagles rushed in and started swarming around the kitchen and living room, barking and looking for cats. Marie. Trying to enter my house. A disaster.

"Vanessa," called Win, as he pulled some things out of the station wagon. "Have you met my daughter? I think you might recognize each other from school."

I stood there and stared.

"Marie, have you two met before?"

"She's in my class."

"In your class? Why didn't you tell me?"

Marie shrugged. We stood, staring at each other, me indoors in pajamas, her outdoors with her breath showing in the cold. How long had she known?

"Debbie!" Win yelled, wiping his boots off on the mat and ushering Marie through the doorway. "Debbie, did you know the girls are in the same class?"

"No!" Debbie came out of the bathroom. "I had no idea!" She bent over and shook Marie's hand. "Very glad to meet you. I've been hearing a lot about you from your daddy."

Marie didn't say anything.

It turned out that because she was nine already, and I was only eight, neither Debbie nor Win had thought we might be in the same grade.

"Vanessa," said Debbie. "Marie and Win and I are going to take the dogs outside to look at the woodpile. Do you want to come with? It's your choice."

"Come with."

"Then go get dressed. Why don't you show Marie your room?"

No way.

"Vanessa?"

"I don't want to," I said.

"Miss Brick, where are your manners?" My mother put on her warning voice.

Who knew what Marie might do to me and my stuff once she got me alone? She might get a hold of my diary with its special lock and key and see all my lists and drawings. Or she might shake my stuffed animals until their eyes popped out, and their seams ripped. She might scratch the records or jump on the bed, there was no telling what she was capable of.

I wasn't going to change my clothes in front of her, either. She was the flasher, didn't they know that? She was the one who had forced her unwanted ass upon me. She was the one who made me afraid to go to school, made me throw my lunch in the garbage and go hungry, made me vomit on the merry-go-round. Just because she was a kid, just because she was a girl, no one seemed to recognize what violations she might perpetrate at any moment. It was Marie who ruined my diorama, Marie who hit me in the face with snowballs, Marie who turned me into a cruel popular girl that I barely even knew or liked.

I couldn't be alone in my room with her. Couldn't, couldn't, couldn't.

"Vanessa, what's got into you?" my mother wanted to know.

"I don't want to!" I said, and buried my face in her skirt.

"She's shy," my mother explained to Win and Marie. "Ever since this whole thing started, she's been shy."

I didn't feel shy. I felt angry and terrified and totally weirded out that Marie was in my house. I had no idea whether she might smother me with a giant snowsuit embrace or slam me into the wall and wave her ass at me, but I didn't want either one to happen.

"I'm not showing it," I said.

"Vanessa, don't you want to be polite to Win's daughter?"

"No," I said, and got behind Debbie's legs.

"Well, you need to change your clothes if you're coming out with the beagles."

"No, I don't." I felt perverse, self-protective. "I'll go in my pajamas."

"That's not an option."

"I'm not showing her my room! You can't make me."

"Why not?"

"It's my room. I don't care what you say!" I yelled.

"Vanessa."

"I won't do it. Leave me alone!" I was stomping off toward the bathroom with a vague idea of locking myself in, when Marie began to cry. A second later, she peed her pants. A thin trickle of urine leaked from her green rubber boot onto our carpet. The cry turned into a wail, and Debbie ran to get a towel from the cupboard.

Win apologized, said he'd given her lots of juice this morning. Probably she was nervous, God, she must be terrified, because this never happened. She was nine years old. This never happened.

Debbie said snowsuits are hard to get out of in time, and it's hard to ask where the bathroom is in a strange place, isn't it? Don't worry, it could happen to anybody.

Win asked for tissues, and Marie blew her nose, whimpering quietly while boots were taken off and emptied into the toilet, soaked snowsuit and blue jeans removed and put in a plastic bag. Wet underwear, too. She stood in my living room with nothing on her lower half, plump white legs clamped together.

Debbie took Marie's hand and led her to the bathroom so she could wipe herself off with a damp washcloth, then brought her to my room and left her there. "Lend her some clothes, Vanessa," she barked at me. "And be nice."

There was Marie, half naked. Exactly what I had feared. Her butt looked small and cold. She was in my bedroom, not touching anything but leaning up against the bedspread to cover her crotch, wiping a leftover tear off her cheek. I remembered that she didn't have a mother.

"I peed," she said with a sigh, as if I needed to be informed.

"Everybody pees," I said.

"Like a baby."

"Our cat Pompadour pees in the closet."

"Do you clean it up?"

"Debbie cleans it."

"I feel dumb." Marie giggled a little and buried her face in my blanket.

"I have days of the week panties," I told her. "And Saturday is the best one because it has butterflies on it. You wanna wear those?"

"Can I see?" she asked, so I got out all the days of the week, except Thursday, which I was wearing, and Monday, which was in the laundry. She picked Saturday, and I gave her some pants and clean socks to wear.

"Are you gonna put my jeans in your washer?" she asked.

"We don't have one."

"How do you do your wash?"

"We go to the Laundromat."

"What's there?"

"Machines. You put quarters in them like for soda."

"Do you get to put the quarters in?"

"Sometimes." Patrick Threep came mewing out of an open drawer. I picked him up and put him on the bed. "We have seven cats. Did you know that? Patrick, Dirigible, Deluxe, Pompadour, Pretty Kitty, Button, and Fuzzy."

Marie cracked a tiny smile and patted Patrick on the head. I'm not sure I had seen her smile before, because I noticed her teeth for the first time.

"Seven cats," Marie repeated. She did that sort of thing a lot. Repeating what people said.

We took the beagles out back on leashes. The woodpile was under our eaves, so it didn't have any snow on it, and the dogs sniffed over the area where the flasher must have stood in order to get his ass up to window height. It looked like the man had rearranged the wood to get a nice stable foothold.

"Do you think he might have masturbated?" I heard Debbie say to Win under her breath. "You know, after he was done at the window?"

Win grimaced. "Yeah. I think it's possible."

"Man."

"Fred used to be a hunting dog," Win said. "I got him when he was already old and rickety, but he chased foxes in his day. He knows what he's doing."

Fred, Robert, Sandra, and Allison found areas of interest all over the backyard—exciting cat pee and smells from neighborhood dogs—but Win kept calling them back over to the woodpile. They sniffed a lot at the side of the house, too, where the guy might have stood while getting ready to show his ass.

I guess Debbie and Win were hoping that Fred would lead us around the side of the house and off in some direction after the flasher. But he didn't seem to get any clear line of scent; and after a while the beagles started shivering in the snow. We gave up and went inside for hot chocolate.

Terry Mandible watched us from the upstairs window.

21.

MISS CREAM AND BUTTER

Katty Sherwin turned out to be a lesbian.

One morning, right before New Year's, she came over bearing a poinsettia plant and holding hands with a tall woman who was dressed in black. "I'm so sorry," said Katty, walking boldly into the kitchen with her flowerpot, "I was such an uptight asshole. About the whole queer thing." She pushed the poinsettia toward my mother. "It was all my fault."

Debbie looked stunned, but she took the plant.

"This is Sylvia," Katty said, rubbing the tall woman's back as the words tumbled out of her. "I wanted you to meet her. Everything's different now. It was all about repression. Repression like you wouldn't believe." She was excited and nervous, bouncing on her toes and exuding an anxious warmth. Sylvia smiled and sat down quietly at the kitchen table.

It turned out—and I only really understood this later, because I was sent out of the room to play with the cats during most of their conversation—that Katty had become increasingly disillusioned with the teachings of the Alexian Ashram. Her participation had been waning for quite a while, but in recent months Katty had totally disassociated herself from everyone she knew who was a part of it, because she had begun to the see the supposed freedoms of the Alexians as restrictions: the insistence on public nudity, for example, in the hot-tub ritual.

Alex had told Katty that smoking cigarettes kept her enslaved to an addiction, and she could never be enlightened if she continued enslaved. Well, yes, Katty wanted to quit smoking, but she didn't want to be told she was an emotional Neanderthal because she liked her menthols. She said she could be just as open a human being whether she smoked or not. In fact, *not* smoking made her bitchy.

And frankly, Katty said, she felt more comfortable with a bra on, and there was no pretending otherwise. When one friend of hers from the ashram suggested that Katty was succumbing to a tyranny of male oppression because she couldn't see the beauty of letting her body flop around freely in its natural state, Katty had simply lost it. "I yelled and screamed at that poor woman," she told Debbie. "I told her my breasts are about six times as big as hers, and she had no idea what it's like to carry these things around. They're heavy as all hell, I told her, and thank God for bras! They're the liberator of all womankind as far as I'm concerned, and I don't want anybody telling me not to wear one!" Katty paused. "We're not friends anymore, she and I."

So Katty had set herself adrift and found herself alone with her title of Miss Cream and Butter 1955, her loom full of hand-dyed wool in pretty patterns, and a son who kept putting on her dresses whenever she let him out of her sight. And now that the ashram wasn't there telling her to find a loving place in her soul for Randy (that cheating sexist bastard), now that there were no Receptacle rituals to help her channel her anger, she had found herself absolutely furious with her ex-husband.

The day after Thanksgiving, the day after she caught Luke in his Captain Hook dress bouncing on my bed, Katty got tipsy and drove round to Randy's house. It was empty. Everyone was gone on a skiing holiday; her three eldest boys and her ex-husband had piled into a van to hurtle themselves down mountainsides a couple hours north, and Katty had left Luke at Malcolm's house while she went over there. She let herself in with her key and trashed the place. She cut all Randy's queen-size sheets in half with scissors, and took all his perishable items, shoved them in the oven, and baked them for an hour and a half at 450 degrees before putting them back in the fridge. She left the children's rooms alone, but she broke all Randy's dishes, poured orange juice on his sweaters, and generally vented her rage on his favorite possessions before getting back in the car and driving herself home. She even sliced the trampoline into quarters with a butcher knife.

Two days later, Bart, Turner, and Pal got back from skiing and called her up to tell how a burglar had broken into the house and smashed all the plates. He had ruined the food and cut the towels into shreds. There was shaving cream all over the bathroom.

Now Katty was horrified at what she'd done. Twelve-year-old Bart was miserable about the trampoline and had thrown up for two hours after taking a big bite out of a rotten, half-baked apple. Fourteen-year-old Pal had to spend two full days helping his father clean up the mess, and ten-year-old Turner started having nightmares every night, screaming that someone was trying to get through his bedroom window to rob the house. Mommy, he asked, could I come sleep at your place?

Randy had driven away with a loud screech of tires before Turner even got up the steps. He knew what Katty had done. She was the only one who could have done it, the only one with a key, the only one who knew how he hated the smell of orange juice. Randy, who had written her love letters even that very year, who had said she could come back to him any time she wanted, in the days after Thanksgiving became the kind of ex-husband that most women had: the kind that never looked you in the eye. He didn't accuse her, and he didn't call the police, but all the love seemed to have drained out of him. He took on the air of a martyr, and Katty—who had played the part of the betrayed wife ever since Randy had that affair—was suddenly the guilty one.

She wasn't even sure why she'd done it. She was mad at Randy, sure. She felt wronged by his infidelity and pressured by his love letters even as they flattered her. He bought the boys BB guns and action figures, and she felt he was teaching them a stupid, manly way of behaving that made her not even like them very much sometimes. So yes, Katty had wanted to unsettle Randy's domestic sphere, the zone he turned over to his housekeeper, in such a way that he'd have to sort it out himself.

But she hadn't meant to disturb Turner, had never thought about how it would affect the boys. The kid was waking up four, five times a night, asking her to check the windows and relock the doors.

Katty lived in daze for most of December, and then she saw an ad in the paper for a weekend workshop on women's sexuality: The Eros Inside. It was a retreat, with lectures and slide shows about the beauty of the human vagina and the mating practices of other cultures. There would be role-playing exercises about communicating with your partner, group discussions of sexual problems, and an introduction to tantric rituals. Katty signed up and spent the weekend learning to masturbate herself to orgasm in a group setting. A group setting! She also bought her first vibrator and learned the exact location and function of the clitoris.

"It was such an eye-opener, Debbie, I can't tell you," she enthused. "And the best part of it all was that during one of the encounter sessions, they were almost like group therapy really, I realized why I was such a raving bitch to you about Luke playing dress-up. I was uncomfortable about my own homosexual impulses! I had been repressing them for years. I couldn't stand anything that made me think my son might be queer, because it made me think about the lesbian feelings I had myself. Even when I was at Radcliffe."

"You're a lesbian?" Debbie lit a cigarette.

"And I never knew it. Imagine what kind of repression I'd been transferring onto Luke, trying to make him a masculine little boy when really he might be a budding homosexual just yearning to express himself!"

"Luke's a fairy?"

"Well, he's only eight. But the point is, it's bad karma for him to be limited in his choices. I have to let him be himself. No one ever let me be myself that way. My parents always wanted me to marry a nice Harvard man. My big rebellion was Randy because he went to MIT."

Sylvia laughed.

"I was never fulfilled," Katty went on. "Never. Don't you see?

That's why I trashed Randy's house. I was resentful of my enforced heterosexuality. Randy symbolized that, and Luke symbolized my fear of my true feelings." Katty wiped her eyes. "I don't want my children to be repressed. The workshop made me realize that. It was so free. And afterward, I went up to Sylvia and asked her to go for coffee." Katty reached over and patted Sylvia's knee. "Sylvia has always been in touch with her feelings for women. She's so open about these things."

"You were at the workshop?" Debbie turned to Sylvia.

"It was an enlightening experience."

Katty nodded. "Debbie, I want to make it up to you. To be friends again." My mother got up to make tea, and Katty followed, hovering over the stove while the water boiled. "I stood up for you at yesterday's PTA thing."

"Did I need it?"

"Alyssa Bent, you know her, she stood up at the meeting, which wasn't even supposed to be about Vanessa, or the Super Duper Spellers, she stood up in the middle of us planning bake sales and skate rentals for the Holiday Ice Party and announced that she felt Cambridge Harmony should institute some kind of reparation for the damage done to children's respect for one another on account of Vanessa's play."

"She didn't!"

"What a bitch, right?"

Mrs. Bent had proposed a series of Sensitivity Seminars. All the kids could go to them and learn about respecting other people and not making fun of big bottoms and diseases like syphilis. She proposed, and Mister Bhaduri stood up with her on this one, that there be a monthlong special curriculum about the different colors of skin and loving one another. The children could be evaluated as to their particular level of need for the program, so that the less sensitive kids, the kids who make butt jokes and things like that, could be put in one classroom to do role-playing and behavior modification. The regular kids could just cut out paper dolls that represent the rainbow of humanity and sing "This World Is Ours to Share."

"Malcolm Bent is the one who made fun of Vanessa being on scholarship," Debbie said.

"You're telling me!" Katty crowed. "I carpool with those children."

"How would they decide who went in what program?"

"The teachers would give the students a one, a two, or a three. One would be insensitive—kids who hit other kids, make fun of people, make racist jokes. Two would be an average kid who still needs some sensitivity education, and three would be a perfect angel kind of kid, who loves everybody and understands about the rainbow of humanity."

Katty lit another smoke before continuing. "Somebody raised a hand and said she was worried about teacher bias, like what if a child acted up in front of one teacher, but behaved really well in front of another; or what if a teacher had it in for a particular kid? Alyssa said they would solve that problem by having three different teachers evaluate each child, but that it was an invalid question anyway because sensitivity wasn't about behavior in the classroom, it was about an attitude that a child had toward other human beings, a respect for personal differences. A child could be loud, or have trouble concentrating, and still be very, very sensitive. Also, they said, sensitivity education would not be a punishment. It would be a wonderful opportunity."

"Then what?"

"Jay interrupted Alyssa by reminding everybody that the issue was not so much the mode of evaluating the students, but the school taking action to heal the wounds that had recently been created in the community."

"Oh, God." Debbie sighed.

"That's when I stood up." Katty giggled. "Before they could even get started on their wounds. I said this was hysteria. All kids are insensitive little assholes if you ask me, always teasing each other and yelling. It's perfectly normal, we shouldn't worry about it, we should leave them alone to do their little kid stuff without interfering so goddamn much. I said Vanessa was the nicest child you'd ever want to meet, and that all she did was express herself. I said the play she wrote was funny, and the PTA members were a bunch of humorless, oversensitive squares if they didn't think so, too. 'Show me the damage!' I shouted. 'Stand up right now and show me the damage to your precious little monsters! My kid thought it was funny,' I said. 'He only wished he could have written it himself.' "

"Did anyone stand up?" Debbie wanted to know.

"Well, Jay did, saying he felt the content of the play would have been very upsetting to Anu if she had been allowed to read it. But she hadn't."

"She did too read it," I said, having ventured back into the kitchen. "We acted out the parts in Super Dupers."

"Oh, Lord," Katty cried. "That proves my point. All those kids read it, and nothing happened."

"Did anyone else stand up?" Debbie asked.

"Not a soul. The entire auditorium was silent. I said they were persecuting a girl like Vanessa and demanding reparation from the school for something that really happened to Anu Bhaduri on her walk home. For something that happened to Patrick Threep hundreds of miles away in New York City. I said they should grow up, drive their children to school if they were worried about flashers and molesters, and stop worrying so goddamn much about what words the kids were learning to spell. Then I volunteered to run the Hot Apple Cider stand and walked out!"

My mother burst out laughing, and she and Katty were friends again after that.

22.

Fred Finds Something Interesting

The Cambridge Harmony Holiday Ice Party was two days later. We weren't planning to attend, what with my scholarship being taken away, but Katty said she needed moral support for going with Sylvia, and Luke and I hadn't played together for more than a month, so we went, even though snitty Alyssa Bent would be there, and the Bhaduris, too, probably.

We spent the evening before it making salt-dough ornaments for the tree everyone would be decorating, even though Christmas was over. Debbie couldn't resist any kind of craft opportunity, and part of her also wanted to show Stuart and all those PTA members what a valuable member of the community she was, and how much they would miss her. She made fat snowpeople ornaments; plump, curled-up cats that she colored all different ways; and smiling sunshines decorated with glitter. I made some abstract shapes that I painted minty green.

It was a gorgeous day. Icicles hung from the tree branches, and kids broke them off and sucked on them like candy. The lake shone slick and bright. People in plaid jackets and snowsuits circled around on the ice. There were baked goods and chili, hot apple cider, and a huge pine tree covered in decorations. The cool, slicing sounds of skates. Boys in winter jackets crying to take them off: "But I'm hot, Mommy! I really am!"

Luke and Turner were there, plus Sylvia and Katty, but none of them were skating. They were stirring apple cider on a portable burner and handing it out to kids in foam cups. The boys had had their faces painted. Luke was a pirate with a big black circle around his eye that was supposed to be an eye patch but looked more like an injury; and Turner was a tiger—black and orange stripes.

I had never skated before, but Debbie rented me a pair of skates, strapped them on me, and sent me off anyway. She would have done the same with tennis, skiing, horseback riding, or roller skating, assuming the fun in them was intrinsic for anyone under the age of fifteen. It was incomprehensible to her that I might not know how to skate, or hit a tennis ball, or play Keep Away. These were things kids liked to do, she was sure I'd like them, they would just come naturally.

I wobbled onto the surface of the lake. Summer and Angelique were there, skating hand in hand. They rushed up and circled around me.

"She doesn't know how to skate!" Summer announced. "You don't know how yet, do you Vanessa?"

I shook my head and immediately fell on my ass.

"It's easy!" crowed Angelique, spinning herself around. "You have to bend your knees." They were standing over me.

"I remember when I couldn't skate. I was a baby and I had

to hold on to my Daddy's leg," Summer smiled. "Oh! There's Didi!"

"Bend your knees, Vanessa!" Angelique shouted, and they raced off to where Didi was practicing her stops, wearing a short pink skirt and a hat with matching pom-poms.

The Bhaduri kids had all had lessons. Ram, Samir, and Anu were whizzing around the open pond. Anu could go backward, and she had a purple skating skirt like Didi's. On Didi it had seemed stupid and affected. On Anu, I thought it was about the neatest thing I had ever seen—so official and confident. I got back on my feet, wobbling uncertainly, looking back to Debbie, who was talking earnestly with Sylvia.

I longed for Anu right then. In situations like this one, she used to protect me, would have held my hand and pulled me along on the ice, the power of her personality glowing around us like a halo. Now her brothers circled round her, teasing her gently. She skated well, but she kept her head down and made a big show of helping Baby, who still fell about once every four steps.

She couldn't have lit that halo round me now, anyway. Even if she had been willing to skate with me and hold my hand. That part of her didn't exist anymore.

I pushed forward on the ice, my heart hitting hard in my chest. Still, I told myself, if the Squirrel of the Universe had won the dreaded snowball fight—had later faced the enemy and given her the Saturday panties with the special butterflies on them—I could certainly wobble around an icy pond without protection. I hadn't had it for months now, anyway. I bent my knees.

When I was halfway around the lake, I saw Win arrive with Marie and the beagles. He kissed Debbie hello, his old lips pressing her young, shiny ones. I had never seen them do that before. It was kind of gross and also kind of cheerful. Win let the dogs off their leashes, and they leaped around, barking and rolling in the snow.

No one ran up to Marie. Luke didn't even say Hi to her when Katty brought him over, I could see. He acted real distracted, waved briefly, and ran off with Turner, yelling like a maniac. Marie clomped toward the skate rental on her own, a dollar bill clutched in her fist. I was standing still on the ice, watching, when one of the bigger kids zoomed past and hit my shoulder. I teetered and fell sharply on my tailbone.

My face was hot and the ice was chill on the heels of my hands. I started to cry, more with surprise and embarrassment than pain. The other kids were whipping past me, colors bright on the white, white background. Voices shrill and oblivious.

A swish of skates stopped by my feet. A small brown hand reached down. My heart surged. Anu?

It was Ram. "Vanessa, you fell!" he said, with his slightest of Indian lilts. "Need help?"

I put my bare hand in his, mine frigid from the surface of the ice, and he pulled me up to standing. Ram's lips were red and chapped with the cold. His heavy black brows shadowed his eyes, and his skin looked like it would taste of burnt sugar. He had on a ski jacket that must have been a hand-me-down from Samir; it was still at least a size too big for him.

I was in danger of toppling over again, but Ram grabbed on to me. I had not held hands with a boy except on field trips when we were assigned buddies, or in circle games when most of them would twist and wiggle their fingers constantly to convince themselves they weren't doing anything intimate. Ram held my hand simply, not because he had to, but because he wanted to—sometimes pulling me forward as he skated backward, sometimes skating side by side.

"Push off with your back foot," he said. "That's it. You're doing good!"

His hand was a little sweaty, and our palms stuck together. It didn't last long. He skated with me only back to the side of the pond where the teachers and parents were, sitting on benches and manning bake sale tables. "You okay?" He smiled and there was that gap between his two front teeth.

I told him yes.

He was so pretty. Such a pretty boy.

And then he skated away.

He wasn't Anu, anyhow.

I bent my knees, pushed with my back foot, and skated twice around the lake without falling down.

An hour later. People were full of warm drinks and sweets. A few kids were crying, saying they didn't want to go home, they didn't want to, they weren't tired! A couple of clouds had appeared in the sky, and the tree was decorated with lots of Debbie's ornaments. No one talked to her, though, besides Katty and Win. The grown-up Bhaduris kept discreetly on the other side of the Ice Party area, pretending like they never noticed us at all.

Suddenly, all the dogs began going crazy. Fred, Sandra, Allison, and Robert, plus a husky and a number of mutts that belonged to other people. Robert, whom I recognized because he had a spot over one eye, was racing back and forth in front of Win while the others were barking furiously at a cluster of bushes and trees on a nearby edge of the lake. Fred was in the front, wagging his tail and barking himself hoarse.

Win rushed over, skidding across the ice in his work boots, to see what the commotion was. When he saw what was in the bushes, what was leaving the bushes and pushing into the woods, he called loudly for the other parents to help give chase. Three or four grown-ups crashed through the trees with the dogs, yelling and pushing and tripping over themselves. The animals were barking and wagging their tails with excitement; the people were cursing as they tried to run across the iced-over snow. Finally, one of the moms grabbed hold of the target and toppled him to the ground.

Ron the teacher had been caught behind a bush with his pants down, his dick out and everything. He was wearing a red cotton shirt with a cigarette burn on one cuff.

When the dogs started barking, he had yanked up his jeans and tried to run, but there was a lot of underbrush and his pants hadn't buttoned properly, so they were hanging down and impeding his progress when Alyssa Bent hit his shoulder and knocked him over. He didn't struggle once she got him, and seconds later, the other parents were swarming round.

Somebody found a pay phone and called the cops. The beagles ran in circles, yapping and sniffing. They recognized his smell from our woodpile.

After a few minutes, the police arrived. They beat Ron with nightsticks until he bled from his nose and his arm hung limp from its socket. Debbie tried to cover my eyes, but I saw some of it anyway.

23.

DAMAGE

Debbie unboarded my window to let the sun shine in, and I started public school in mid-January. The halls felt gray—no bright colors like at Cambridge Harmony—but I had my own desk with a top that lifted up. I could keep my diary and my minty green pen in there if I wanted to. And best of all, nobody paid. Not one single person. And when I went to play at their houses, they were small, like mine and Debbie's.

There had been some talk of my skipping a grade, but I was so short that Debbie worried I wouldn't integrate socially, and my math skills were really not so good, so I was still a third-grader. The teacher—there was only one—was a tall man with a receding hairline named Mister Fishman. He wore plaid shirts a lot, tucked tightly into his pants, and liked to tell us stories about when he was the handball champion of the city of Boston. When he came into the room, we had to say, "Good Morning, Mister Fishman."

I made some friends, but nobody special, and I liked the gym program, which had swimming lessons every Wednesday. We all wore these official school bathing suits that were handed out to us at the start of the hour. Sometimes you got a good one, one that fit, and other times we girls had to pin our shoulder straps together at the back with barrettes.

I turned out to be a rather aggressive swimmer. A lot of the kids had never been to the beach and were scared of the water, even in the spring semester after having lessons all fall. But I could do a passing crawl stroke with my face in, and so was allowed in the deep end. We had races some days at the close of the hour, and although I was timid at first, I pushed off the wall with my feet and kicked as hard as I could. Sometimes I even won, beating the tall boy who called me Shrimpy in the hallway.

Landis continued to be my mouse-sitter, even though I didn't go to her school anymore. The play, *Oliver*, had five performances one week in February. Debbie and I sat in the front row of the Cambridge Harmony auditorium for the Saturday matinee, and I don't think I've ever clapped so hard in my life as I did that afternoon. Landis wore a red dress with a corset that pushed her jumbo breasts up high, and when she sang, her voice was so enormous it seemed like it wanted to fly out the windows of the theater and run up the street. She even did a flirty kind of dance where she picked her skirts up over her knees, and the sad song about "not betraying his trust" made the lady next to me sniffle and search for a tissue in her purse.

I wanted to burst with pride, explode all over the state of Massachusetts. She was my baby-sitter, my wondrous Landis, my someone to be proud of. We brought her a bouquet of flowers, and she seemed to really appreciate it, and Debbie took me back to see the play again that same night, because I liked it so much.

Pretty soon after that, Landis's heart unbroke. The guy who played Bill Sykes asked her to go to the movies with him. He had a car, and he kissed her in the parking lot before they even saw the film. She hadn't expected that. She had figured kissing only happened at the end of the date.

Landis began to realize that a boy might like her more than she liked him; that a boy might have a car and be able to drive you around at night; and that some boys will put their mouths on your breasts. Like they were kissing them! (She didn't tell me that part. I overheard it.) "Who ever thought?" Landis crowed, laughing, on the phone to Connie while I was brushing my teeth one night. "I swear to God it never crossed my mind until he put his head down there and started smooching around! I had no idea what he was doing! Does that count as oral sex?" Connie must have said no, because Landis said, "I didn't think so," and then, "No, he didn't use his teeth. How gross would that be?" Then she speculated that she might break up with him because he was always calling her up at night and she just didn't have time to be chit-chatting on the phone. And then she hung up, made Lopey do some funny poses, and read me four bedtime stories before kissing me good night.

Ron Trafalgar lost his job at Cambridge Harmony, and in March he had a trial in criminal court. The state of Massachusetts accused Mister Trafalgar of lewdness and indecent exposure. His lawyer was claiming Ron was only in the bushes for self-gratification; a mistake certainly, a bad idea, definitely—but he hadn't intentionally exposed any innocent children to the sight of his private body parts. Therefore, he was innocent, even though there was no denying that Alyssa Bent had tackled him on the grounds of the Holiday Ice Party.

The prosecution was claiming that it was impossible for someone to think no one would see him in the bushes. It was a public place! Besides that, he was a recidivist offender executing a signature crime in which he purposely exposed his body with the intent of shocking and offending somebody else. He was wearing a red shirt with a cigarette burn, the same red shirt that had been noticed on a flasher who had exposed himself perniciously and repeatedly to a young girl in the community. These other events were to be presented as corroborating evidence of prior bad acts.

And that meant I had to come in and tell some people in suits what had happened.

I had a long meeting with the lawyer and the police detective who had interrogated me about the bottom. I found out later they wanted to determine whether I was telling the truth, and I guess they decided I was, especially since Debbie had seen the same thing one time. Then I testified at the pretrial hearing, where I answered the same questions over again and wore a fancy pink dress with bows that Debbie bought me for the occasion. Afterward, she took me out for pizza and to see a cartoon festival in a movie theater.

By the time of the actual trial, I wasn't nervous. The lawyer was friendly enough—a young guy with pimples who didn't look old enough for his job, even to to me. He gave me sour cherry candy that he always kept in the breast pocket of his suit and told me not to get confused if the defense attorney asked me complicated questions with words I didn't know. Just keep repeating the detail about the red shirt with the cigarette burn if ever I wasn't sure what someone was asking me.

When we got to the courthouse, me in my pink dress again and Debbie in her respectable blue one, I saw Anu in the wide hallway of the building. It was the first time in more than three months. Her hair hung in tight braids, and Mister and Mrs. Bhaduri were each holding one of her hands. Anu's testimony was already over. They nodded to us politely.

"Hello," Debbie said, as if she was testing them.

"Hello," Mrs. Bhaduri said. "You won't have long to wait. They finished with us very quickly. The lawyers are looking for you."

"We had a flat tire," Debbie lied. Really, we were just running late.

"Too bad, too bad." There was an awkward silence, then Mrs. Bhaduri went on. "Well, we are glad this is almost over. It seems certain there will be a conviction."

Debbie sighed. "I hope so."

"Good luck in there, Vanessa. It's not too scary."

"I know," I said. "The lawyer told me."

"She knows!" Mrs. Bhaduri laughed a laugh that told me I'd been rude. Anu looked down at the floor.

"Well, you all go do something nice. Go get an ice cream sundae or something," Debbie said, forcing a smile. The edges of Anu's mouth twitched.

"Thank you, we will."

Mrs. Bhaduri shook my mother's hand, as if they were business acquaintances. And then they left the building.

That was my last sight of Anu—wearing clean white knee socks and holding both her parents' hands for protection. Small in the giant hallway of the courthouse. But it is not how I remember her.

I remember the girl who was sometimes nasty, the girl who

staked out territory on the tire swing, who looked tough in her ski jacket. How she decorated her locker with a million stickers even though the teachers told us not to; how she let me play with the best of her toy plastic horses. How she gave me her chicken slices every single day. I remember the patient way she let me stroke her long black hair. How she made Marie stop destroying my diorama. Called people Fucker behind their backs. She told me once that she liked to imagine the whole universe would disappear if she snapped her fingers a particular way. A pushy, urgent, generous soul. A great speller. Such a pretty girl.

I have never had a best friend since Ron Trafalgar flashed Anu Bhaduri. No one else has even come close.

The courtroom was not like the ones on TV but more like a whitewashed classroom with scuffed floors and scarred wooden chairs. On the advice of the lawyer, Debbie had explained to me about the judge, the jury, the defense, and the prosecution, so I'd know what was going on. She told me multiple times that I wouldn't go to jail, no matter what I said.

"Vanessa," the lawyer began, "will you tell us what you saw out your bedroom window on several different nights in November of 1970?"

I knew certain things he wanted me to say. "I saw the bottom of a white man," I said. "It was naked. He had dark hair on his legs."

"Are you certain it was a man?"

"Yes."

"What clothes was he wearing?"

"He always wore the same red shirt with a cigarette burn on the cuff."

"Are you sure about the cigarette burn, Vanessa?"

"I'm sure. I saw it every time."

Then he pointed at Ron Trafalgar, who was wearing an ill-fitting blue suit and staring earnestly at his hands. "Do you know this person?"

"Yes."

"Who is he?"

"He was my teacher at Cambridge Harmony. He helped me put my diorama back together when someone broke it."

"What is his name?"

"Ron Trafalgar."

"Did Mister Trafalgar ever behave inappropriately to you, in school or outside of it?"

Again, I knew what I was supposed to say. "He called me a Crumpet a bunch of times. And he taught me how to spell words that some parents didn't like us learning."

"Such as?"

"Fornication. Gonorrhea."

"He was teaching eight-year-olds the meaning of words like that?"

"Some of the kids were nine and ten."

The lawyer smiled.

"We wanted to know what they meant."

"And do you know what they mean, now?"

"Fornication: noun. Intercourse between a man and woman not married to each other."

The lawyer looked significantly at the jury. "How old are you, again, Vanessa?"

"I turned nine in February."

"Did you see him doing anything else inappropriate at school?"

"He talked to my friend Anu. I overheard him in the hallway."

"What did he say?"

"He said it was okay to be aroused."

My interrogator raised his eyebrows. "Vanessa, tell me. Could the posterior you saw out the window belong to Ron Trafalgar? I'm not asking what you think, but just if it is possible that it was him."

"Yes. It could have been him."

"Was there anything you saw that would make you think it *wasn't* him?"

"No."

"Nothing at all?"

"No."

"Thank you." The lawyer turned and told the jury very simply that the perpetrator of these signature crimes against Vanessa Brick had worn the same clothing that Ron Trafalgar had worn during the case of indecent exposure for which he was on trial. It was not an ordinary red shirt, but a shirt with a distinctive burn on the cuff. Mister Trafalgar had no alibi for any of the times the signature crimes had been committed, and there were witnesses who had testified to seeing him in the neighborhood of Vanessa Brick's house on several occasions, late at night. He warned the jury that although the defense attorney was going to tell them that the person Vanessa Brick saw wasn't Ron Trafalgar at all, the signature nature of the offenses should be enough to indicate that this man *was* the perpetrator of said prior bad acts. He was a repeat offender, and therefore it should be clear that he was up to no good when he was captured in the bushes of the Holiday Ice Party. This man had inflicted his perverted desires on at least two innocent children, Vanessa Brick and Anu Bhaduri, damaging them deeply in an act that verged upon sexual assault. It was imperative that he be stopped, and it was in the hands of the jury to make sure that happened.

"No, he didn't." My voice sounded loud in my own ears.

The lawyer looked at me in surprise. I was interrupting. "What?"

"He didn't." I said. "Damage me."

"What do you mean?"

"It was just a bottom." The court stenographer giggled nervously.

"Thank you, Vanessa," the lawyer said, and turned forward again. "The evidence presented earlier proves there is no doubt that it was Ron Trafalgar's bottom, which he exposed indecently, in addition to displaying himself lewdly on January 1, 1971, in the Sleepy Pond Park."

"It didn't hurt me!" I cried.

"Vanessa," Debbie leaned toward me from her seat. "It's not your turn to talk now. The lawyer is talking."

"Okay, but I have something to say!"

The lawyer looked exasperated. "You can't say it here, Vanessa. You can talk to your mother in the other room."

"It was just a bottom," I repeated in my loudest voice.

"Vanessa!" Debbie hissed. "Please be quiet."

"Don't say I'm damaged!" I yelled. "You don't know what's in my head."

The lawyer looked at me again. "Vanessa, this isn't about you.

It's about a crime, a bad thing that someone did. You're too young to understand."

"It was just a bottom!" I insisted. "Everybody has one."

The defense attorney, when asked, said he had no further questions for this witness. And they took me out in the hall.

Ron Trafalgar went to prison, but only for thirty days. Then he packed his bags and disappeared. After he got out, he sent me a postcard. "Thank you for sticking up for me in court," he wrote. "You're a very intelligent girl. Yours sincerely, Ron Trafalgar."

I hid it between the pages of my diary before Debbie could even see it. I knew she would freak out if she knew, but it was the first piece of mail I'd ever received that was addressed specifically to me, and I wanted to keep it. The postcard had a picture of a kitten, one of those misty photos with the animal sitting in a flower bed. It was pretty thoughtful. He was like that, Ron, even if he was a pervert. He always remembered stuff you liked. Cats, or horses, or playing on the tire swing. He knew certain kinds of things were important to kids—like being told you were an author, and putting together a really neat diorama that no one else could mess with.

I wished he hadn't interpreted what I did as standing up for him, though. I had only said what the whole experience felt like to me. It wasn't a defense of anything.

Pompey saw a walrus, and he knew what he had seen. No Doctor Eng, no Debbie, and no pimple-faced lawyer was going to tell me the bottom wasn't what I thought it was.

I was the one who knew what had happened to me. They couldn't possibly know.

24.

Jordan Benjamin Brick

Jordy died.

He committed suicide. We found out two days after I testified in court. He had been dead for almost two weeks, but they hadn't known to call and tell us until someone looked at the will and saw that my father left every penny of his estate to my mother. It was quite a lot of money. Jordy's own parents were dead, had died right after the divorce, and they had invested in tampons when they first came out. They left all their stocks and cash to their only son. Jordy left it to Debbie and me. Half a million dollars.

Jordan Benjamin Brick died alone in an apartment in Boulder, Colorado. Not in the state of California at all. He had never been there in the first place. He killed himself by hanging from a lighting fixture with a piece of plastic cord tied around his neck. Before dying, it looked like he'd consumed nine-tenths of a bottle of gin with nothing but a lemon for garnish. Eyes bulging, mouth slack, feet dangling, face turning blue. No one found him for three and a half days, and there was nothing in his apartment but a drum kit, an old mattress, and six science-fiction novels. He left a note, but it was such a short one that no one was sure that it was really meant to be read by anybody. It might just be a fragment of a song half remembered:

Down, down baby,
Down by the roller coaster

Jordy wasn't a meat-eater, either. Well, he was, but that wasn't the problem between him and Debbie. It wasn't why Grin and Pompey disapproved of him. Jordy was a drunk.

He had been one when Debbie married him, and he was one when they divorced. He had tried going cold turkey, had tried switching to wine or beer, had tried drinking only after 5 P.M. on weeknights. Nothing had helped. He couldn't stop. He liked gin in his morning OJ and gin in his afternoon root beer. He liked martinis with fruit peel. He liked these things more than he liked Debbie, and he liked them more than he liked me.

When my mother couldn't take it anymore, she kicked him out. Jordy tried going to a drying-out joint in Connecticut, but as soon as he got out, he started drinking again right away. He went on a binge that involved tipping over a pinball game, punching a well-known member of the Hells Angels, and getting arrested for being drunk and disorderly. He phoned my mother, slurring his words and protesting his innocence, at quarter to four in the morning.

She bailed him out but told him she didn't care what happened to him anymore after that. He could rot in hell, and he shouldn't bother to telephone. Not ever again. Let her live her life in peace.

He took her at her word and never once called. He went on tour playing drums in a mediocre bar band. After they kicked him out for sleeping through a show, half comotose on the floor of his hotel room and stinking of gin, Jordy had settled in Boulder and tended bar.

There was no one to tell us why he killed himself, no one he knew besides a crew of regular customers who said he was always a happy drunk and they were surprised as hell.

When Debbie got the news, she cried and cried. She cried for hours, the cats sitting vigil on her bed in the darkened room. She used up all the tissue in the house. We had to put on our jackets and trudge to the corner store, where she bought three more boxes of Kleenex and some licorice for me.

Her crying made me cry, though I didn't know the whole story then. I probably don't know it now. We sat crying together on her bed, snuggling the cats and throwing the used-up tissues on the floor. Sometimes we watched TV. Sometimes we sat there in the dark.

"He was the silliest man, your father," Debbie said to me. "He used to put on funny voices that made me laugh so hard I almost peed my pants." She traced my mouth with her hands. "Your lips are the same shape as Jordy's. Did I ever tell you that?"

I shook my head.

"Your lips and your eyebrows, too, sugar." Her eyes welled up again. "I can't believe he died alone like that. It's so sad to die alone."

I didn't say anything. I just scratched Fuzzy's flaccid tummy and put my head on her shoulder to listen to the purr. Debbie blew her nose.

"Nothing happened that Jordy couldn't laugh about. He was never afraid of what people thought. He just said things, strange things, like the world was one big circus." She reached over and turned on the light by her bed. "That's why I married him."

We ate peanut butter sandwiches, and cried, and watched TV until we both fell asleep. Debbie let me stay in her bed that night. I didn't even have to brush my teeth.

A couple days later, my mother went out and bought herself an expensive set of china. There were matching cups and saucers, salad plates, and serving dishes. They had a soft pink floral pattern all around the edge. There was even a teapot with a sculpted rose on the lid.

"Why do that?" said Grin on the telephone. "You know you could have had my extra set, the one with the gold rims. It's sitting in the garage collecting dust."

"I wanted my own set, Mother."

"You were always so strong-headed," Grin said, meaning it as a criticism.

"That's right," Debbie answered. "And I still am."

25.

Which Is Not Caused by Cigarettes

I need to remember this story, have needed to remember it, because that third-grade year was the first time I found myself actually in the world, not hiding in the corner by the mouse cage. I went in a person defined by her mother and her best friend, but I came out defined by my own ideas. It was my first step toward adulthood, the first time I thought to myself, *I, Vanessa,* in any kind of way that mattered.

I am thirty-eight now, and my mother died last week. Debbie Brick Gifford, born Deborah May Delancey.

She wasn't that young for dying, but it wasn't her time, either. She always thought it would be lung cancer, used to laugh about it when she put her cartons of cigarettes away in the kitchen, but that wasn't what killed her, after all. One Sunday afternoon, a winter day with a sky so dark it felt like night before the kids were even out of school, she drove to an unfamiliar neighborhood to buy craft supplies. She did her shopping, loaded her bags into the car, and got behind the wheel. Before she could put the key in the ignition, she had a stroke. Knocked her tiny paintbrushes and jars of glittery enamel paint all across the passenger seat.

It shouldn't have been fatal. Wouldn't have been, had someone rushed her to the hospital—but it was a couple of hours before anybody noticed she wasn't moving and called an ambulance. They tell me she didn't feel much pain.

I need to tell this story now because I am in the world without her, and the process of separation that began when I first kept secrets from her, when I first disagreed with her, when I first wrote something I knew she wouldn't understand—that process is over. She is gone.

My Debbie, my mommy, my one, my only.

She is dust in the garden, where the kittens of Deluxe's kittens can roll in her at will.

I have not had this empty feeling since Anu Bhaduri hissed in my face that I was keeping secrets from her, thirty years ago on Halloween night. Since she swam out to sea and never came back. It is right behind my sternum and spreading up my spine with a dead chill. Because I miss them both.

Miss them, so.

The Bhaduris left town at the end of the school year in 1971. Mister Bhaduri took a job at Yale, and his wife got some kind of research grant, so the family packed up and moved to New Haven.

We didn't hear anything more about them. Nobody asked us, and we didn't ask anybody. But just a few days ago, I saw Ram at the Greenwich Village Halloween celebration in New York

City. I was alone, my kids and my husband fast asleep after a night of trick-or-treating. Had stepped out to look at the crowds and think about Debbie without the warm jabber of other people's sympathy crowding my thoughts.

It was a balmy night. The streets were packed. People wore ornate feathered masks and rubber monster faces. Some carried plastic pumpkins. I saw Glinda the Good Witch of the North drinking out of a bottle wrapped in brown paper.

Ram was in drag, as many people were that night. A smooth, tight dress and a long black wig. Hair like his sister's. His body had a wiry look to it, and his high heels made him very tall indeed. He was laughing and dancing with some friends, and his pouty lips were covered with heavy red pigment.

I had an urge to go up to him, to kiss him even. He was still so beautiful. Such a pretty boy.

But I didn't. I didn't do anything. I just sat on a stoop nearby and watched the dancers swaying their hips to music from a portable radio.

He came over to me, then, asked me for a light, smiling and showing the gap between his two front teeth. I handed him my book of matches, touched his fingers for a second. He had polished his nails a shiny pink.

He didn't recognize me. Lit his cigarette and was gone. I watched him dance up the street with his arm linked into someone else's. Teetering a bit on his heels.

I know nothing of what happened to Anu. She vanished from my life as surely as she had once dominated it. But part of me never stopped looking for her.

My Debbie, my mommy, my one, my only.

On street corners and in restaurants, from the corner of my

eye I catch a flash of thick black hair and milk chocolate skin, a striped ski jacket or the angle of a jaw—and I breathe in sharp and think it might be her.

Because I miss them both. Miss them so.

But it isn't Anu, after all. It is always a stranger.

26.

What I Need

Ron's conviction caused Cambridge Harmony a serious period of financial hardship until the scandal wore off and he became something of an urban myth for the kids there: the creepy teacher that flashed his butt at someone's window and played with himself at the Holiday Ice Party. No one was really sure if he existed, but they passed the legend down nonetheless: a cautionary tale for the young. I heard it from Luke Sherwin's kids a couple years ago. They asked me if it was true.

Luke turned his palms up in apology, as if to say, Sorry, the kids have no tact—but I laughed and told them nothing like that had ever happened to anyone. It was only a legend, like the story of Peter Pan. There were lots of tales about strange things coming to children's windows in the middle of the night. None of them were true.

I see Luke sometimes when I'm back in Cambridge on holidays. He got married young—to a pretty, faded woman who bakes her own bread and plays folk songs on guitar—and disappointed his family by becoming a building contractor. I think they felt that someone who was once a Super Duper Speller should have lived up to his intellectual potential. His brothers all went to graduate school, so Luke is something of a black sheep. But I think he likes his work.

It is difficult to tell, though, with Luke. He is either in massive denial, or he's very happy. He never was one to wish for what might have been, never seemed to pine away for something lost and not recovered. He has always bounced through life, coming at small things—Christmas presents, a good pie, a song on the radio—with such enthusiasm that it is impossible to know whether some deep disappointment or frustration lurks inside. When we were growing up, he never seemed particularly affected by his parents' separation; he accepted Sylvia as easily as he would have accepted a gift of some cool new action toy. And he didn't appear to miss her when—after a year and a half—Katty dumped her and returned to Randy.

"Being with Sylvia was such a growth experience for me," Katty told Debbie, smoking on the porch steps one summer afternoon in 1972. "She opened up my heart. But the person I love is Randy. I've always loved him. I wouldn't have trashed his house if he wasn't the center of my universe." So Katty moved Turner, Luke, and her big wooden loom back to the house with the trampoline. And never left again.

She sent me a card last week, a condolence note on handmade paper. "Life is a bitch, Vanessa," it said. "A bitch and a half, even. And there is hardly anything in this entire bloody world that I love as much as I loved your mom. Peace and kisses, Katty Sherwin."

* * *

Marie is my family, now.

There is Grin, of course, who moved to a posh retirement community when Pompey died of a heart attack, and now drinks cocktails every evening at six with a woman named Doris Ann. And I do have kids of my own, and a husband, and more cats than most people would find respectable. But Marie is the only person left who remembers my childhood.

She is the only person I know who has lost her mother.

And now she has lost my mother, too. We are talking every day.

From third grade on, Marie and I saw each other all the time because of our parents—though our relationship was never easy, never full of confidences. We had no whispers, no shared jokes, no secrets. Instead, we'd poke things with sticks and squirt each other with water guns. Our Barbie dolls would beat one another senseless, and fairly often we'd end up pummeling each other on the ground, the beagles yipping and circling around us.

"I'm having chocolate," Marie would announce definitively, when our parents took us out for ice cream on a hot weekend afternoon.

"No, I'm having it," I'd say.

"Don't copy."

"I'm not. I called it first. I said it in the car."

"No, you didn't."

"Yes, I did."

"I didn't hear you."

I'd look upward. "Debbie, didn't I say in the car I was having chocolate?"

"Yes. You said chocolate with rainbow sprinkles."

"See? *You're* copying *me.*"

"I don't want chocolate anyway," she'd announce. "I'm getting mint–chocolate chip."

And suddenly, the minty green ice cream would be by far the best ice cream, the only one to have. "But that's what I always get!" I'd wail.

"You're not getting it today. You said chocolate."

"I can change my mind."

"Yeah, but I already said mint chip. You can't say it now. You can change to rainbow sherbet." Rainbow sherbet was a hated flavor.

"You girls can have the same thing," Win would usually interrupt. "It doesn't matter."

In the end, we'd get double scoops: mine with mint on the bottom and chocolate on top; hers the other way around.

Even after Debbie and Win had been dating for years, Marie remained something of a mystery to me. I didn't have the sort of physical appreciation of her that I had with Anu and Luke, or even with Angelique. I didn't want to wear her clothes or touch her hair. Didn't want to hold her hand, sleep next to her, or trace my finger down her cheek. Her body wasn't the sort to inspire that sort of reverence. She was a simple soul, I think, who liked pretty things, wanted to hold them in her big hands. She liked math. She liked dogs. She liked making cookies and riding bicycles. We fought because I wanted to shake her up, jar her into something more alive. I felt small and complicated next to her.

Debbie finally agreed to marry Win the year I turned fifteen. She had spent some of the money Jordy left her on going to art school, and by that time had started a small business making cleverly painted furniture: pretty toy boxes, colorful rocking chairs, that kind of stuff. Win's hair was completely gray, but he still gushed over my mother like a teenager. He announced the engagement one night when we were all four sitting around the dinner table in the Arlington house, an apple pie Marie had made cooling on the sideboard.

"I love Debbie very much, as you girls know," Win said, raising his glass high in the air and smiling so the lines creased his face. "I love her unconditionally."

He liked to say cheesy things like that. It took some getting used to.

We all made toasts, and said congratulations, and then Marie and I took our plates of apple pie out on the back porch to watch the dogs cavorting in the yard while the grown-ups cleared the dishes. Marie had grown tall, with breasts and hips and a tousled head of hair that told boys she didn't care about them and still made them think of the bedroom. I was slight, with strong shoulders from swimming. Arms still a bit too long for my body.

"Just what I need." I sighed.

"What?"

"You in my life." Marie's reactions to sarcasm were always unpredictable. I wanted to see what she'd say.

"It's way too late," she said.

"Too late, they've sealed the deal, or too late you're in my life?"

"Too late, I'm in your life."

"True."

"I can make pie," Marie said simply, as if offering up one of her skills in hope of acceptance.

"It's good," I conceded. "You added lemon juice or something this time."

"The crust needs to be thinner."

"Yeah, but I like it doughy. It's like pastry."

"It is pastry."

"Duh."

"I would add more cinnamon." Marie poked an apple with her fork. "I'll add more cinnamon next time."

"You will, will you?" I wanted to bother her, to diffuse some of the touchy-feely happiness that was going on indoors.

She socked me on the arm.

"You can't hit me!"

"Yes, I can." She sat back down and ate some pie. "Sisters can hit each other."

"It's battery."

"No, it's not."

"I can beat you in a snowball fight," I said.

"Oh, tough girl."

"You know I can beat you."

"So?"

"So?"

"So eat your pie," Marie said. "Flies are landing on it."

"Will the cats come live here?" I wondered. "Debbie's not moving without them."

"Then they'll come."

"Allison will chase them."

"She'll probably try."

"Dirigible will rip her to shreds."

Marie laughed. "Allison drops rats on the porch all the time. Half-dead rats, only a little smaller than that cat."

"Dirigible has claws of steel."

"Allison has jaws of iron."

I poked Marie with my index finger. "Be nice to the cats. They're going to be new here."

"You're always nice to the new kid, is that it?"

She had me there. "Dirigible can chase Allison all around the yard. Allison's legs are so stubby."

"You're not always nice to the new kid," Marie persisted.

"Thanks for reminding me," I said sarcastically.

But I meant it. She was right to remind me.

I have not forgotten again.

27.

Old Haunt

Yesterday I went up to Massachusetts for Debbie's memorial. I tasted another of Marie's pies—pumpkin, this time. I stroked Win's wrinkled hands, and kissed Katty's menthol-smelling hair. Afterward, I drove to Cambridge Harmony and looked through the wire fence at the playground.

It has changed a bit over the years. In the early 1990s, the main climber was replaced by bright plastic playground architecture, and the wood chips gave way to sleek rubber matting. The old metal merry-go-round is long gone. But the tire swing still stands, and the third-grade girls are still spinning on it, round and round with their heads tilted back, singing naughty songs. Making themselves dizzy and staring at the sky. Because it is funny. And because they are young.

Acknowledgments

My beloved husband, Daniel Aukin, gave me the benefit of his faith, patience, and unconditional enthusiasm throughout the writing of this book, even though I wouldn't let him read it. Elizabeth Kaplan represented me with great skill and unflagging determination; I can't thank her enough. She is the agent I always dreamed of. And Allison (the editor, not the dog) McCabe has been a wonderful and insightful aide. She pushed me to make the book better, pushed me some more, laughed at my jokes, and knitted booties for my baby.

Thanks to John Zilavy for legal information, and to Bellamy Pailthorp for connecting me to him. Editors Sally Abbey, Laura Mathews, and Elizabeth Mikesell all provided much needed encouragement when I embarked on a novel. Eliza Block helped me remember the lyrics to numerous playground songs. Susan Carey and Ned Block submitted to my questions about Cambridge in 1970. Dalton Conley read an early draft and gave insightful suggestions, as did Andrew Blauner. Jessica Green,

Frances Foster, Jonathan Bing, Betsey Schmidt, Maria Russo, Adam Fisher, and Laura Miller generously shared their contacts. Hilary Liftin gave good advice. The Centrum Arts Colony in Port Townshend, Washington, gave me time and space in which to write. Thanks to Sarah Benolken for her support. To my family, especially: Ivy, Johanna, Len, Zoe, Ramona, Joan, and Bea. And to Raine, Sasha, Ivan, Lizzie, and Becca, wherever you are, for being childhood friends I'll never forget.